MW00905559

Swift River

R.C. Binstock

Books by R.C. Binstock:

The Light of Home
Tree of Heaven
The Soldier

cover painting and illustrations by Katarzyna Maciak

R.C. Binstock Books
copyright R.C. Binstock, 2014
all rights reserved

ISBN: 978-1501097249

Library of Congress Control Number: 2014917787
CreateSpace Independent Publishing Platform, North Charleston, SC

for Mahalia, my daughter

and for the discontinued everywhere

It does not appear to us to be a very important objection to our plan that certain mill sites will be 80 feet below the surface of the basin, nor that the homes of many industrious people dependent upon these mills for their living will also be submerged, because all these can be paid for, and an equivalent will be given...

— Massachusetts Board of Health
on its Nashua River reservoir proposal
1895

You don't impound water where people live anymore.

— Ray Raposa
director, New England Water Works Association
1994

We are the victims of an unfortunate necessity.

— J.H. Johnson
selectman of Dana, Massachusetts
1922

the last

I keep thinking about the dog. The one who disappeared just before we heard the news. For a while I figured he was killed by an automobile, then I decided he left us to stay with someone he liked better. But even later, after that, I wondered if he knew. Somehow knew what was coming. And maybe got clear away—you know I raised him, not them—out of the valley to someplace safe.

But he was an old dog even then and not the smartest, if I'm honest. Stuck close to home for protection, more likely, as any simple beast would.

Still I keep thinking about him. If it trapped him in the end. It's so damn unlikely—odds are he was either long dead or long gone by the time they closed the gate—but I keep wondering. I can see him, that dumb old dog, all dirty feet and burrs in his hair, poking around in some forsaken cellar hole that still smelt of horned pout from the summer before, too caught up in his nose to see what was happening. I see him jerk his head up in surprise.

The truth may be that my ma ran him off. And wouldn't ever admit it. Which was peculiar. Because I loved that stupid dog. He was a bad dog but I loved him. I've had a lot of dogs since then; I've worked hard to forget him. They're all just dogs to me now.

I keep thinking about him, though. The last one, maybe. It could be. The last one in the valley.

Part I

What in God's name can we do to get water for the Metropolitan District?

— Leslie Haskins
state representative for Dana and Athol, Massachusetts
1926

(1925)

Last night it snowed, good and hard. First time this winter. Most folks won't make it to church at all. What can you do, says Papa. Not much. It's the Lord who chooses the weather.

There is snow all over the whole white world. Right now I'm looking out my window. It's Sunday and there are no foot tracks but for Cal's, no smoke from the mills, no automobiles or trucks or wagons trying to use the road. The Rabbit has already missed a run. The stock are all in. Early last week the river froze solid over, now you can't tell it from the bank.

The snow is everywhere, everywhere, everywhere. Everything I look at has snow on it. Mama likes to say it covers up our sins but even I know a snowstorm can't change a thing.

2

(1926)

In the first week of December Ma took me to Springfield to do the Christmas shopping. She said I wasn't to tell Papa because she wanted to surprise him—she had some money to spend for once—but we stayed a long time, longer than she meant to, and we barely beat him home. Mrs. Pearson gave us a ride (I love to watch a lady drive!) and we saw Pa's train heading towards the station as we came past Mount Lizzie. Ma said, Do hurry, Charlotte! but Mrs. Pearson only laughed.

Before she picked us up we went to visit at the Hornigs. They used to live in the Plains; all their children are grown now. I had an awful lot of cake. We were on our way out when Mama said, Just a minute and went back through their heavy black door for some reason. It was closer to five and while I waited I walked up to the corner. It wasn't so very cold. It had started to snow a little and the street was very quiet, especially quiet, the whole neighborhood, as if no one really lived there. As if they'd all gone away. It was twilight and I could still see everything—the doorknobs and the mail slots and the fences and hedges and the round metal plate in the sidewalk with SMWD on it, when I cleared it with my foot—but it was all fading fast, everything turning purple and dark, and I could hear the snowflakes falling. The street lamps hadn't been lit.

I looked at this big yellow house on the corner, a nice house with a wide garden, watched it steadily disappear except for the lighted windows, and then I heard a bird's call. It made no sense but it was true. I looked all around. When I finally stepped closer and peeked through the curtains I saw a cage in the parlor. There were two of them there. Canaries or lovebirds, I'm not sure which, but they were singing. On and on. I could hear them through the glass.

3

January 2, 1927

So here's Polly McPhee. Eleven and two-thirds years old. New diary, straight hair, pale eyes, weak smile. Too smart for her own good, too big for her britches. Reads more than she should. Got a wristwatch for Christmas exactly like she asked for, on condition of wearing it only to church until she's thirteen. Wants to have more friends but doesn't know how to do it. Wants to not be called names. Sleeps with a big orange cat older than she is, feeds and brushes the dog. Treats her brother real nice most of the time. Washes her face and says her prayers every night without fail.

I suppose it doesn't matter how I got here. Everybody gets somewhere somehow. Sometimes I'm surprised my parents had me but then sometimes they are too. I know I catch them looking from me to Caleb, both of them, wondering what was the difference. But you can't expect life to give you reasons, Pa tells us whenever he gets a chance. Events happen now and then that make no sense at all.

January 22

Our schoolhouse in the village is almost full up these days. Makes it seem even smaller. We're as jammed as could be.

In a really big school each grade would have its own room. I think that would suit me better. As it is the big ones are mad at me for being caught up with them, the ones my age for being ahead.

I'm not so fond of Miss Thomas. The grownups favor her because she comes from the valley but I'd just as soon we had someone foreign like Miss Miller again, someone from Orange or Pittsfield at least. Miss Thomas is as stirred up as anyone. I see her looking at the clock and I think she's like a woman who means to catch the last train. Wondering if she should take the next-to-last, just to be safe.

January 27

Our town is Greenwich, Massachusetts. Only a name but it's ours. Just say it like the color: *green witch.*

We have lots of ponds and lakes in our town, and river branches running through. Farms and orchards and mills. Make all sorts of things in this valley, most anything you care to have. Not so much anymore but they used to, Ma says. Musical instruments. Panama hats. Shoes, buttons, brushes and brooms. Bricks and whetstones and matches too. Most of the factories are on the lower center branch, down in Enfield or up in North Dana, but Greenwich still has its share. We make good pitchforks in this town, for example, and scythes.

And we grow all kinds of food. Here on our farm there are chickens and cows and maple candy that we make. Vegetables and berries and some honey. Use most of the eggs and milk ourselves but Ma takes a few gallons to the cheese maker now and then and we've been known to trade in the village. Mostly we sell berries and honey, though, and the candy. How much of those things can the four of us eat?

And I suppose I should mention the ice. "Ice capital of America" — that's what they call us. Every winter the strongmen of Greenwich cut it up and ship it out. Some of it goes as far as South America. A funny idea. But as long as they're willing to pay.

5

January 31

I wish Maisie liked me. I'd do anything if she would. I don't know what she has against me. She showed us a pretty new doll this afternoon—she left it hidden in her coat sleeve in the hallway all day—but she wouldn't let me hold it. She let everyone else.

February 11

I don't much mind the chores in winter. Caleb hates them, or claims to; says he can't stand to rise from his soft warm bed and go down to light the stove and then out in the cold and dark to milk the cows and pitch down hay. I can't say I agree. I expect I don't like getting up any more than he does but for a start I keep fresh socks by me while I sleep, under the covers, so they're warm when I put them on. And leave my slippers next the bed—he runs down barefoot to get his shoes. I've told him a million times he ought to dress himself better when he goes out, but he won't. But mostly it's his attitude. Of course there are days when I'd as soon stay in bed, or just have breakfast and go to school, but the trick as I see it is to not mind so much.

So while he grumbles and complains I have a special time. I could do without the cold but I like crossing the yard to the hen-house, just before dawn, to find them all huddled and drowsy. I like reaching under a warm hen to pull out an egg. The way the pump works even during the worst freeze. Because there's less to do in winter I can go a little slower. I especially like when the old moon is failing and rises an hour or two before the sun. I say goodbye to the fading stars. And Mama waiting in the kitchen, breakfast all made, the smells of Pa's coffee and of butter and eggs drifting around in the air. I like walking slowly with my pail towards the window and seeing Ma's backside through it, or the top of the stove if she's not in the way, or Pa's shoulder as he sits down.

7

February 20

They say this is the year. It's hard to believe but that's what they say. Most think it was settled a long time ago, though some still say we have a chance. Mr. Partridge scoffs at that. How do we stand up in Boston today, Mr. McPhee? he asked my daddy last week when we were getting us some nails. How do you think they like us up there on Beacon Hill? After we left my father explained that at the meeting in Enfield he and Mr. Partridge had had words. Mr. Partridge wanted to give up, he told me, and try to work the best deal, but he wasn't ready for that yet. Didn't matter whether there was a real good chance of winning, he said; everyone would feel better if we fought it as long as we could.

There's no question that most folks have come to believe it. It has certainly changed the town. A few families we know of have already left. Businesses closed up. It's a long way off if it happens at all but some people act fast.

I suppose facts are facts. They filed the bill last month and it'll pass, everyone says, just like the one before it. I heard they already bought some land.

March 9

Roy Ralston. What a name. Bad enough they're still sending state boys here. But with a name like that on top of it! I doubt they'll ever let up on him. Not that he doesn't seem able to take it. And I guess this must be better than where he was before.

In only two months I'll be twelve.

March 15

Now I'm reading "Treasure Island" by Robert Louis Stevenson. I got it from the library. Mama saw me with it and started to speak but Pa jumped right in. If she can manage it good for her. It's a boy's book, isn't it? No such thing, Pa said. So I took it out of the room.

8

March 19

Last night we saw a man from the Commission. He was small and harmless-looking but Pa says he's the main engineer. We were coming out of the Inn and he walked right past us on the sidewalk, followed by a whole mob as if he were President or something. That bastard used to fish here, Pa said after they'd gone by. He used to eat our goddamn trout.
Then he apologized for his language. You'd think he'd be more careful. As it is I'm tempted to cross out those words, now that I've written them down.

March 27

One last good snowfall yesterday. We figured it would probably be gone by Tuesday so we all grabbed our sleds and headed out for the hills, just as soon as it slacked off. It looked like the entire south end of town was out there. Lots of older ones too.
It started out pretty cloudy but later on got very clear. I could see the whole valley, getting ready to be spring. And I could see Mount Monadnock, plain as anything, from the top of the hill. The summit was all snow and probably very windy too but I wondered if there was anyone up there, facing south, looking at me.

April 6

Bad dreams last night. Spooky and awful with a pain in my stomach. Had to sleep with my parents. I haven't done that in years but I wasn't going back to our room, Cal or no.
It was dreams of a fan, or a giant hand. And of acres and acres of ice.

April 12

Roy Ralston fell asleep in school today. With these quiet little snores. At first I wanted to laugh but when Miss Thomas noticed I felt bad. She worked him over something awful. She wouldn't do like that if he had parents, that's certain. When he tried to explain

9

she wouldn't let him talk at all, then once she'd made a fool of him and his face was all red she told him to state his excuses. He said he stayed up too late reading and got up early for chores and just didn't sleep enough. She asked And what, pray tell us, were you reading? He said The story you gave us last week about the railroad. She said You were to have finished that already. I did, he said, but I wanted to read it again. And I read kind of slow. My brother's buddy Augie snickered but Miss Thomas paid him no mind. She wasn't near through with Roy.

Master Ralston, she said, real sharp, I don't know what your habits were before you came here to Greenwich from wherever it was, and I don't care why you stayed up late, but from now on you will not sleep in my class. If I catch you again I will wear you out. Do you understand? He nodded and she got pretty upset. You open your mouth and speak to me, Roy, she said. You say yes ma'am. Yes ma'am, I do understand, he said. It won't happen again.

It had better not, said Miss Thomas.

After school I wanted to talk to him but he hurried away. What makes her so hard? All he did was doze off, even I have done that.

April 16

Can't find the dog. I've looked everywhere. My heart is broken. Caleb seems to care for once and has tried to give me comfort. He claims the dog will come back but it's three whole days now and I'm starting to not believe it. He isn't the sort who goes away for long stretches. In fact he comes in every night. He prefers to stay by me.

I know Ma is glad though she pretends not to be. She never liked him for some reason, nor he her. They just never got along. She tells me we'll get another but I really dislike for her to give up on him like that. *And I want my old dog back.*

She has never said a bad word about that dog. Not a one. Just gone on hating him, is all.

I went out looking today. Of course it did me no good. I can't stand to think about what might have happened to him. So I'll assume he's coming back.

April 19

Another school year soon to end. Another year of too much by myself. Today Edna asked me to come to her house and I got real excited until I remembered promising Ma I would help her with the planting. I didn't know what to do. I thought if I didn't she'd never ask me again but I couldn't break my word to my mama that way. And Edna lives in the village, in a big house near the church, and hasn't any chores at all.

At last I asked could I come another time? She said, Well we'll see Polly. If you have better things to do I wouldn't bother you again. I almost started crying but was able to hold it back. You don't understand, I told her, it's my mama. I just have to go home, you must know what that's like. It isn't better, I just have to. She looked a little less mean.

And I so want to see your house, I said. I hear it's just beautiful inside. And everyone knows your mother's so pretty. Well why don't you come over tomorrow instead, she said, you can meet her then and maybe she'll bake us cookies. Then I could smile.

April 22

The dog is gone. There isn't any question. If he were alive and within five miles he would have found his way back. I know he loves me. So he must be dead.

April 27

Ma says they finally decided. The bill was passed and the Governor signed. Pa is out in the yard kicking dirt. Ma says we have to leave our homes, every one of us. It's finally true.

11

"Listen to this! Listen to this!"

"All right then, dearie, read me the rest."

"'So life goes on, tragedy mastered, grief controlled and disciplined, but underneath the calm face lies the aching heart and wounded soul.'"

"You stop now! Just stop it! You're killing me!"

"'Step by step this drama moves towards its close; a pageant of many moods, but one theme—the eternal conflict between the old and the new, the struggle between the needs of the many and the rights of the few, the endless enigma of human existence.'"

"That's her *essay*?"

"A swell one, huh?"

"Her *yearbook* essay?"

"Look right here. See it right here."

"Oh that Maddie! Oh that girl!"

"When I first read it I thought I'd die."

"I'll bet she's so proud of it."

"Mister Chronister thinks she's God."

"He might think I was too if I fed him stuff like that."

"The thing is it's in the 'Echo'. It'll be there forever."

"That's just exactly what she wanted, isn't it?"

"Fran? What's an enigma?"

"Like a riddle."

"Oh."

"Give me the city part again."

"OK. Here we go. 'But a need has arisen, a necessity to satisfy the growing demands of a great city, and this beautiful river, the nestling ponds, the long established homes, the cherished cities of the dead, all that American culture, ideals and civilization cherish and nurture must be laid waste, be uprooted, be destroyed and be utterly removed…'"

"Oh Maddie! You kid! I'll uproot *her*."

"I could never write like this."

"You wouldn't want to, 'retta honey. 'Cities of the dead'!"

"I guess she's all shaken up about it, huh?"

"I guess she is."

"Aren't you?"

"Who, me?"

"Not a little? Not at all?"

"Why? Because we have to go somewhere real? Somewhere with tar on the roads and lights and toilets in the houses and no more stinking pigs and chickens? Fat chance!"

"Still, Fran."

"Still nothing. The sooner the better. And you can tell Mister Chronister I said so."

5

My mother's fingers were long. I will never forget them. She was not a tall woman and grew stocky as she aged but her fingers were elegant, long lovely and slender, the fingers of a queen. No matter how dry and callused, how work-worn they became. They were long and I admired them. I much preferred them to my own.

To watch her play the piano was to see her secret guise. At other times her fingers were the part that didn't match but on the keyboard they ruled and the rest of her faded. Those fingers. Those fingers. My mother the queen. Mama's fingers playing gently, playing sadly in our parlor.

I thought they would be with me forever, those fingers. That's what I honestly believed.

6

July 7, 1927

It's a very strange thing. The more it sinks in—about the project, I mean—the less I'm surprised. As each day goes by I understand a little better that it had to end this way. Once the proposal was made.

It's been my whole life, you know, and sometimes it makes me angry. But I could just as well be angry that I'm not a millionaire with Chinese carpets in my house.

July 18

All these high-horse engineers, with their surveys and their drilling. With their cars and Boston clothes. Always polite to our faces but from a distance you can tell they're having fun.

July 24

Roy Ralston is quite an athlete. He can really play baseball. I was watching some little kids play—Fox and Geese, I think it was, and one of the girls had a hoop—and it looked like such fun I wanted to join in, but of course I'm much too old. So I went looking for something to do.

They were having a game out in Peterson's pasture. When I got there Roy was pitching. He throws hard, very hard. Only the two oldest, Jamie Hancock and Amos Carter, could even get wood on the ball. And Roy can hit too—he whaled it—and he runs like the wind. He wasn't so good at catching but the glove he was using was an old chewed piece of nothing barely holding together. I think he had it tied to his hand with a cord. Must have been a cast-off from a boy who had better; Roy naturally wouldn't have a glove of his own. He probably came to town with just the shirt on his back. If that.

Most of the others refused to like him or be his friend. No matter how good he was. And it's not that he's a state boy—Frankie Duncan was there too and they treated him just fine.

As an example, they were all kidding with each other, calling each other by ballplayers' names. You know, good ones for their own team and poor ones for the other. They were calling Jamie 'Hornsby' and Augie Roberts 'Cobb.' And Caleb 'Handy Andy' when he dropped an easy throw. But Roy was just 'Ralston' or 'he' or 'him' no matter who it was talking. Even after he struck out the side.

It was a beautiful beautiful day. The kind you always think of when it's deep dark cold in winter. They hardly noticed me sitting on the fence in the sun and after a while I got so sleepy I fell right off. They noticed me then. They all laughed but Cal came over to see if I was OK. I told him I was but my ankle hurt lots. I couldn't walk at that moment so I got back on the fence and pretended to like the laughing. To be a good sport.

The game was tied at two when Roy said he was leaving. They all yelled and even cursed but he just said he had chores and walked away. Augie threw a glove at him that hit him in the back but he never even turned.

July 27

Since I'm twelve I made up my mind that I have got to be more helpful. It isn't right that Caleb and Pa and Ma work so hard and I still live like a child. I asked Mama to give me some new chores. She acted surprised (don't know why) and said she would think about it.

This getting older is kind of funny. Sooner or later I'll be grown and there are times when I can plainly see it coming. I stood at the mirror with no clothes on today, when everyone was out. I know my flesh is supposed to change and there it was right on schedule. Maybe even a little early. I hadn't studied it so carefully in a very long time. Don't think I'll ever be buxom like Mama but not a skinny pole like that Estelle either. My breasts (Cal calls them teats) are standing out from my chest and the nipples are all sore. And I'm starting to have a waist.

August 3

Several men here in Greenwich have taken work with the Commission. It's a little surprising. I'm sure some people need the money—since the mills started closing good jobs are getting scarce, and they're not paying too high for farmland—but even so.

Town people don't care so much, Papa says. It's the farmers who love this land; to the mill hands it's just rocks and mud. And they're collecting OK on their houses. Stands to reason they're just as glad.

He talks about it all the time.

Actually folks are all mixed up. Like if you had a hundred diaries they would all say different things. Some seem to be so glad to know for sure, one way or the other, that the actual fact of it doesn't bother them at all. Some seem to think we're being punished. A few are walking around mad. And some others have no real intention of leaving, not even of making plans.

But most of all we're just waiting. What do they say?—sitting on our hands. Years and years to go. That tunnel, for instance, won't even be started until I'm at least fifteen. Who knows when it'll go through, straight from here to West Boylston? I could be married by then. I could be in another state.

When they finally get around to it the intake shaft will be right here in Greenwich, not that far from our farm. A big hole in the land for anyone who comes looking. And they'll take down our

17

house, probably, along with the fences and the trees and every other thing nearby.

Last night in getting off to sleep I tried to imagine diving in and swimming all the way to Coldbrook through the tunnel, my eyes closed in the dark. I got a very little way but then it turned horrible. Dark horrible and endless. I was trapped in all that water and I couldn't make it back.

August 11

Saw Edna at the pond today. She waved at me in a friendly way, then left the boys she was talking to and walked over to say hello. I admit it made me nervous. They all watched me as she came. But when she got real close she said for goodness sake, Polly, can't you do better than that dress? Don't you want to look pretty? She was wearing a fancy bathing outfit with bows on it but I don't think she had any plans to go in the water. She's already thirteen but in my view she's kind of ahead of herself. If you think well of a particular boy it's one thing but who wants them crowding all around you like that? Especially the older ones. They just get out of hand and push you over into the hay or the snow, and then run. I know that makes Maisie giggle but I don't believe I'd like it. I don't even want to try.

Where's your bathing suit? asked Edna.

At home, I said. Hanging up on a hook.

She looked at me as if I'd spilt milk on my shoes.

But then she asked me to come over in the evening and work with her and her sister and Maisie, cutting up the fruit and melons for her mother's big social tomorrow. I couldn't help but say yes.

She had one of those paper fans they were giving out at the store up in Dana last month. With the fancy lady on it. In the big drooping hat. I never got one because I heard about them late. Anyway you had to buy Coca-Colas to get it and I have better things to do with my nickels. But it's a really nice fan. Edna kept waving it back and forth but not enough to stir a breeze. Just to show me.

18

August 20

Hot. Hot hot hot. You'd think it'd be cooling off by now. Worked in the garden this morning—like to faint from the sun— then spent the afternoon at the pond with all the other kids, but before going home I went walking in the woods. Needed to get away from that sun, I suppose. Just for a little while. You can't feel as if you're dying in the desert like some Arab when you're under the maples and pines.

As I walked the path I pictured a very, very cold place—so white, so still that it was like frosted glass. The South Pole, I thought. Or the North Pole. Or the South. But somewhere cold, somewhere icy. Far away from this sun furnace. Somewhere other than this town.

Then I found an old leg bone. From an animal, I guess. I wonder how long it was there.

August 29

Disputed with my ma about the dog yesterday. In the beginning it was just chatting. I asked her where she thought he was and she said she hoped he was with some nice people. I asked if she thought he was dead and she pretended to be annoyed but then allowed it might be so. I asked if she sent him away and then she was angry. What put a thought like that into your head, she said, I don't honestly know. Where do you come up with these ideas? If not one thing it's another. And so on in that way, with her voice all raised and tight. As if it was the most terrible thing in the world for me to tell her my mind. As if she didn't already suspect me of thinking it.

I know you didn't like him, so I was wondering, I said. Polly, she shouted—and I want to put this down just in our own exact words—that is the silliest and most rude of all the silly rude things you've ever said to me. I haven't raised my hand to you in years but I'm tempted to do it now. Go ahead, I told her. I will keep silent from this day on.

19

She sat down in a chair then, and put her head on her hand. It was all of a sudden quiet. I felt awful for what I said.

Later on—I was feeding some scraps to the cat—I heard her playing the piano. Generally she waits until evening but this time she held up her chores. First she played a song I didn't know—it sounded like an old one, maybe one they danced to—and then she played one of her favorites, called a sonata I think, that she plays very seldom. It was so beautiful, even on our lousy old piano. Just beautiful. It made me want to go in to her and tell her how sorry I was, simply throw myself at her feet. After she finished she sat there for a long time, a very long time, and then I heard the piano bench creaking as she got up and went back to the kitchen to start the washing again.

September 6

First day of school. I'm so glad to have lessons. All the other kids complained but that was just talk, I think. Summer gets sort of worn out by its end.

Roy Ralston was there. I was so happy to see him. I don't think we'd laid eyes for a whole solid month—they must have kept him working real hard on the farm, we've had a lot to do ourselves—and when he came in through the door I understood I'd been fearful. That he was gone, who knows where. Sent to another town, maybe. Or maybe back with his mama who turned out not to be dead. It was bad of me to be so glad he was still in Greenwich, because I don't believe he likes his place very much and if he weren't an orphan after all that would be wonderful news, but I was glad anyway. I waved hello, just a little with my fingers, but I don't think he saw. He hitched his pants up and sat down without looking. His shirt was old and kind of thin.

I can tell Roy is smart. Not so good at school but smart. Miss Thomas was lecturing to a few of us in her usual way, about long division, and the thing she was explaining she didn't need to explain. Even Maisie had seen it already. I really wanted to get started but I held myself back, kept my hand from my pencil, so as

20

not to make her angry. I looked over at Roy and this time he did see me. I could tell he was thinking the same.

September 11

Caleb is getting a little strange. Harder to talk to. He still takes good care of me and he's usually polite but when I go up to him, sometimes, he doesn't seem to really see me. I have to speak to get his attention and even then he might not answer. Only every so often but it makes me feel bad.

It isn't just me. It happens with Ma and Pa too. Like he's watching something different, something moving far away.

September 15

After school Roy waited for me. I'm almost certain he did. He was tying his shoe as I came up behind him and then he stood up so fast he almost knocked me on my bottom.

Hi Polly, he said.

My real name's Rebecca, I said. Those were the first words from my mouth, I can't think why. Probably Ma and Pa and Caleb are the only ones who know.

You want to be called that? he asked.

No one asks me what I want.

Polly's fine, I told him. Is Roy OK for you? It's the only name I got, he said, it had better be. Unless you want to call me Mister. We both laughed at that.

The wind had picked up and it was a tiny bit chilly but we were walking very slowly towards the corner. I was dizzy and wanted to run. Where have you been? I asked him. Working hard? I haven't seen you at the pond or playing ball for a long time. And you weren't at the Dana band concert last week.

Yeah, working hard. They run me ragged. Want to get their money's worth, I guess, especially in summer.

Doing what?

Mostly stomping on the silage, he said. Along with my regular chores. They got a silage mill on wheels. Steam powered. Draw it around with a horse. They run the corn through and when it comes out it has to be stomped down in the silo. Or the wagon. They set me doing that a lot.

Sounds hard, I said.

And risky. You can drown in the corn. Fall under a wheel if you're not careful. Nearly lost a leg last month.

Other than that do they treat you OK? He looked at me like I was silly.

Miss Thomas, you shouldn't be bothered about Miss Thomas, I told him. You shouldn't mind it when she's strict. Just that kind of teacher I guess. But he kept looking at me.

No they don't, he said. They make me eat by myself, in the kitchen.

They do? I wonder why. Most state boys are just like family.

But not this one, said Roy. And then walked quickly on ahead.

September 24

A few of the farms have started making their cider. You can smell it. Later on it'll be everywhere but today it came to my nose as I was cutting across the Atkinsons' wood lot. Guess they have some early fruit they have to take care of.

Sometimes I think this should be called the cider valley. Everyone keeps a barrel or two. Drink it fresh, drink it hard, freeze it off and make jack brandy. Or leave it go to vinegar. And feed the pulp to the pigs. Papa says apples are nature's gift to America; in old times they couldn't have got by without them. When he talks that way Mama gets a look on her that I have never figured out.

Last winter Caleb and Daniel snuck into Daniel's daddy's barn and took the plug out of a barrel of hard cider, then stuck a piece of macaroni in and sucked a bunch out between them. Caleb was looking very queasy when he got home. In fact I had to cover for him, tell Ma he was sick to his stomach from slipping on some ice on the slope and having the wind knocked out of him, keep her occupied and away so she wouldn't smell his breath before he had a chance to wash his mouth out with soap. I even fed the cows for him. That's how come I know what happened. I made him tell me, as well as give me three sticks of chewing gum and a picture of Valentino. That was the price of my silence. And of my not laughing when Mama pulled his chair out for him, at supper time, and asked if he was all right.

October 9

Indian summer, it's called. And I can't imagine why. I'm sure they liked a warm October but of course so do we.

In the orchard this morning I was looking for drops and a breeze blew soft and warm. *Indian summer*, I thought. I straightened up slowly and then took off my jacket, stretched out my arms. The breeze flowed all around and brought faraway places. Greece and China. Timbuktu. Places I will never see. The leaves above me rustled and I wondered where it came from. The soft breeze, I mean. Where it first started out.

There were Indians here once and they felt those breezes too. Waited for them every year. Some Nipmuc girl, same as me, was standing in that spot with her arms held out wide about a thousand years ago. Stopped in what she was doing. Surprised the air was so warm. Wondering about the wind, what she would have that night for supper, when she would see the first snow. And before her were the trees and the rabbits and deer, and the chipmunks, and the otters in the east branch. Forever and ever. All of them here before we came.

But all those Nipmuc are gone and soon the rest of us too. Gone, long gone. The orchard, the henhouse, the pasture long gone. The otters and the chipmunks and the maples. Once it's done we're long gone. Just the fishes and the turtles where Rebecca used to be.

7

"Let's get out."

"I don't think so."

"Why not?"

"Because your family has been here for five generations?"

"Does anyone care?"

"I do. Me. You too I'd hope. But me."

"And the rest of us?"

"The children are happy here."

"What about their futures, David? And ours?"

"What about their home?"

"A home with no future."

"But we've been making a go of it, damn it."

"Only because of your salary."

"I'm the one rides that train to Ludlow every day, Sarah. It's no skin off your nose."

"Working yourself to death."

"You make it sound like something bad."

"I admire all your effort. I really do. But now it's pointless."

"I hate your saying that."

"That's fine. This is silly. It doesn't matter anymore. They're taking our land, so let's get out now."

"It'll be years yet. We can enjoy this place for a long time to come."

"We'll find somewhere else to enjoy."

"Like my mother's house in Lawrence?"

"I mean another farm. A better one."

"I want this one."

"It isn't just the reservoir, David. I've felt it on and off since we came. My grandfather used to talk about the good years, I remember. When the valley was full and lively. But that was a long time ago. And it's a lost cause now, darling. There's really nothing left to take."

"So you're ready to just lie down?"

"David. I'm an Armstrong. I'll survive no matter what."

"An Armstrong, yes. Exactly. This is your own blessed farm you want to give away so easily."

"That's just not true. It was both of ours. But as of last April it isn't anybody's. In fact it doesn't exist at all."

"Is that you, children? Go back to bed."

8

(1923)

My daddy took us for boat rides. For rides out on the pond. He made us sit in the middle and pledge never to stand. His friend Larry had a rowboat and lived close to the shore and Papa borrowed it from him. Took us out on summer evenings while the sun was still bright. First he ordered Shove us off! and Cal heaved hard against the bank. And then we coasted on the water. Sometimes Papa pushed too with his oar on the bottom, to move us faster toward the center. Other times he just waited. But as soon as he could, as soon as we were deep enough, he always started in to row.

9

December 29, 1927

If I were a boy I'd choose to work as a milkman. It seems a fine job—bring people what they need, say hello to your friends, plus a lot of time to think. A mix of company and quiet. Along with being out of doors. And there's this: a milkman harms no one in the course of his employment.

Quite a few men here have work like that. The meat man and onion man, for example. And the blacksmith. Even old Mr. Brooks the photographer. Out and about. It seems a shame that women don't get to do likewise.

January 3, 1928

Papa should have been a preacher. He cares so much, and he sure can talk. New Year's Day was a Sunday and some people came over after church for a small party, I guess you might call it, to wish each other the best. They drank the new year in with cider (Pa got out a fresh jug) and ate some cakes Mama made. There were the Marlowes and the Atkinsons and Mrs. Schuble and the Webbs. Quite a crowd for our house.

When Mr. Webb brought up the project they all got sort of quiet—it took the steam out of the new year's wishes, really—but then my father took over. He was very persuasive. Told them not to worry, it was just sticks and dirt after all, what they cared most for wouldn't be flooded. Your loved ones, your faith and your principles, he said. Your good names. Said houses were houses and crops were crops, those things could be replaced, but here we all had a golden opportunity to understand what really mattered. What no earthly authority could claim. Mattered to whom? asked Mrs. Schuble. Not to those people in Boston. To God, he said. To yourself. The things that make a happy life.

Look, he said, I'm not saying we aren't losing. You all know I fought this thing as long as anybody. I went all the way to the state house two years ago to testify, you remember that. I believe to my soul it's a crime. But the Lord won't reward bitterness. He won't reward anger. What's done is done and now it's up to us to decide what kind of 1928 to have. And '29 and '30 too.

Know what you're going to do yet, McPhee? asked Mr. Webb from the corner. He didn't mean any harm.

My folks looked at each other. I'm going to live and work and farm and take care of my family, Randolph, said Pa, tend to my business every day. The rest will come to us in time.

January 14

We had a snowball fight today. Me and Roy against Cal. My brother started it himself, he hit me right in the back when I wasn't even looking but he got more than he could handle. For a while we were all laughing but Roy can throw so well, you know, if it's snowballs or baseballs or rocks or potatoes, and I'm not too bad myself. It wasn't near fair to Cal and every time he went to pack another, one of us would hit him or at least come pretty close. Roy even got him in the side of the head. It didn't take too much of that before Caleb was good and mad. You kids! You kids! You stop it now! he shouted, his hair all wet and his face all red. It struck me as sort of funny but I managed not to laugh.

Hey Cal, Roy said then, you want to use my double rip?

Sledding is for kids, said my brother.

Not if you find yourself a fast enough hill, it ain't. Or one with a whole lot of stumps and boulders.

Caleb came over. You haven't got any double rip, state boy, he said.

Do too, said Roy. Come look here. He led us round the sugar shed and there it was by a tree. A nice one too. Old but nice. Good sized, big enough even for a big boy like Caleb. Fresh rope on the front.

Where'd you get it? asked Caleb.

Traded for it.

Traded what?

Never mind, said Roy, it ain't none of your business but you want to use it or not?

My brother looked him in the eye. Sure, Ralston, he said. He lifted it up. I'll bring it back here when I'm done and you can come and get it later.

OK, said Roy.

I won't run it into no stump or boulder, though.

It's fine with me if you do.

After Caleb had gone I asked Roy where he got it.

I found it around the farm, he told me. What of it? No one was using it far as I could tell.

Later on we watched them cut ice on Greenwich Lake. It was peaceful. I explained about the weather and how iffy it can get. They might have spent close to forever laying out a big field and then a turn in the temperature can wipe it all away. Have to work like crazy to get it cut.

We talked about the prices they probably pay in southern countries. Here it's just a cent a cake. But after they've freighted it to Boston and loaded it onto a ship and sailed it somewhere hot it must be awfully dear. Roy said maybe a dollar a cake and I said that sounded high but maybe. Whatever it is, he said, must be only rich folks who can buy it. The sheiks and rajahs and like that. That must be so, I agreed. I guess it's something that all the swells do, he said. Invite the whole town over for the holiday feast and serve them big cold drinks with ice. Just to show how much money you got.

January 19

That Maisie. What a chatterbox. Has words to say on every subject. Usually the same as the ones she said a minute ago, just in a slightly different order.

Today she was going on at lunch about their trip to New Haven over Christmas and some restaurant they ate at. I simply *loved* it, she said. Over and over. I had to work not to laugh.

But later on I thought, well what *does* it mean, anyway? We all of us use it all the time, and in so many different ways. Love Jesus, love your parents, love your country, love chocolate candy. Love love love. There are times when I love Caleb, times when I love a doll or a book, times when I love a stone or stick of wood I find lying by the roadside on the way back from school. Times I don't even love my own mother. Cal loves Babe Ruth, my pa loves his friend Hank who drinks all that whisky, a dog loves scraps from the table, Louise down the road is in love they say although no one has seen the boy.

January 28

We made popcorn last night. It was really very jolly. Cal insisted on being in charge and for once Pa was in a good mood and told him to go right ahead. It turned out he had picked up the knack, as Ma put it. Each batch came out so nicely, not burned, all ready for the salt and the butter. It was delicious. And it seemed to make my brother happy.

While we ate it with milk Mama played the piano. She played a bunch of songs Pa asked for and even blushed when he mentioned one. She didn't want to play it at all but he made her and in the end they sang it together, him standing there behind her with his hand on her shoulder. She kept glancing back at him. She was so pretty in the gas light. Caleb grinned at me and winked but I felt proud.

January 31

Mabel Hutchins died of pneumonia yesterday. A week ago she wasn't even sick. Now her parents are all bent over and Anna May's an only child and Bobby Bolt will have to marry someone else. As soon as the news got round they all went rushing over there with dishes of food. For all the good it did them.

February 7

I love Mount Zion. It never changes. No matter what the time of year it's just as long, just as rounded, sitting quiet there and waiting while the wide world goes on by. With the village at its feet. Today it's pure white and later brown and then green but always ripe to be enjoyed. A place we're fortunate to have.

I heard a story once, though. About an ox killed by lightning. Right there on the hillside. I have never seen the spot but they say it was beneath a big old broken chestnut tree.

Summer people like Mount Zion. Like to go up there for picnics. You can get pretty far from the road, if you're willing to climb.

February 11

We heard they started on the first tunnel. From the Ware to the Wachusett. Heard it at the Inn today, in the barbershop. Cold out and very windy—a lot of men were there, keeping warm by the stove. There was barely room for us. I don't see how the crews can work a bit in this weather but I suppose if they waited they wouldn't ever get it dug.

Someone's bound to get hurt doing that said Mr. Murphy. Dynamite and tons of rock. Bound to get killed sooner or later, said someone else. Yes and that makes it serious now said Mr. Murphy. No turning back at all. Soon as one of them falls or is buried in stone the Devil himself couldn't stop it. It'll be written out in blood.

Once the contracts were written out that was enough, said Papa. Black ink was all they needed. And the promise of cash.

31

That's so, said Mr. Murphy, but that old tunnel is still the beginning of the end, don't you think?

10

"I think we'd better."

"I'm not so sure."

"We've got food enough and plenty of space. And we could certainly use the cash."

"Still you're do-gooding aren't you?"

"I'd call it common decency but all right, guilty as charged."

"It isn't as though we need him."

"I think we do. Or will. Caleb is almost sixteen, he'll have other interests soon. We can't keep on tying up all his spare time. And you and I are getting older."

"I'm only thirty-eight, you know."

"With the boy here to help Polly won't have to work so hard."

"Work hasn't hurt her."

"It hasn't, dear, but she's growing up too. She's a young woman, not a farmhand."

"I've noticed."

"And she thinks so well of him, David. Says he's an awfully nice boy."

"That's for us to decide."

//

I remember one cold day when I was small. Maybe seven. Papa came home like he never had before. Sarah you won't believe it, he told my mama. They posted a map. Put on your coat and let's go down to Enfield.

I remember everyone standing and staring. I got just the one good look before the grownups crowded us out. Maybe they simply didn't want us to see. Or thought we couldn't understand it, I suppose, but I did—there were houses under all that blue.

12

Mama told me today that when Papa first came here he knew nothing about farming. Not a single blessed thing. That surprised me because he's an expert by now or anyway acts like one. But Mama said no, he was a city boy who never grew a plant or tended an animal other than a dog or cat until the day he set foot on our place. It was quite a job, she said, to get him learning. You must have done it right, I told her. You'd never know it of him now.

Being married is like that, Polly, she said, drying off some dishes while I worked the butter churn. You have to make up for what's missing. You have to pull each other's slack without allowing that you are. Everyone else in the world is to think that your husband doesn't need you, that he could do it all alone, but you always know better.

I don't even remember what started her on the subject. As far as I'm aware she grabbed it out of the blue.

Didn't he know anything? I asked. He's real smart, isn't he? You'd think he'd have picked something up on the way.

Nothing at all, dear child, she said. Not a thing. The first March we were here, before Caleb was born, I sent him out to tap the maples. I took him over to the shed and showed him all the equipment, explained just what to do, and went back to the kitchen. Ten minutes later he was knocking on my door.

What for? I asked.

35

He wanted to know which were the maples, she said. I had to show him that too.

April 19

A fairly nice spring so far. Not too cold. Things are mostly wet enough but we've also seen blue sky.

April 25

There was an incident today. One that upset me very badly. My hands are still trembling—please forgive the poor writing—and my head and stomach hurt. It was typical, I suppose, or at the worst just plain stupid, the kind of thing boys always do, but even so it simply shook me.

I guess it was just another scuffle. I'm making something out of nothing, as my mother often says. Maybe no one else thought so very much of it. Maybe not even Roy. I'm not too worried about him, really, though it makes me good and nervous that he can't settle in. But he'll be fine. It's what his troubles do to me that makes me panic for the future.

It happened after school. Everyone was on edge on account of a rainstorm that never arrived. I was off a ways with Maisie—we were watching some men who were painting the church—when we heard the angry words. We rushed back to the yard to find Roy and Harry Smith practically shouting at each other. They were standing in the center of a circle of boys and Harry's face was all red. Roy was talking really loud. Maisie looked at me as if something wonderful was happening.

Ain't my fault you never been out of the sticks, Smith, said Roy as we got close to the circle. You wouldn't know. But your ignorance ain't my problem.

Harry took a deep breath. You're a liar, he said. I don't think you ever been anywhere but whatever town you come from.

What would you know, said Roy.

Whatever town your ex-house was in that your mama kicked you out of, I mean.

Of course Roy got real mad. I swear he grew an inch just then.

By that time all the girls were crowding around too. The whole school was crowding around.

Why don't you just fight me then, said Roy. You rotten son of a bitch.

Hey Ralston, said Jimmy, sounding mild compared to them, you know he's got a bum leg. He can't fight no one. You know that.

He ought to fight me, said Roy. Say a thing like that. And if he can't fight he ought not to say it.

They watched each other for a few seconds. The whole mob of kids was as quiet as anything. I waited for Miss Thomas's high straining voice to come calling and break it up.

He ought to fight me, said Roy.

Say whatever I want, said Harry Smith.

Then fight me, said Roy.

Dollar a day, said Harry. That's what you are, state boy. Got no mama, no home. Just a dollar a day.

So Roy reached out and shoved his shoulder.

That did it. Harry stumbled—he really does have a bad leg, he had polio, you can see it when he walks and he can't play ball—and one of the others caught him. Roy should not have done that. In a second they were all shouting and he just closed his eyes. They were shouting different things but then it all turned the same. Dollar a day! Dollar a day! Separate at first and then together. Dollar a day! Dollar a day! Don't cry now, I thought, don't cry Roy. If you cry now you'll have to go far away from here. But he's much tougher than that. He just stood there with his eyes closed. In the middle of that circle. The boys were all yelling it, every single one—Dollar a *day*! Dollar a *day*! like at a basketball game—and a lot of the girls were smiling. I wanted badly to run but I knew how wrong that would be. I wasn't brave enough to stop it, so I just stood.

I wondered again about Miss Thomas. I turned around and you know something? There she was. In the window. Just watching.

Harry pushed himself off the boy behind him and punched Roy in the chest. It was a pretty good punch and everyone shut up then, waiting for the fight. He hauled his arm back, swaying a little on his feet, and punched Roy again in just the same place. It must have hurt a lot—nothing wrong with Harry's arms—but Roy didn't hit back. In fact he didn't react at all, didn't even open his eyes. He just stood there like a tree.

Hey! I'm fighting you, said Harry. Just like you said you wanted, huh? Hey! Dollar a day!

Roy opened his eyes. Yeah, I guess that's what I am, he said.

Then he pushed through the circle and went over to where his books were, picked them up and walked away.

The whole crowd of them watched him go. I thought for sure Harry would say something else, or another boy, or even that one of them would stand in his way. He turned the corner and was gone.

The thing is I suspect he does know very well. What it is that makes them hate him. Just like he knew what would come of pushing Harry. And it did.

May 6

Prescott's going. I don't mean just the people; I mean the whole entire town. I heard they filed a bill to turn it over to the Commission. To give up running their own affairs. I can understand why; Prescott was always half empty and now they're down to so few they just can't manage, I suppose.

Still I wish they'd keep trying. At least another year or two.

It's only temporary, Polly, said my pa when I complained. Before you know it there'll be no more decisions to make.

May 16

In a year I'll be in high school. I still have eighth grade in the village but then it's off to Belchertown. Cal is already there, been there nearly two years. We'll spend just the one together, with him a senior. I suppose it will embarrass him to see his little sister.

Get there on Route 21. A full twelve miles on the bus. They built a whole new school just a few years ago for the sake of us pupils here in Greenwich and Enfield, at least partly. Kids were going all the way to Athol on the Rabbit, leaving early and getting back late and still missing some of the day. So they switched us to Belchertown.

May 26

My birthday. I'm thirteen. Somehow I'm not so excited. I'm writing this early, before school, because the girls are coming over for a party today and Mama made a pretty cake. Probably by then I'll be happy. Right now I'm still waking up.

I almost forgot: I'll put my wristwatch on now. That's what they promised when I got it. It's one of my thirteenth birthday gifts—being able to use it all the time, I mean. It's not as special anymore as it might be, I've been wearing it every Sunday for a year and a half, but the point I suppose is that they trust me now to take care of it.

It can't have cost them much money; it's just a very basic watch. But it does keep good time.

June 1

Spoke to Roy about high school today. Seems like I have it on my mind. Roy is a year and a grade beyond me so I asked if he felt ready. For what? For Belchertown, I said. I'll miss having you here but I think you'll enjoy it.

We were sitting and holding hands, watching the Rabbit Run steam through the valley. Or waiting for it anyway. The 3:57 was late. It's fun to get up on Parker or Curtis Hill and watch the train

39

go by. Especially on a bright warm and breezy spring day. I mean it shouldn't be fun, we've all seen it a thousand times, but it is. Even if it's just the same old B&A it's heading out of the valley. If you wanted to travel all the way to San Francisco, to get on a boat to go to China or Japan, you'd take the Rabbit to Springfield first.

You know where I wish I could have been? he asked me. All this time? He had a peculiar expression. That school that moved to Marlboro last year. You know? The one the lady runs.

The Hillside School?

That's the one.

But they're all orphans there, I said.

I guess they are, he replied. And then took his hand away.

But why wasn't he with Mrs. Drinkwater? I wondered. Most of the state boys have parents who can't keep them. So why a state boy instead of landing up there?

No more school for me, he said. You'll tell me all about Belchertown.

You've got to go to high school, I said. You'll never better yourself otherwise.

Polly, don't forget who I am. No one cares if I'm better. They want a full day's work is all.

Just then the Rabbit's engine—the Whistler, they call it— finally chugged into view up the track, coming round Mount Zion and pulling through Morgan's Crossing.

Dollar a day. That's all I am.

That's not all, I said.

And I don't blame them, said Roy. Why should the taxpayers pay just so I can go to school?

June 4

I keep thinking about this short story I read. In an old magazine. Someone left it in the parlor of the Inn, in that rickety little letter-writing table, and I read it straight through while Pa was waiting for a haircut. I wanted to take it home but didn't see how I could. It wasn't a children's magazine.

I never read anything like it. Not so long but it was simply filled with sadness. Sadness and a sort of mourning you can't really feel, can't give in to, because no one has died. A man does die, in the end, but the mourning starts before. When he gets sick. And someone else gets divorced, and there's a little boy involved—oh, it was so difficult. I don't know why I kept on.

That mourning—it isn't just the sick man and his wife, or the failed marriage. It's a lot more than that. It's in the writing. In the story. I don't see how you could write it without being sad yourself. A genius, maybe, but very sad. I'm not sure why you'd want to.

There are two parts I think I will remember forever. When the man finally does die, at last, in the dark of a night in May, and "the scent of the syringa hung upon the window-sill." That's one. If I tried to I couldn't forget. "The scent of the syringa." And the other is at the end: "The gathered kindness in their eyes."

I had to look up a word so I could understand the title. "The Lees of Happiness" it's called—and it turns out "lees" is "dregs." Something that settles out of wine. So the lees is the part you try to avoid, but it's always there waiting. I think that's what he meant.

June 7

Roy is coming to our farm! I can barely believe it. At times I think I'm going to faint. I had to try hard as anything not to show Ma how I felt and even so I nearly jumped into her arms.

Why that's wonderful! I said. Oh, you'll like him so much. But what for?

The man he'd been staying with didn't need the help any longer, she explained, was on the verge of sending Roy back to Boston when she and Pa heard of it and went to see him. So they made an agreement that Roy would come to us instead.

But what for? I asked again. We don't really need him either.

She sat down then and took my hands. I prayed she wouldn't notice the speed of my heartbeats. I think we do, Polly, she said.

41

It's time for you to stop working so hard. It's time for all of us to stop working so hard. Roy can pick up a lot of the load.

I nodded, though I didn't exactly follow.

And the fact is he needs a home, she said. He's simply got to have one. Somebody has to provide.

Can he go on to high school? If he gets his chores done?

Of course, she said. Of course he can if he wants to. What makes you bring that up?

Some state boys go right to work, is all.

I don't want you using that term, Polly. You'll embarrass him. He's a member of our family now.

When I grabbed her neck and kissed her she giggled out loud.

He's going to like it here, I said.

Of course I rushed right out to find him. Which wasn't easy. At last I spotted him in the village, waiting for something outside the mill. Can you believe it when I tell you that he didn't even know? He almost fainted himself! We almost fainted together.

Do you mean it, Polly? he asked me. Do you really honestly mean it?

How come he doesn't want you at the other place? I asked.

Why do you bring that up, he said. Can't you just be glad I'm coming?

Roy Ralston, I'm as glad as I could possibly be about anything in the whole wide world, I told him, up to and including Mr. Charles Lindbergh landing here beside me this instant and taking us up for a ride. And you know it. It was just an innocent question and I really want the answer. Now what happened?

I hit him, said Roy.

My hand went to my mouth.

I'll explain it some time when you're old enough, Polly, he said. I don't feel like telling you the whole story now.

It hurt to see his frown.

Aren't *you* glad you're coming? I asked.

He looked at me.

You can go to high school after all, I said. You can stay in school, Roy. My mama told me you could.

June 15

A stranger's car stopped on the road. License numbers in the valley all come from one sequence so we can tell if an auto is local. This was a pretty green coupé and it stopped just up the road as we were skipping the rope. A very slight rain was falling but we'd decided to stay outside. I was turning one end, wishing Jeannie would miss already so I could take a quick peek at the arrowhead I'd found—she's very good for her age—when I heard it slowing down. I mean the change in the sound. When you live in this place you get used to the sounds of motors and you know right away when they slow or drive on.

We all looked over together. Jeannie missed her step of course. Whoever was driving sat and stared back through the windshield—we couldn't hardly see them, because of the way the light was and anyway it was too far—as we watched them watching us. After a little while of that they reversed a few feet, then turned across the road and went back the other way.

Kidnappers, said Edna.

Oh Edna, said Jeannie.

Kidnappers, said Edna. Too many of us is all. Good thing it wasn't just one. She'd be rolled in a blanket by now.

You read too much trash, said Jeannie.

That's all right, said Edna. Wait until you see it in the papers, won't you? You'll know what I mean then. And be glad we were with you.

Stop scaring her, Edna, I said. I had my hand in my pocket, feeling the arrowhead. The sharp edges. It started raining a little harder.

I suppose *you're* not scared Polly.

You know who it was? I said. An engineer. Wanted to do some surveying or something but figured he'd come back when there was no one else around.

Why would they care? said Jeannie. Why would they care who was here?

Just awkward, I said. Wouldn't you be? Or maybe it's a secret. He'll be back at five a.m.

Very soon after that I began to figure out why I keep thinking about Belchertown. I'm getting older now. Old. In a way it's all at once. Roy is coming next month and he makes me feel grown up. And the way Caleb talks to me. My father too. I feel done with these childish games. Jump rope and hopscotch. Making wreaths with the other Girl Scouts. All those things are simply girlish to me now.

It's not just the way I'm treated. It's something starting from my middle. Something reaching out and pulling me along.

June 23

I'm to have my own room. Roy and Caleb will share. I'll miss lights-out time with Caleb but only a little. This is long overdue.

June 26

Prescott is gone. They had their meeting yesterday and turned the whole town over—gave the keys to the Commission. After a hundred and six years.

I find it makes me fairly sad but things'll get even sadder, I imagine, so I'll just put this from my mind.

13

This old lady spoke to me early that summer. On the sidewalk, down in the Plains. Didn't know her—said she knew me. Said she was Martha's grand-aunt and had seen me around. I asked after Martha but she said would I mind helping her with her packages? She was old and her bags were heavy. I had nothing else to do. She lived close to the village and we got there soon enough though of course she was pretty damn slow.

When we went into the hall she said to drop the bags there and go out on the porch and she would get me some lemonade and a brownie she baked. I said No thank you ma'am but she said you can forget your nice manners, young man, I know you really want a snack. You just sit down I'll go and get it. So I waited on her glider, looking over her straggly rose bushes and the little statues by the steps, until she came back with a tray. She had a lemonade for herself too. I took my glass and my plate and kept them in my lap.

Oh my, she said after we had sat there a long time. Seemed long to me anyway. Oh my, oh my. This is hard for you children.

What is, ma'am? I asked her.

All this talk about the project. It doesn't matter much to me, I'll be gone by the time it comes to anything, but you must be very troubled.

I suppose so ma'am, I said.

She looked at my face then. I'm sorry, she said, I see you're younger than I thought. Don't you pay me any mind. You just eat your brownie boy.

I always mind my elders, ma'am.

After that we sat for another while. The lemonade was good—I had been thirsty from the heat. Had nowhere else to go. Her clothing was all black or white, every bit of it. Not a single speck of color. I watched her stare into the day as if the lord struck her blind.

When she was my age, she told me, there was a rising of the river in her town in Vermont. A big spring flood. Her mother had been sick and finally gone to the hospital and the day after they took her the river overflowed and flooded their house and she and her father and little sisters had to move up the hill to stay with friends. While they were there her mother died. In the hospital. Her first time back in her own front parlor was for the funeral. There were water marks on the walls, she remembered, marks way above her head, and a big old beat-up coal stove they'd dragged in to dry things out.

Her voice was slow and strange—kind of hollow—while she told me. She looked at me when she was done. I am so sorry, she said again. Now I'm sure I've upset you. Please don't mind me, young man. I can't help it. I'm just too old.

You left your brownie, she called out but I kept going.

I don't know what happened to her. Passed on soon after I expect. As she said she would.

MONTHLY PROGRESS – REAL ESTATE ACQUIRED FOR THE SWIFT RIVER RESERVOIR

COMMONWEALTH OF MASSACHUSETTS
METR. DISTR. WATER SUPPLY COMMISSION

DATE	TOTAL APPLICATIONS LISTED (Acres)	LISTED BUT NOT REQUIRED (Acres)	PLACED UNDER OPTION (Acres)	TITLE VESTED IN COMMONWEALTH (Acres)
December 1926	1,629	174	586	16
January 1927	1,704	1	876	1,007
February	1,597	0	204	728
March	4,441	57	1,103	493
April	2,772	90	2,088	563
May	2,373	217	1,591	513
June	3,948	151	974	830
July	1,747	174	1,647	1,337
August	2,490	347	1,325	1,765
September	3,847	502	1,675	2,045
October	2,221	330	1,856	873
November	825	240	1,444	700
Total For Year Ending Nov.30,1927	29,594	2,283	15,369	10,890
Total to Nov.30,1926	2,608	185	216	
Total to Nov.30,1927	32,202	2,468	15,585	10,890

Acreage is based upon estimates obtained from deeds or other information and not from surveys.

from the MDWSC annual report, 1927

R.C. Binstock

Part II

Yet this section, almost midway between Boston Harbor and the New York border, is more wild and rugged than the average urbanite supposes any Massachusetts territory can be. Motor cars which easily cover any roadway in the White Mountains must exert themselves to conquer the back roads in the Swift River country. A traveler might assume the neighborhood to be abandoned, so wilderness-like does it appear.

— F. Lauriston Bullard
"Reservoir to Cover 3 Bay State Towns"
New York Times
July 31, 1927

14

"No they don't."
"Yes they do."
"Not really."
"Even yours, smarty pants. I read about it in a book."
"I thought you heard it from your cousin."
"Uh-huh. First she told me then she showed me. Her brother brought it home from college."
"I can't believe it."
"You'd best start trying."
"Don't think I want to."
"Didn't you know about any of this?"
"I knew you had to do something."
"But you didn't know what."
"No I didn't."
"Well now you do."

15

July 1, 1928

I want to keep this diary better. I've been studying all the rules. I want to be a good writer and it's important that I make this as proper as I can.

It's also important to read a lot. I have done that right along but now I've got to keep it up. It's harder than you might think because I'm only thirteen and a girl and it bothers some people, the way I like books.

Maybe at the high school I'll have a teacher I can show this to. For help with writing. I can't wait.

July 10

Prescott people are moving over. I try to make them feel welcome. They generally take the empty houses, the ones owned by the government. The Commission rents out all the property it's bought, to the workers or to visitors or to anyone who wants it. Some have even turned around and leased their own places back.

Lots in this business is backward. Prescott, for example, will be mostly above the water line, and we'll be mostly drowned, and yet they're coming over here. From the driest to the wettest. By rights we should all be heading west, to higher ground.

July 24

Roy tried to kiss me today. I don't know why I wouldn't. Just plain nervous I guess, thinking what Mama would say. I've been much more alarmed about the cuddling we've been doing since he came to stay with us. Behind my parents' backs. Same as always I suppose but much harder to forget when we're inside our own sugar house or picking the Armstrong patch.

We were resting on a log in the woods when he did it. It was natural enough, my head was on his shoulder, but it somehow struck me wrong.

"I'm sorry," he said.

"You just be patient Roy," I told him. "I'm going to kiss you soon enough."

"That's all right," he said, all mild and relaxed. He stood up and walked a little ways. The fallen log was very big but when he left it I worried it might roll and throw me off. "I wanted to right then," he said, "that's all. But I can wait."

"Maybe we should be more careful."

"You know we're special," he said. "You and me."

"I'm not yet thirteen and a half, Roy Ralston."

"And I'm not quite fifteen."

"I don't feel old enough sometimes."

He smiled a funny smile and even laughed. "I'll tell you a secret, Polly," he said. "If you're honest with yourself you'll admit that you never feel old enough for anything. I can promise you that's so." He came over and reached out his hand. "You learn to go ahead anyway."

"You want me to go ahead anyway."

"Your choice," he said, still smiling.

But later on he got gloomy. While we were walking down a path. And I thought: there's my Roy.

"I'm sorry I wouldn't kiss you," I said, and he looked away. "You're my sweetheart without a doubt. But it's going to take some time."

"A man wants to feel wanted," he said.

53

Mrs. Spiller died last week and we all went to the funeral. I hadn't seen her in months but her only daughter, Rachel, is friendly with my mother—they make pastries sometimes—and anyhow everyone went. Everyone in the village, almost everyone in town. She was that kind of person: very old, well known, involved in all sorts of things and generally looked up to. "I remember her husband, now there was a man," said my father as he buttoned up his shiny black boots, but even though it was Pa talking I wondered if that was the real Mr. Spiller or just the echo of the fact that everyone was at his funeral too, a year before I was born.

We got there late because Caleb couldn't find his black socks so we had to sit in back. Roy as far as he could from me, as is usual these days. We could hear Rachel's words and her brother's and the minister's but I felt removed from them all, in the next to last pew, staring at the hymn book and thinking about something that had come to me on the way. It was purely a good thing for Mrs. Spiller, I'd realized, that she'd died. Wouldn't have to leave her home, after eighty-two years. Wouldn't have to see her neighbors leave, her family. Nor sit in some room in Shutesbury or Ware, missing her house and garden. And her children were spared too, and her grandchildren and the rest of us—spared the embarrassment of doing nothing to defend an old lady.

Walking home I lost my handkerchief. My very favorite one that I have loved so for years. With the embroidered roses on it. I wasn't expecting to cry but after the burial we went to pay our respects and then I started. So I had the handkerchief out—my daddy bought it for me in Hartford—and somewhere between town and the farm I must have dropped it. I was talking to Ma. I realized just outside our gate. I ran back a long ways but there wasn't any sign of it. It blew away or got picked up or something, but it was really and truly gone.

This upset me very badly but it didn't seem right to mourn the loss of some linen when a person had died. Mrs. Spiller never got tucked into my bodice, though. That kerchief was close to my heart. Finally I told Ma, expecting the worst—expecting to be instructed to grow up, Polly—and she was very sympathetic and understood just how I felt. But said it's a blessing I attended, all the same.

August 22

Finished "The Three Musketeers". Pa said he loved it as a boy and I can see why he did but it didn't seem real. Not to me I'm afraid.

August 31

Roy won't go to school. In fact he flat out refuses. We all argued with him, Ma and me and even Cal, and Papa more or less ordered him. But he wouldn't give ground.

"It wouldn't do me any good, Mr. McPhee," he said. "I'm not up to reading any more books right now. And there's too much work for me here."

"We had every intention of you getting your diploma when we brought you here, Roy," said Pa. "You are part of our family." It sounded almost like a threat. "In this family we watch out for our futures." He looked like he might start to stamp or shout. "Don't you see how important high school is, Roy? Can't you see?"

Roy was upset too. "I can't explain, sir," he said. "I'm just not ready for it now." He looked at me and then away. "If you'll allow me to stay home—to stay here for this year only, I'll go to high school next fall. When Polly does. If that's OK."

"You'll have Caleb with you now, you know," said Mama. "You won't have to go alone."

"Not in the same grade, ma'am," he told her, "and anyhow that isn't really what's holding me up. I just can't do it." He seemed as desperate as my father. "I don't think I could pass my courses, tell the truth. I want to do right by you folks. I need a year to work hard here and to think about things. Then I'll go to Belchertown with Polly. I promise."

55

So what could they do? They agreed in the end. Not much sense in trying to make him. They knew he'd just run away.

September 9

Not a week goes by now that we don't see someone leaving. In a van or a wagon. Heading down the road on foot. Or a whole house on a truck with livestock herded behind. My ma rode up past Millington the other day with Mrs. Pearson and described it as eerie. Thought it would need a lot longer, she said, for everything to start to slide.

September 12

I've been relieved of all my chores. Caleb as well, except one or two. "Roy wants to work the farm," said my pa, "so he must have his opportunity. He can just go ahead and prepare to be the best damn farmer in Massachusetts."

We still don't talk much. He won't be friendly. Sometimes I see him working around the yard, all dirty and sweaty, and I feel like I'm the guest.

September 24

School this year is unbearable. Impossibly slow. I miss Roy. I want to be in high school. Maybe he really will come with me. But I'll be going either way. Though if I make it through to June with Miss Thomas on my neck it'll be strictly luck.

October 5

My parents are fighting. Not much, just a little. But more than ever before. They have always gotten along but now the edges are ragged. I have noticed all the signs. The way they glance at each other at the table. Their voices talking late at night. The way my father has more trouble getting ready to go in the morning, fussing with one thing or another. And the long, close embraces when he comes home.

October 17

Roy's 15th birthday.
I really like him.
We're over our trouble.
I gave him a flower.

October 22

First hard frost. Somewhat later than I expected. I don't know exactly why but I've been bracing for the cold.

While Miss Thomas told this morning about the produce of Spain I was thinking about last summer. When the senator spoke, at the big celebration—Greenwich's 175th birthday, minus one. What a peculiar event. A town gathering, for what? To remind us we haven't the time left even to wait for the proper year?

That was a fiercely hot day. Even the band played limp and slow. No one listened very hard—to the senator, I mean—but his speech made the whole crowd jumpy just the same. When he finished I heard somebody yell, "Do they really need it all?" But by then he'd turned away.

November 6

Went with my pa to vote today. I dared to ask how much it mattered and he got slightly overwrought. As if I were a Bolshevik or something. A few passing people noticed.

There was a small crowd of people in the town hall lobby, looking at some poster from the Commission. I saw my pa's face get cloudy. "Al Smith could put a stop to this," he said, but under his breath. "I swear it's not too late."

Once we got down to the basement he was all worked up. "You know, I'm damn good and sorry I ever voted Republican," he said, very loudly, as if speaking to me. Everybody turned to look. "All those loyal years and now they've gone and sold us out."

"No electioneering in the polling place, please, Mr. McPhee," said Mrs. Rutger from behind her table. "And no profanity, if you don't mind." I doubt that anyone in that room had ever voted for a Democrat. Ever even considered it.

"This isn't electioneering, Doris," said Pa.

"You know the rules, Mr. McPhee."

"Please don't make a scene," I whispered. I grabbed at his hand, though I knew he'd shake me off.

"Well why don't we just let the foreigners run the state, McPhee," said a man in a heavy overcoat in the corner. "The country too. Turn it all over to them."

"How'd your folks come over, Kreisler?" asked my father.

"On a ship same as mine, didn't they? But more recently."

"Gentlemen, *please*," said Mrs. Rutger. "I won't have it!" Her face was all red and she was standing in front of her chair. Her shirtwaist was askew. I was mortified and so was Pa.

Everything was quiet after that.

When Pa came out from behind the curtain he looked pleased with himself. I knew he'd voted for Smith. Before turning in his ballot he went over to the table and spoke to Mrs. Rutger, his hat in his hands. I heard her say, "No hard feelings, David." The overcoat man had left.

Mrs. Wilson was at the exit. The ballot box said PERFECTION in big black letters on the side. She turned the crank a couple of times and Papa's votes were gone from sight.

16

(1925)

The waning summer sun gleams. Caleb goes in a car. Through the pines the gentle rays find the children, call them out. Caleb goes in a car with some boys who are older and his sister stands watching, waiting watching, heart rising, mounting terror (he won't come back, will not come back, won't come back ever she knows) growing up and spreading limbs, like an overarching tree, like the elm of dismay, and its roots bind her down. She is held to the spot. Caleb goes in a car and she watches him enter and be lost among companions and the old rattletrap slowly moves down the slope with the dog right behind and she thinks she can see, can see his face for a moment at the tiny rear window though of course he can't see her, the sun is bright at her back and as she stands and sadly watches she hears footsteps knows she's lost but it means nothing. Nothing at all. Caleb gone in a car. Gone to the Plains. Gone away. Hughie Kliner has the wheel and her Caleb has gone and the steps come closer closer then a hand on her shoulder and "you're it!" she knows it's true.

17

The first time I saw her was when she started at Belchertown. On her very first day there. In 1929. I was ten years old. Riding the bus with my father like always. High school started early so I could ride along with him and then make it to my own class in plenty of time. My mother worked in a lunchroom and had to be there before dawn, serving breakfast to the mill hands. So I went with my father. I was the only child they had. Later on when I was older I could have stayed home but I always rode that bus, all the way up to Greenwich Village and back, twelve miles each way on old route 21. I liked my sleep plenty but I liked my dad more. We always talked, he and I, and I could never stand the thought of him riding out alone.

So September '29: we pulled over to the shoulder and Polly got on. By the shore of East Pond. We weren't supposed to stop like that but I found out later my father made an exception. I guess they lived halfway between the village and the Plains and there wasn't any sense in making her walk to one or the other.

She had an older brother who was still at BHS but the funny thing is he always got on at the Plains. With his pals. He didn't once that I remember get on where his sister did. It wasn't as if he was ashamed of her, and I know they lived on one of those small valley farms so he must have had chores in the morning. He must have been plenty pressed for time. But he always walked down to the Plains. His sister went with him on a number of occasions (I would sit there good and worried if she wasn't at the roadside until I saw her next to the church) but he never went with her. Just his habit, I guess, like my riding the bus.

Anyway the point is if she'd been at one of the regular stops I might not have picked her out. Might never have noticed her at all. She wasn't so much to look at, certainly not then anyway, all shy and skinny at fourteen. And I was too young to pay attention just because she was a girl. There were lots of other girls on that bus in those days, some of them very sweet and pretty (valley women always were) and I never thought too much about any of them.

But Polly came up the steps all by herself, kind of slowly, my father calling her by name—I guess her folks must have phoned— and smiled at him with the sun in her hair. It was coming through the window to his left and it went past his head and sort of fell all over her. She blinked and squinted but smiled anyway. He said "Good to have you with us"—by God he was a nice man, my father, they don't come like that anymore—and she kept smiling, couldn't say anything, and just sort of stood there instead of moving to the rear. I was in front, on the right, only a foot or two away. She didn't know I was there. My father said "Take any seat you like, I hope you don't mind the bus because you'll be riding it a lot" and he laughed his nice laugh—Jesus I miss him—and she more or less woke up then and said "Thank you" and blushed and turned to go and sit down. When she noticed me watching she blushed even more. "Hi Maisie, hi Tom," she said as she joined them—I could see her trying hard to relax—and all I could do was stare at her back.

For the rest of the ride to the high school, the whole eleven miles, I wished she were sitting with me.

18

Smooth smooth skin was and hair so fine, softer even than my own as I reached up reached up to press him to me. Smooth skin soft hair dirty summer boy smell the strength I'd been seeking and the sweat on his forehead falling into my eyes. Sweet pain everywhere the need to shout and shove him off, horrid weight pressing on me I wanted an end wanted to hold him keep him there with no exit no leaving forever. The mark on his hip what's that I asked he opened his eyes then laughed I love you no I adore you didn't know he knew the word but there again I adore you and his eyes closed breath rasped lips tight I felt him grow and reach deep reach deep. No woman I longed to tell nothing there for you no but it had it had to reach deep very deep its mission in the deep and Polly gathered what she could to offer up for the reaching bones limbs too thin too frail to withstand hold steady be strong don't tear come apart your duty to contain him. You are in me she said he grunted yeah yeah his arms strained and tight more sweat falling you stay she said don't go don't leave me not empty can't stop he said can't stop don't stop she said keep going go on go on don't leave me can't stop! he said and faster faster reaching growing deep so more full pain never empty again you *stay* she shouted can't I can't reached UNBELIEVABLE deep and faster than any fastness ever fell on her, all the way on, arms gone rhythm gone collapsed onto into her and going away more pain burning pain don't LEAVE ME she told him fist striking you STAY you STAY I can't do it! he cried.

19

March 31, 1929

My pa was disturbed by a rumor this morning, that he heard after church. Said his old friend Larry Sherman had decided to go. Had already sold, in fact. So right after dinner he set out to track him down. I asked if I could ride along and he said to hurry up. But when Roy made as if to join us I shook my head no. I figured I was the best company available. Especially since my ma has started pressing to leave.

"You don't see Mr. Sherman as often as you used to, do you?" I asked as we headed down the road.

"I don't," he said, "and to tell you the truth I don't feel much like talking now."

As it happens when we got there he was standing by his gate, the one with the horseshoes on the posts. He was reaching into his mailbox though it was Sunday. I was happy to see him. It was a dim and cloudy day but even so he shaded his eyes as he studied us coming. He had no coat and I could tell he was cold.

"Well I done it, Dave," he said, as we pulled up. "They make you fill out a form." He looked away, at his house and then his fields and then the road. "It was easy," he said.

"Good price?" asked my father.

"Not too bad," said Larry. "Better than I expected." He turned to me then. "Polly, you're so pretty. How old are you now?"

"Almost fourteen, Mr. Sherman."

"I was always Uncle Larry to you before," he said. "I hope you won't get all formal now you're grown."

"I'm sorry, Uncle Larry. I didn't mean to be."

He smiled. "A regular lady." He held his grin a second more and then dropped it as he stared at the pond across the way.

"I got some things for you people," he said. "A couple things I want you to have."

"That's very thoughtful of you," said Pa.

"Look here, David," said Larry, still staring at the water, "the fact is I see it this way: if I'm going to work a farm again I better get started now. I don't have no other line, like you. Dirt is all I know." He pulled his eyes away from Sunk Pond and looked right at my pa. His face was misery. "I got to get moving, don't you see?"

"No need to explain, Lawrence," said my father as he picked up the reins. He turned to me and I nodded. "When do you plan to set out?" he asked. "And where? If you don't mind saying."

"Don't know yet," said Larry. "I'm looking right now. When I find a place I'd like to get there quick as I can."

"Stay in the state?"

"Maybe. I'd like to."

"Well," said Pa. "I'll be back to see you soon. We'll talk. Just wanted to know if it was true." He lifted the reins again. "I'll miss you," he said.

"I'll miss this valley like anything," said Larry. "Specially these pretty girls." He put his hand on the wagon rail, gently, then took it off again. "Best of luck to you all," he said.

It wasn't until we were halfway home that I noticed we'd never stepped down.

April 11

What Maisie said. About what the grownups do. Kind of awful in its way. But good to know.

April 27

He did leave us some things. And one of them's a victrola! Pa brought it all home in the wagon today and there it was. My mama asked what on earth a man like Larry Sherman was doing with a victrola. "To each his own," Pa said. "He had no family after all." It looked almost new as he lifted it out. He explained how to work it—I like the way you make it louder by opening up little doors— and showed us the records too. There aren't very many, mostly songs and one symphony, by Mr. Johannes Brahms, on a set of four disks. My mother clucked over that. "Must have come with the machine."

Then she grabbed hold of Papa. "How could you accept this, David?" she asked. "It cost a great deal of money."

He shook his head. "I tried not to," he said. "Believe me. He swore he'd break it up and throw it on the pile." He pointed at me. "Then he said it was for Polly, and Caleb."

"Can't we keep it?" I asked.

"Oh Polly," said Ma. "Of course we can."

May 3

I have listened to that symphony at least five times already. I have discovered a new world. It sits in a corner of the parlor, next to the brown easy chair, and I just trim the lantern low and then curl up and listen. I know exactly how many turns it takes to go all the way through each movement. It's incredibly beautiful. I'm so excited I can't sleep. The whole family looks as if they think I've lost my mind, even Roy, but I don't care.

Mama found me in tears last night and didn't know what to do. She was all flustered and nervous, as if something had gone wrong. And her a musician herself, crying over her old sonatas! I know deep down she understands.

I went so far as to ask Miss Thomas about Brahms and guess what? She was very nice. She had me wait after school until she got out a book and showed me a picture. Of Brahms at the piano, with his long white beard. She said he lived in Germany and died about thirty years ago. She said he didn't write that symphony, his First, until he was over forty, that people had been waiting on him for years. She told me a few other interesting facts but the most important thing she said is that he was a very great composer and if I'm fascinated by his music it isn't surprising, and I'm not alone. I should follow my instincts, she said. She might even be able to lend me more victrola records if I promise to take good care of them. She's going to see what other Brahms she can find.

How do you like it?

Roy is jealous. That much is clear. As if I don't kiss him and hold his hand and let him hug me all the time. Jealous of a dead man! And says it's just scratchy fiddles. What does he know?

May 21

Businesses closing all around the valley now. That summer camp west of Dana Common, for example, won't reopen this season. Also the big hotel in Enfield. Even some in outside towns. Our whole section will be permanently changed.

Listened to the Brahms again. He must have been an angel.

May 26

My fourteenth birthday. And what a fine one it was. Caleb made me a comb. Roy gave me *eau de cologne*. And Papa handed me an envelope.

"What is it?" I asked.

"You've got to open it and find out."

Three tickets and a concert bill—*that's* what it was. And they were playing the First Symphony! How was it possible? I just stared.

"Your teacher saw the notice," said Ma, "and wrote a note. Your father skipped four lunches to make up the time he took to go over to the box office in Springfield."

"Thank you, Pa," I said. "Thank you, Ma." Then I looked at the prices. "We can't afford these," I said.

"That's our worry, not yours," said Pa. Roy was grinning from behind. "You turn fourteen just the once."

"Tell me how I can help to pay for them."

"Hush up," said my brother. "I mean it, Polly. Everyone wants you to have these."

I looked at them smiling. "But you all think I'm silly."

"It's still your birthday," said Roy.

"We still love you," said my pa.

"Even if we do have to pry you off the victrola," said Cal, "just to hear Irving Berlin."

I turned to my mother. "Mama, you'll go with me, of course. Who else? Papa?"

He shook his head. "Not for German music, Polly," he said. "Hasn't been long enough for that." Trying to keep a straight face! "When it's British you count me in. Or even French."

"I think Roy wanted to come along with us, Polly," said Ma.

"I don't *want* to," put in Roy. I looked at him. "I'd be honored to."

I simply had to sit down.

June 1

I'm scared by what I heard today. What Roy told me. Couldn't help himself, I guess.

We were walking by his old farm and as usual he frowned and I got ready for him to shut up for a while. I've learned not to ask about that place anymore. But he surprised me and stopped, at the top of the hill, and pointed toward the farm—toward the big old red barn with its crumbly little cupola—and poked my arm.

"See there?" he said. "That's where he did it."

"Where who did what?"

He frowned even more. "You know who," he said. "Him. That bastard. And it was there, right there in that barn."

67

"I don't know, Roy," I told him. "But don't say if you don't want to." He just stared back with his mouth shut. I was lost for words, really. I had never seen that sort of look on his face before. "The day after I came," he said. "My first whole day here. He just took me there and did it. Wasn't any way to stop him."

He looked me over and saw me shaking. "Don't worry Polly," he said. "I feel bad and full of hate but not at you." He sat on the stone wall and patted the place next to him. "Come on," he said.

"What'd he do to you?" I asked. I sat down. He didn't answer. "What'd he do?" I asked again.

"What he did you don't want to hear about," he told me. "I hope you never have to hear about it ever in your life."

I grabbed his right hand with my left, then. He looked down at it as if he'd never seen it before and seemed about to give it back but I squeezed hard and he squeezed too—more like a clutch but I was glad—and held it in his lap instead.

"What he did destroys you," he said. "You can't ever be the same. It's like to eat you alive."

"I wish you'd tell me," I whispered.

He looked away from me toward the barn, toward Connecticut, toward a place long out of sight. "Won't let no one do me like that ever again but I can't never forget . I'm not about to ruin you the same so you'd better quit asking." He looked down at me and was crying. "It was evil, that's all. That's everything you need to know."

"Oh Roy," I said. He let go of my hand.

"I was a *boy*," he said, real low. "I thought I was grown but I was still just a boy and I was pledged to his care. I know I'm just a damned orphan but it's no excuse to hurt me."

I kneeled at his feet, grabbed his leg and hung on for dear life, hid my face in his dungarees. I felt his fingers on my head, in my hair for a few seconds, plucking gently, but then he took them away.

"He *made me*," he said.

68

I held on tighter than I thought I could. Then somehow I was able to take one hand away and reach up for his, and hold on to that too. His flesh was terribly cold. My knees were in damp soil but I'd have kept them there forever if they were rotting away.

He pulled me to my feet. "Come on," he said, wiping his face with one quick movement and starting up again in the direction we'd been going. "Let's get far away from that son of a bitch."

I fell behind in brushing the dirt off and had to run to catch him up. In a minute or so we were into the forest and the barn was out of sight.

"Last winter I was down at the Inn," he said, quiet but fast, the same way he was moving, "and they were talking about the war. They said there was a truce in the very first year of it, right around Christmas. All up and down the line. Because the soldiers wouldn't fight. They came out of their trenches and played games and swapped pictures. One man has a nephew in England and this fellow told him a German soldier gave him chocolate from the Kaiser and called him 'my English *kamarad*.'"

He looked at me then and saw the tears in my eyes.

"That's what I want," he said. "That's all I want, Polly. A truce. You understand?"

June 9

The concert was last night. It was my idea of heaven.

First of all there were the people in their fine outfits, getting out of the taxis, parading past the tall pillars and through the grand doors of the Auditorium. Standing around in the lobby in groups, laughing with one another. The men were near as fancy as the women, with their watch chains and silk ties, their cufflinks and slick hair, not nearly as colorful but as just richly turned out. Even the folks up in the balcony with us looked as if they came from a magazine; the swells below hurt my eyes. I felt like a country mouse. Ma said my gown was very nice and she had put on her best but even so I was ashamed. And Roy was perfectly hopeless,

69

in Caleb's suit that didn't fit. We had walked from the station and I'm sure they saw us coming a mile away.

But I soon forgot all that. I was caught up in my senses. That hall smelled different, for one thing, from any place I'd ever been. And the sound of the audience—we were early and we sat there watching them come in, Mama to my left and Roy to my right—was like nothing I'd ever heard. A single giant sound made of a million little pieces. The big electric lights were terribly bright and the ceiling gleamed with gold. I could hardly sit still.

Then I heard music noises, little ones, and looked down to see the musicians taking their places. They drifted onto the stage, a bunch of men in white and black, except for the lady flute player who had no white at all. After a while they all started playing the same note and adjusting their instruments and then the chief violin (the concertmaster, my mother whispered) stood up and started gesturing and the audience got quiet. Then the lights were turned down and the conductor came out and he bowed to our applause.

I can't write much about the music. It makes me forlorn just to try. All the words I can think of are much too small for what I heard. But the concert was nothing—*nothing*—like listening to the victrola. *Nothing like it.*

The first half was Schubert and Mendelssohn. I wanted to ask my mother about them but didn't know how to say the names. I think I opened my mouth and then shut it, that was as far as I got.

Those two pieces were very lovely but they rushed by too fast. As soon as I thought maybe I had an idea of what was happening the music had moved on. There was a great deal of applause at the end of Mr. Mendelssohn's, which was second, and I clapped so hard my palms hurt. Mama reminded me to breathe.

During the intermission we worked the cramps from our legs. There was a space behind the balcony and we stayed there, though many others went down. Ma was enjoying herself, I could tell, but she also missed my father. I was all jumpy and impatient and then angry at Roy for looking sleepy and bored. When we went in again

I saw him sitting up straight as he could and biting his lip. Then they started the Brahms.

I won't try to describe it because I can't—someday maybe, but now I can't. Although I knew the piece so well and listened fiercely as I could it went by even faster than the others, cruelly fast. Like someone was pulling treasures out of my hands. I longed for them to play each movement again. But also I knew how it all fit together, how it built to the finish, and I devoted myself and when it came to the last part, the last wonderful part—where all the horns blow at once and the drums beat so loud, and then the strings start up again and then more horns with strings also and drums rolling, and then the race to the end—I knew just where it had to go. I knew it. I was stunned all the same but I was there waiting for it. Waiting for it to come home.

The silence when they finished, as the ending notes faded, must have been about a second but it seemed like fifty years. No one wanted to applaud; no one wanted to spoil it. But then one brave person did, and then another, and then me, and soon it was like a roaring rush, a waterfall of clapping pouring down on the players. The conductor bowed to us and then again, very deep. He made the orchestra stand and bow. We applauded so loud I thought the hall would fall around us.

Just then Roy touched my arm. I had forgotten he was there.

As I stood by him and clapped I imagined an orchestra— Brahms's orchestra—cheering and cheering, the first time they ever played it. Cheering in amazement, shouting his name. I pictured him weeping in embarrassment and pride, the concertmaster rushing to shake his hand. I felt bad that he was dead.

June 20

Last day of school. My last in Greenwich. I looked at the schoolhouse my own mama went to, that my children never will, and wondered if I was sorry.

I *am* sorry to leave Miss Thomas. Honestly sorry but also glad. She's really not a bad person and she truly loves music—she made me tell her about the concert—but she's not a good teacher. I think she might have been happier in another profession. Maybe the project will lead to some sort of helpful change.

Edna and her family are moving out next week. She told me just before school the other day. According to her I was the first one to know. She kept it all a big secret. It's hard to see why—I could have organized a party if I'd had enough time—but that is clearly what she wanted. Now I can only wish her well. "Why don't I come over this weekend, to say goodbye?" I asked her today as we strolled down the lane that cuts through to the store. She had a ribbon in her hair.

"Why don't you say it now?" she said.

"Don't you want me to come?"

She surprised me by stepping quickly into my path and taking my hands. "My father got a job out in Buffalo, New York," she said. "That's a fairly big city and a long way from here. I'm scared, Polly. I want to pretend we're still friends. I want to imagine I'm staying in this county. I want to pretend you'll visit me."

"I will visit you," I told her. "Just as soon as I can."

She shook her head. "No you won't, Polly," she said. "There's not the slightest tiny chance. But if you just walk away now, like we'll meet again in the morning, I can pretend for a little longer. I can pretend you'll be nearby."

I was puzzled and speechless.

"Walk, Polly," she said, like ordering a dog. "Walk away!" So I did.

June 29

One hundred and ten islands—that's what they tell us. Scattered across the surface, like jewels on a tray.

July 13

I don't honestly know if I should write it down at all. Thank God I have my own room. I put a quilt along the door and hung a bonnet over the keyhole, in case anyone comes by.

In the morning, if I want to, I can rip the pages out and slip them into the stove.

He led me by there today. That's why it happened as it did. He took a notion I suppose. We were going through the forest and when I saw him turn right I started to speak but he said, "Come on." He was walking fast and steady like he had a job to do. My heart rose in my chest. I tried hard to keep up until I tripped on a root and by the time I had my feet he was two dozen yards ahead. But when I got to the edge of the pasture he was just standing, looking down.

"He's gone," said Roy.

"What?" I was brushing the leaves off my skirt.

"He must have sold out. There's no one here."

I looked down and he was right. The farm was quiet and still. It was a bright sunny day with a strong July breeze and no sound other than the birds and the tree limbs moving and from down around town a cranky engine not quite catching. We knew the place was deserted. Nothing you'd really want was still there, aside from the buildings; it was a small farm stripped clean. Since last we'd passed by. He must have been packing even then.

"Come on," said Roy again, and started quickly down the slope.

The gray old farmstead waited grimly as we came. When we reached it there was nothing to make us think any different. There were crops in a couple of fields—he must have sold them to a neighbor—and I even found some feed around the henhouse, but that was all.

It was strange to be standing on an empty farm like that. Still it will look the same as any other, I reasoned, from a boat over- head.

While Roy was staring into a window of the house, the kitchen I believe, I walked across to the barn. The door was left wide open and it was cool and dark inside. The smell of cattle was still strong. I had tried to forget what Roy had told me—That's where he did it, right there in that barn—but I had failed. Failed completely. I looked over to the house and there he was in the yard, his hands deep in his pockets as he studied the pump.

"Hey Roy," I called out.

He looked up. "Get away from there!" he shouted. But I shook my head and waved. He stamped but I just waved for him again.

So he walked over, scowling, and stopped a few paces distant. "You get away, Polly," he said. "Right now. You know I won't go in there."

"You have to."

He shook his head. "Never will."

"What happened?"

He turned completely around, toward the house and then back. I think he hated me just then.

"Don't you ask me," he said. "Don't you ever, ever ask."

"I'm asking," I said. "I'm asking and you should tell."

He spun again and then stared hard.

"You've got to tell me," I said. "You can't keep it to yourself forever." He shut his eyes. "You've got to tell me," I said.

"Well, you asked," he said softly. I kept my mouth shut and waited. "There's a thing men do to women."

"Yes, I know."

"You do?"

"I heard all about it, Roy."

"Oh."

"So what of it?"

"He did it to me."

I knew my eyes were staring wide, my mouth hanging open. On account of those words my purpose up and ran away. *His* eyes were still closed and if he'd looked at me then or said another plain sentence, made any other little sound, everything might have been different. I probably would have headed back to those woods as fast as I could go. Or better yet down to the Plains to find some grownup to tell. But he just stood there with his eyes shut breathing deep, not moving, and little Polly climbed inside and this other came back out. Who knows it all or thinks she wants to. I had to ask him. I had to ask.

And he told me all right. With his eyes closed, stock still. It took him very few words to give me the idea. It was hard to believe, almost impossible, but underneath it all I knew. As sour and ugly as it seemed.

"He ever do it again?"

"Just the once."

"You still hurt? Your body I mean?"

He breathed so deep and slow I thought he would never stop, and his voice got very tired. "That went away pretty quick."

I figured out just then that my jaw was aching tight. In picturing my face I saw a horrible frown. As if Roy had harmed *me*. The wind picked up strong and I tried to let it wash me, let it wash my features clean. I relaxed every muscle and a good thing I did because he opened his eyes.

"How can you ask all these questions, Polly? Don't you know how bad I feel?" It sounded as if his throat might be closing on him. "How can you shame me this way?"

"So now you do it to me," I said.

"What?"

"Then you'll be even."

No reply.

I walked a few steps into darkness. "Come on," I said. "Right now."

He stood there shaking and breathing. His face was wild.

I said: "It's now or never, Roy." And moved all the way back.

It was cool and dark and damp there and it smelled to high heaven. But I found a heap of straw. When he came to me at last I held his arms and I kissed him. I made him open his eyes and then kissed him again.

"Here is your Polly. This time you will be the man."

He would not believe it yet. So I took off every stitch. I knew he could see by then and I wanted him to, to really see me, to see what I was giving. I had to think it would help. "Here I am," I said again. I stepped back and let him look—shivering naked in the air—and then came closer and embraced him. Undid the buttons. We were both breathing fast. I held tight and I kissed him and when I thought it was time I dropped to the straw and pulled him down there with me. Pulled him down by his center. I know I never let him go until the last possible instant, he started right from my hand, and then I held his ribs tight—I couldn't bear my palms empty—and tried hard not to scream. The pain wanted to take me but I looked up to see its match, which was there in his eyes, and then I knew I was safe. I simply lay on the straw and let the hurting grow weaker, let Roy begin to understand that this was his act to do, his fate to follow, let it continue from there.

And in the end there was a flood.

July 15

I dreamed I met Brahms. He showed me mountains and castles. Then he sent me away.

20

"No sleep."

"It's time now darling."

"No sleep."

"Yes daughter it's late. Even Caleb's asleep."

"More book."

"No more storybooks my lamb. Lie down. Here's your blanket."

"A sing."

"You want a song? Which do you want?"

"A baby."

"All right. Do you have your dolly? All right."

"A baby!"

"I gave my love a cherry that had no stone; I gave my love a chicken that had no bone; I gave my love a ring that had no end; I gave my love a baby with no cry-en. How can there be a cherry without a stone? How can there be a chicken without a bone? How can there be a ring without an end? How can there be a baby with no cry-en? A cherry when it's blooming, it has no stone; a chicken when it's pippin, it has no bone; a ring when it's rolling, it has no end; a baby when she's sleeping, there's no cry-en."

21

I don't know what would have happened if the sequence had been different. The order of the revelations. If Roy had spoken before Maisie. Had I not been prepared. "I know a secret" she said and then my innocence was gone. My final innocence was gone completely gone no more to be affronted by him nor anybody. So when he told me what had happened I wasn't frightened or repulsed; I simply wanted to make it right. I wanted to save him, I suppose.

I did some good but none that lasted. I feel worst about that.

And then after there was shame. His fear and shame and my distance. Distance pain coldness numbness maybe shame for me too and a sense of betrayal. By whom of whom I don't know — perhaps I betrayed Roy, perhaps Maisie sold me. Perhaps Roy's farmer, Uncle Larry, or the head of the Commission. At this lengthy remove it's still all wrapped up together and could never be otherwise.

I took my chances as they happened. And had to live with what remained.

I felt so sorry. Don't you see?

22

August 3, 1929

My brother thought he'd give advice. I was sitting with the cat, reading a story by Herman Melville. About a man called Bartleby who won't do anything—only says, "I prefer not to." I had read it twice before.

Caleb sat down next to me on the sofa. That was unlike him. So was the way he touched my arm. I looked closely at his face and noticed his dark whiskers. He'll be seventeen this month. I don't think he's shaving yet but he'd better start soon.

"Polly, I have to talk to you," he said.

"About what?" Roy was picking corn and Ma and Pa were down in the village. It was a still and cloudy day, not very warm for early August.

"About Roy," he said. "About you and Roy I mean. About the way you're spending time."

"Caleb, what are you talking about?"

"Don't be clever with me, sister. I know what you two have been doing."

I was very angry then but I kept my mouth shut.

"You don't know about boys," said Cal. "You don't know what they think. You don't know what they want."

"Roy is a very good person," I said.

He laughed for a second. "Sure he is," he said. "I agree with you. Heck, I'm a good person myself, but that doesn't stop me thinking what I think."

"Which is?"

It gave me some satisfaction to see him turn red. He stopped for a moment but then pushed on. "It's a man's job and duty to want to have children, Polly," he said. "Without that it wouldn't happen. I mean, it's the woman wants the babies but the man who wants to make them." His blush was very deep and he avoided my eyes. I knew he'd planned the whole speech. "A man wants a lot of things a woman doesn't necessarily like."

"That's nonsense, Caleb," I said.

"It isn't Polly. You'd best listen. I'm talking for your own good."

"It is nonsense," I told him, "and I appreciate your help but I can take care of myself."

He stood up and looked down at me. "I see you," he said. "I see you holding hands and kissing. If he didn't live here I wouldn't worry but you have lots of chances alone. He's going to lose his head someday and try to take too much."

I closed up my book, which had been open in my lap. "All I have to do is refuse him," I said. "Isn't that right?"

"You're not as old as you think you are, Polly," he warned, and then was gone.

August 15

A man in Boston says the new lake should be a memorial for the dead. From the war. That seems fine as far as it goes.

Heavy rain today. I wish it would keep up forever.

August 28

The way we live now isn't pleasant for me. For any of us I don't think. Roy and I hardly speak and since he let my folks know he wasn't going back to school—I could see Papa getting ready to tell him to pack up, then, and I could see him getting ready to do it—they don't talk to him much either. Cal has been quite touchy since he lectured me in the parlor and I'm beginning to believe he blames himself for me and Roy. (I could ease his mind but why should I? Up until he butted in I was making steady progress at forgetting what had happened—both to Roy and to me—but now near every man I look at puts it back in my mind.) My parents fight a lot about whether and when to sell and in between they're quiet too. The result? Very little conversation at all. But we'll get over it in time.

September 3

Listened to the Brahms last night. Hadn't in a while. It's still beautiful enough but not the same anymore. Not surprising really. It was a passion that came and went quickly, is all.

September 9

Belchertown at last. I'm glad Roy isn't coming. And I'm just as glad—really—to state the truth about that.
So we made a mistake. *I* made a mistake. It was Polly's fault, my fault, mine mine mine. Must we all be sad forever?

September 13

A little boy rides the bus. I guess he belongs to the driver. I don't like the way he looks at me. I'm probably four or five years older, but he looks like he thinks I'm a grown lady ready to tell him what to do.
Belchertown High is not at all what I expected. Or rather it's just what I expected—separate grades, harder lessons, the big impressive building—but I feel very different from the way I thought I would. I just knew I'd be shy and worried about what others thought but no. It's not as if I go around yakking my head off or bossing people around but nothing bothers me much—not the

town kids, not the teachers, not the things I don't know—and nothing puts me off for long. I just shrug and move on.

This morning some older girl stopped me in the corridor and said "Valley freshman eh? Where's your pocket money?" I just looked at her and waited, which was not what she thought I'd do.

"Oh, I get it," she said. "Too poor to pay. Mud farmer."

"I had plenty of money with me today," I said, "but I threw it in your yard on my way here this morning."

Her friends laughed. She just stared. I pushed past and moved on.

The good thing—the best thing, there's quite a number of good things, I don't mean to sound like I'm not happy there—is the reading. They give us lots and lots of books. And so far I like them all. The history book is interesting, every page, and in English this week we got a biography of Louis Pasteur (although he was French). We also have texts in geometry, of course, and in Latin. Anyway, it isn't just the books but that everyone in school is *expected* to read. Even Maisie can be seen with her head in a book. (Which takes some doing.) So I feel somewhat at home.

September 22

A balloon came to the valley. A real hot air balloon. They are touring the country. They were supposed to come last month but I guess their truck broke down. Anyway they finally made it and they came to Greenwich yesterday, offering rides at half price on account of the delay. Ma said someone made them do it, probably Mr. Murphy. Pa said it wasn't really half price, they told us that to draw us in. But I didn't really care; I just wanted to go. I had enough saved for a trip—enough for half a dozen trips, I'm a very frugal girl—and I was hoping Pa would let me.

They were set up by the road to the west of East Pond and everyone came out to see. To see the balloon. It was big as a house. All blue and pink and red.

"One ride apiece," said my pa, reaching out his wallet. "Pa!" I said. "Not really."

He smiled—he sort of smiled, it made me feel bad that it wasn't quite a regular smile, it's like none of us has the energy for that sort of thing—and nodded. "Who knows when we'll get this chance again, Polly?" he said. "Might as well take it now. Plus"— he looked over at my mother—"we'll surely never see Greenwich from up in the air anymore."

He counted out the coins. "Caleb," he said, then "Sarah," then "Polly." He looked at us. "Each one can take his own time deciding when he's ready. Tell the truth it makes me just a little nervous. I need to watch for a while."

People were already going up. There was a device of some kind that made fire under the opening, at the bottom. When they wanted to rise they just turned the flames up and hot air filled the balloon. It would billow and get tight and the ropes would creak and the whole thing would rise—pretty fast, too—until it got to the end of its line. It looked at least a hundred feet, though I don't know for sure. They would stay up for a while and then turn down the flames and the contraption would fall. Very gently. It barely bumped when it landed. Then they'd help the people off and load another batch on.

"Hey Roy!" my father shouted. Roy looked up—he was some distance away, on the other side of the crowd—and Pa waved, so he came over.

"Take a ride when you get ready," said Pa, handing him the money.

Roy looked at him. "Thank you, sir," he said. "Thanks. I really want to. I mean I never seen anything like this."

"Me neither," said Pa, and touched him on the shoulder.

Caleb decided to go with some friends and I guessed that my parents might want to be together so I waited and joined the line a few minutes after them. I was just behind Mr. Partridge and his family; he must have closed up the store. As I listened to them talk about some airplane they once saw close up in Pennsylvania I felt someone move in beside me.

"You don't mind, do you?" asked Roy.

I tried very hard to answer. I wanted desperately to say No no no I don't mind but it got clogged up somehow. Probably by all the other words. All the words of three months. So I ended up shaking my head.

It turned out there was room for the Partridges and Roy and me. And the man who was running it. When our turn came at last he fiddled with the knobs and the flames went wooosh! and we started up in the air. I had to hold the side of the basket—there was a bad feeling in my stomach—and when I looked over I was terrified! I understood then why folks were so quiet coming off. It was completely new and different, to look down from so high. With all the people like insects or seeds. And the green and silver valley spread beneath us, roads and farms and streams and all. I could see such a long way: to Enfield, I figured out, through the gap by Smith's Village, and all along the top of the ridge, even up to Pottapaug. Miles in every direction. There was a steady little breeze and it made the basket sway. Stevie Partridge looked sick and the man made him sit and close his eyes.

To see something a new way, something you've known all your life in a completely new way—that is a blessing. I was grateful. I stood in that basket and looked as hard as I could to try to fix it in my mind, grabbing hold of the experience, moving from one side to another so I could memorize each view.

I was in the southeast corner, staring down at our farm, when Roy put his hands on the rail.

"I don't want to be enemies, Polly," he said, really low, so the others wouldn't hear.

"My goodness Roy," I told him, "neither do I."

October 16

I decided to look into more by this Fitzgerald. The one who wrote the story about the sick man and his wife. So I managed to get his novel "The Great Gatsby" at the library. I had to ask Mrs. Fletcher. She gave me a strange look and then sighed and said, "You seem to know what you're doing, Polly. Honestly."

Then she went and got the book. I thanked her and took it but she gripped me by the arm.

"Polly," she said, "if there's anything in there that you don't understand, or that upsets you, you just come to me and ask. All right?" "I will, Mrs. Fletcher," I told her, but she wouldn't let go. In fact she squeezed a little harder. "I shouldn't let you," she said softly. "You're too young." "No I'm not," I told her. "Believe me I'm not." She stared at me then. "I'll come right to you, Mrs. Fletcher," I said. "I won't say a word to a soul."

The reason I wanted it was I was thinking about that story. Most every day. About the syringa, and the biscuits they nailed to the wall. And when I pictured the man I kept seeing Roy's face. But the wife did not have mine.

Anyway I read it. It's a puzzle. I admit that I probably was too young for it, as the librarian said. Not for the intimate parts, I don't mean; not even with the ones who weren't married to each other. That was all the same to me.

But all that "love." That's what I don't get. All that caring for just one person with no recourse. When it seems perfectly clear to me that if you wait long enough someone else will come along. It isn't like parents, where you have only the two. It's just a matter of choice.

And what happens to her—I can't see it as fair. She's sort of shallow and stupid but those really aren't crimes. And now I'll go on for the rest of my life watching her lie there in the dirt, with her body all torn. Bleeding out into the road.

Hopeless, I'd call it.

I'd like to meet him some time. Not Gatsby, Fitzgerald. I'd like to know how he is. And ask him if he writes about death every day, or is it just coincidence?

November 2

The Stock Market has crashed. Wish I could tell what that means. So far a lot of city folks, they say, have a lot less money than they thought they had, which has nothing to do with us. And times are already pretty tough for the farmers—they can't get so much tougher. But there are hints of greater harm.

(1928)

Roy and Caleb at the carnival. Wandering together. They look almost alike. Where one goes the other follows.

At the last booth on the right they give their nickels for baseballs. Roy shoots first, hits a stack but only some of them come down. Shoots again and gets the rest. And all of another with the third. He receives a sorry rag doll and he passes it to me.

Next my brother. Calliope playing. First ball hits, cans fall and clatter. Second misses altogether. The carnie urges him on and Roy calls go get 'em friend. So Cal rears back like Alexander and the pyramid explodes. One dented empty can flies up and strikes the man in the chest. The pitchers smile and clasp hands.

"You didn't!"

"I did."

"Just like that?"

"Oh, it was horrible. Hideous. I wish I hadn't, Sarah. By God. I have no excuse at all."

"But where will he go?"

"I can't possibly say."

"And what will we do without him?"

25

February 25, 1930

Dana Center got together and decided to give in. Figured out they had better take the cash and go now. Instead of waiting until no one will give them a dime.

The town of Dana, Massachusetts wasn't part of the Act, because three-quarters won't be flooded, and at first they intended to keep on living where they were. Going to school up in Athol, shopping at Osgood's, taking money from the folk who come to the Eagle House to drink and carry on. It's a pretty place, the Center, and they meant to keep it that way.

But when you add it all up it's got to go same as Greenwich. All the factories on the middle branch, disappeared with their jobs. No more railroad, no more village to the south. Even Mount Zion on the far side of the water. Their fine big pond drowned in the reservoir—no more swimming or boating—with a fence out their back doors.

And it's goodbye to Enfield and Prescott as well, and Nichewaug on the east branch, and Williamsville and Coldbrook on the Ware. All their neighbors. It's a long way to New Salem and Petersham and Barre.

Plus they can see it clearly now, all the departure and decay. They have a view into their futures. So they're throwing in the towel—petitioning to be included. To join the club.

March 10

Dreamed again about the dog. As I have several times. Kind of funny to have dreams about an animal that disappeared almost three years ago but I don't question what comes in the night. If it's music or a barn rat or the ocean or Caleb or a mutt running fast across a broad and empty field. Running and running, hot on some trail. But never reaching the other side. He runs and runs but doesn't get there. I wake up ready to scream.

March 24

Roy still looks so lost and puzzled. Even though it's been so long. I know he fears he caused me harm but it just isn't so. I simply found what I was looking for, that's all.

April 15

Here it is seven months now of coming to the high school and the fun of it is missing. The excitement I mean. It's only a brick building. Belchertown seems so huddled and gray. The other kids are just other kids, whether I knew them at Greenwich or not, and while the teachers are better than Miss Thomas they all have their faults as well. When I look back on my eagerness I feel mostly embarrassed. I thought Belchertown was New York or Paris, I guess. Thought a high school was like Yale. Thought young Polly's life would change.

But there is still a purpose to it. In working hard at my studies. I'm beginning to get the idea that the world has been divided up according to education. And this will be my only chance. To be more than an ignorant farm girl, that is, as some people might see it.

Oh, that's all a bunch of lies. Just me trying to act smart. The fact is I love books, love classes, love that school, and I'd walk if need be to make it in every day. I think I'd crawl there on my knees.

April 30

Greenwich Plains P.O. closed down. A big change. Mr. Treacher has been running the place for thirty years. Some of his children were born there. Only two things in the world you can imagine him doing: sitting behind that window or delivering the mail.

May 9

I'm glad I saw only the end of it. Else who knows what I might have done. It had to come sooner or later, and life will be easier for me, but it was a bleak and hurtful scene.

Poor Roy is just about bereft now and if he's solidly convinced he'll never get a break in life I wouldn't blame him a bit. I have no idea of where he'll end up but he's close to sixteen which is old enough to get by as an adult, if you're a boy. He's very strong and works hard and will find a way to live.

It'll have to be out of the valley, though. No one here would take him now.

And it's painful to know that this is all on my account. Probably. In all likelihood. That is, not only do I believe Roy, but even if he'd done what Pa said he did it wouldn't be the real reason. Pa is kicking him out because he senses what happened. That something happened between us. That shouldn't have. And he connects this with Roy because his intuition's good. Because he knows, he knows it all, although he doesn't know he does. He can't hate me of course; I'm his one and only daughter. Ruined or no. Therefore he hates Roy all the more. It simply got to the point where he needed an excuse.

The way Caleb told me later he said he found some money missing. Two dollars and some coins he said he left on the shelf right where you come into the kitchen. Missed it while Cal and I were out. So it had to have been Roy. My brother said Roy denied it, turned his pockets inside out and offered to lead Pa to their room and let him search it end to end. Said he actually went to his knees and said, "Mr. McPhee, I wouldn't steal from you. Not from anyone but especially not from you. With all you've done."

"All I've done? All I've done?" said my father, according to Caleb. "Don't you dare to sass me!" And on like that. The sort of thing he never says. Giving Roy no chance at all. This was just outside the barn. Roy kept on denying it and Pa kept accusing him and Roy offered again to let him search and he said Roy could have hidden it anywhere in the house. Or in a hole in the ground. It was an insult—did Roy believe he was stupid?

Just then I came around the corner.

They were watching each other with Cal a few paces off. I saw Papa's twisted face and thought, he's all anger now. Between his hurt over the project and his grief over me the man's been driven from his body. There's nothing left in him but rage.

"I took you in," he said softly, almost too soft to hear. "Might as well have been their brother."

Roy just stood there with his mouth shut. The sun shone down full and bright.

"Look," Pa went on, very carefully, almost calmly, as I tried to ignore the shears I noticed him holding, "I don't want or need any state boy around here anymore. Understand?"

There was a look on Roy's face that I had often seen before. He stared at Pa a moment longer, then turned to Caleb and to me, then to Pa again.

"OK," he said quietly. "Fair enough. It's your farm." And he stepped past Pa and walked across the yard and went through the gate to the road.

The three of us watched him go. At least he had shoes on. But no jacket and of course none of his other things. My brother and I would get them to him but it was hard to watch him leave with so little. Almost worse off than when he came.

What will Ma say when she hears? I asked myself, mostly as a way of not thinking what Polly might do when the truth hit home.

Then I turned to my father. "Have you lost your mind, Pa?"

He wasn't angry. He didn't tell me to watch my tongue. He sort of sank down, is all, like that big balloon last summer when they let out the air.

"I guess maybe I have, Polly," he said. "I guess I have." Then he went on toward the house.

For a while there was just sun and dirt and chickens and not much else.

"You must never talk to him that way again, Polly," said Caleb, when Pa had gone entirely through the door. "From here after. Or Ma either. No matter what they do or how bad things get."

And left me that to think on while he went away too.

May 19

My folks have tried to get Roy, to bring him back, but no one can find him.

May 28

Turned fifteen. If anyone cares.

June 7

Caleb is going. To Boston he says. Just as soon as he graduates.

He announced it very suddenly during dinner last night. It isn't really a surprise—there's no work for him here, if you rule out the project—but it is rather drastic. He doesn't have to go so far. Or so soon. He and Norman have tickets and want to leave a week from Friday. With fifty dollars they saved and borrowed.

Said he means to go to college. I wish he'd discussed it with me. Given I mean to go too.

He and Norman are going to take the best jobs they can find and live together to cut expenses. They have it carefully planned out. Save their wages for school. Boston has several and they figure they'll get places in one or another. Norman wants to learn electric but Caleb isn't sure yet.

"Won't you miss your friends, dear?" asked Mama as she spooned herself some gravy.

"Not as much as you might think," he said. "Mostly I'll miss the three of you." He sighed and looked at his plate. "But I'll come home for visits." Which is what she wanted to hear.

I felt happy for him and when he excused himself I went over and kissed him hard. He blushed but liked it. And I held his hand and squeezed. But later on, when he'd gone out, I thought it through a bit further. Fine for him! What about me? Roy and Caleb both gone and the valley disassembled village by village, family by family. It made me feel left behind and I wanted to give up. To call a strike or something. I felt angry at Caleb and for once found in

94

myself no desire to behave, to be good, to go along as expected. I thought of Bartleby then, as I sat in the parlor staring at the old piano and the victrola. How he said "I prefer not to." Wonder if it would work for me?

June 19

Why did I do it? I don't know. I don't know. Most of the time I can't believe I did. It was another girl, not me.
Circumstances make you older. At least for a moment. And then it's back to being a child.

June 29

Without Caleb and Roy we can barely keep up. The chores are almost overwhelming. Of course this is the busiest season but I worry for the days ahead. I'm afraid it will age my ma something terrible, and Papa isn't getting much sleep. The two of them are ashamed that I'm back to working so hard. As if I minded. They'd hire another hand if they could but my pa's wage was cut and the prices keep dropping—all the farmers are hurt bad, you should hear them down at the Grange—and they just can't afford it. So we'll have to make do.

If I could find my beau Roy I'd drag him back here by the ankle. For their good and for his own. Even for mine.

July 4

This year is the state's three hundredth anniversary. A very big deal. Lots of speeches, as you can imagine. Lots of talk about the past. But here they are holding the past in their hands and mean to wash it clean away.

26

I brought you something, I tell him. He's all dirty and ragged. There's a twig in his hair.

Good God, Polly, thank you, he says. Look at all this. By God I'm grateful. You can't imagine how hungry I am.

You're finding some food on your own, aren't you?

I am, he says, but not enough. I'm half-starved. I need a gun so I can hunt.

You can't stay here forever.

I know that, he says. His mouth is nearly full as he chews on a sandwich. There are those and some fruit and vegetables and biscuits. I almost brought him some tins but the opener would have been missed.

I know that, Polly, he says again when he's finished. I'm just making do now. I'm not sure where I'll go. I need some time to think it out.

But how can you stay here in the forest?

I like it here, he says. It's so quiet. It's peaceful. Nobody telling me I'm bad. Saying how I let them down. And I like never having to talk to anyone. It's a treat.

He smiles. Present company excepted he says.

Winter coming.

Oh yes. That's true. I'll have to have a place by then.

Now he's wolfing a pear and the juice runs down his chin. His shirt is so dirty I can't even see the stain.

There's got to be another farm, I tell him. Or maybe a mill or a store.

He looks at me. Two strikes and I'm out, Polly, he says. They won't ever give me three.

I stay for a while and just sit as he eats. The sun shines through the trees and a chipmunk runs by, back and forth, back and forth, trying for a crust that fell to the moss. I promise to bring him more food soon, and warm clothing; he smiles again and tells me not to get in any trouble. I can manage, he says.

When I rise to go he frowns. He kisses me gently, but that's all.

27

August 14, 1930

I know. It's a while since I wrote anything here. Nothing seems important enough to write about, really.

September 21

I have to pull myself together. My parents are as distracted as I am, in their own ways; it isn't so often they're actually paying attention that I can't put on a face for them, at least reassure them that I am OK. And most of the time at home I'm on my own—doing farm work, doing homework, reading, sleeping.

But the hours at school drag on and on and I simply haven't the strength to pretend every minute. My friends are all noticing. And Mr. Williams actually asked about my health yesterday. Stopped me as I was leaving the classroom.

Maisie, of course, hasn't the imagination to truly be worried, but even she is showing a kindness I've never seen in her before. Last week at lunch I found I just couldn't eat and she kept trying to get me to. Offered me her own sandwich. Went to get me a cup of water. Said, "Polly, you must eat. You're slender enough already. You mustn't make yourself weak." Little she knows.

October 12

Columbus Day. The usual nonsense at school. What are we celebrating? And why don't they just say the truth? Which is this man had a grand idea for making a big pot of money but had trouble finding enough backers until he got to the king and queen of Spain, who were so greedy and desperate that he was able to convince them the pot was even bigger than that. He blundered around the Caribbean for a period of years and never really got what they promised, but Spain piled up gold and the natives suffered and died and pretty soon were all gone. Everybody knows this is what happened, everyone who bothers to read a history book at least. Just won't say it out loud.

The autumn colors are no pleasure this year. Nor the squash, nor even the cider. I expected some hard times, but not like this.

November 27

Thanksgiving, on the other hand, was nice. Just as silly and false a "celebration", yes, at least historically, but family's at the heart of it. And although we missed Caleb a lot—we got another postcard from him a couple of weeks ago, that's a grand total of four in the five months he's been away, you'd think he'd try a little harder, and I can't imagine why he couldn't come home for the holiday—we had a fine time together, not exactly gay but quite pleasant and somewhat cheerful. I'd been dreading my mother's "count up all your blessings" speech, to be honest, but in the event it was actually rather helpful to us all.

What have we lost, really? What do we suffer from? The project and our future are constantly on our minds, of course, and the struggle my parents have been engaged in about what to do, but at this point it would be inaccurate to call it a loss; it's been a fact for so long it's just reality, that's all. People all over the country are losing their jobs, their homes right now. People get sick and die all the time. How can we really complain?

Yes we do miss my brother, but we know he is OK. Roy is on our minds, too, in a harder way really, for Pa and me at least; the guilt and the shame make for a crueler sort of worry. But I gave them a version of what I know—he's healthy, he has shelter and a fellow looking after him, if you think I'm going to tell them I was

sneaking him food before he took up with some strange forest re-
cluse in an eight by ten shack, you are out of your mind—so we
could all relax somewhat about that mess.

The point is we've spent so much time recently thinking and
talking about what's wrong, reviewing what's right did us good.
My folks both smiled more in three hours, I think, than they had in
a month. The food, which I'd spent half the day preparing with
Mama, was all delicious, and there being much too much of it
somehow felt optimistic, rather than profligate or sad. We even
played cards after. It was really very nice.

28

I have this dream. A guy goes back. Have it so damn often. Every year he goes back to this ruined homestead, up on a slope above the water. Finds the cellar, the woodpile, the garden, all just the same as it was, year after year. He stands and looks—he was so young—he tries to grab hold of his boyhood. But he can't grieve despite he wants to. It's all in vain.

And every year before he goes he empties out the spring. Where his grandma got her water. Its winter fill is leaves and stones; he cleans it out and walks away.

29

December 30, 1930

Called on the Patenaudes this evening. Listened to the radio there. A man came on who was kind of gloomy. Said the prospects for next year don't seem much brighter than this. In fact it could be worse, he said. He sounded sorry about it but pretty sure of his facts. I guess the whole entire system is in terrible shape. Something has gone seriously wrong.

Papa is always reminding us we're not the only ones in the world with troubles right now. So I don't let him see me cry.

P.D. 147.

33

	Year ending Nov. 30, 1930	Total to Nov. 30, 1930
SWIFT RESERVOIR DAMAGES:		
Salaries, Engineering	$00.00	$14.58
Consultant Expense	521.90	1,443.37
Purchases and Settlements	8,061.00	14,107.00
Miscellaneous Expense	.80	2.70
Total Swift Reservoir Damages	$8,583.70	$15,567.65
SWIFT DIVERSION DAMAGES:		
Salaries, Engineering	$5,098.48	$14,395.20
Consultant Expense	2,963.27	5,048.96
Engineering Instruments	25.65	555.35
Laboratory Equipment	154.45	174.44
Automobile Maintenance	0.00	1.25
Contracts for Investigations and Surveys	0.00	569.47
Laboratory Supplies	0.00	20.98
Miscellaneous Expense (undistributed)	109.04	2,890.92
Printing and Blueprinting	16.72	63.29
Rental of Equipment	9.00	9.00
Total Swift Diversion Damages	$8,376.61	$23,728.86
CEMETERIES:		
Salaries, Engineering and Clerical	$1,459.30	$2,776.81
Legal and Expert Expense	17.75	43.50
Labor	1,435.76	3,566.64
Miscellaneous Expense (undistributed)	15.09	80.89
Stationery and Office Supplies	0.00	3.51
Purchases and Settlements	1,675.50	3,552.00
Monuments and Inscriptions	8.00	244.55
Materials	641.97	1,525.56
Transportation of Bodies	0.00	45.00
Transportation of Monuments	396.00	778.00
Total Cemeteries	$5,649.37	$12,616.46
PERMANENT CONSTRUCTION — EXCEPT CONSTRUCTION CONTRACTS:		
Installed Equipment	$0.00	$214.78
Total	$0.00	$214.78
Total Swift River Reservoir Division	$1,029,578.18	$4,909,987.73

SOUTHERN SUDBURY EMERGENCY SUPPLY

GENERAL OVERHEAD:		
Administration	$13.04	$8,667.76
Engineering	93.76	33,397.03
Total General Overhead	$106.80	$42,064.79
ENGINEERING:		
Salaries	$0.00	$33,810.46
Consultant Expense	0.00	3,816.25
Furniture and Fixtures	0.00	30.70
Engineering Instruments	0.00	216.06
Rent and Upkeep	0.00	543.40
Automobile Purchase	— 200.00	1,719.00
Automobile Maintenance	0.00	1,514.45
Labor	0.00	173.00
Miscellaneous Expense (undistributed)	0.00	1,575.75

from the MDWSC annual report, 1930

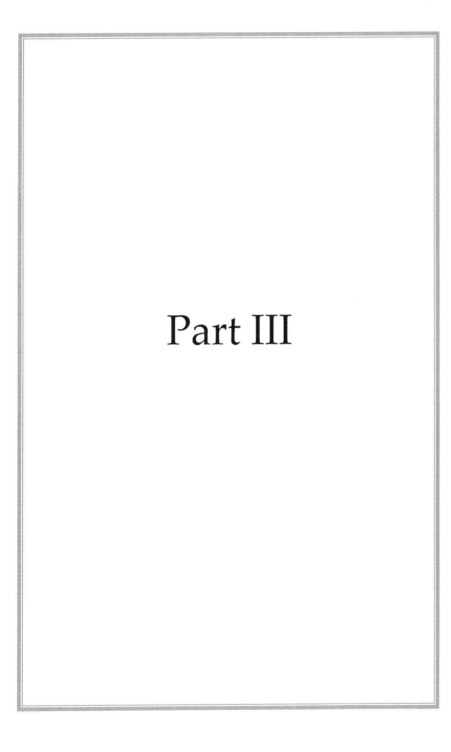

Part III

Village life begins and ends with the presence of an engineer.

— John Baskin
New Burlington: the Life and Death of an American Village
1976

30

January 30, 1931

The valley is full of strangers. They drive our roads, sleep in our houses, eat our livestock and our crops. They've brought a new life to the land but it's only temporary. Like a false dawn, I suppose, except no sunrise will follow.

January 30, 1931

My dearest son,
How are you now? I hope you are well. It is hard to bear your illness at this distance. If you were here I could have nursed you! And Boston is so full of diseases, from all the countryside around and up the coast and overseas. Unlike Greenwich, where at this moment I probably have the same cough my great-grandfather had eighty years ago, passed as it has been from neighbor to neighbor since then. So I would be pleased to hear from you that you are entirely recovered. If you would do me that favor.

How do you enjoy your position? I hope you find it exciting. You were fortunate to get it and there must be much to learn.

I do hope the general debilitation of trade will not affect your firm too greatly. It is very bad here. It seems as if every route by which money enters the valley is at least partly blocked. Except the Commission of course. I am not so very grateful as to say praise God for it but the fact is that without the wages they pay which are spent in the area, and their purchases of materials and supplies, things would be difficult

107

indeed. We are better off right now than many others around the state, although their prospects are considerably brighter.

They treat our town as their property. They see us all as intruders. They're so full of their plans and schedules that when we cross their field of vision they start back in surprise.

We are trying to make plans, your father and I. We are not always in agreement. When we put our heads together—when we're able to talk calmly—we produce the same answers. There isn't much to discuss. We've got to let them have the farm and find a way to stretch the money to buy a decent house somewhere, not too distant from his work. Ludlow, maybe, or Wilbraham. And that's the end of being farmers. We'd need four times what they'll pay to have a chance of buying another. I point all this out to your father and he doesn't say no.

But when it comes to making arrangements he gets very emotional. And I confess so do I. He talks at length about my forebears but refuses to acknowledge how I ache on their account. He seems to think the loyal thing is to remain on the spot until the water's at our chins. But I can best show my respect by having done with it now.

They don't know us, know nothing about us. Just last Tuesday I heard one of them say Grennitch. Grennitch Village.

Your sister is troubled. And I'm concerned. I've tried time and again to find out what might be wrong but she refuses to respond. Just worn out, Ma, she says, from doing trigonometry. Or from pitching down hay. Then let your father pitch the hay, I tell her, and she simply turns her head.

I suppose I am slow to accept her maturity. She is almost sixteen. I was younger than that when I first met your father and just eighteen when we married so I suppose she is old enough to care for herself. But still I take some convincing. It was simpler with you, a boy after all, but she's a girl and my baby. And she's Polly, more to the point.

I want to ask a favor of you. Would you write to her, please? I believe it would make her happy (I don't know if you realize how much she misses you, Caleb, and how hard she is rooting for you to succeed) but more important she might write back. Might find herself more able to set her problems down on paper than to talk of them to us.

Oh son, I won't pretend. I'm very worried about her. She has been blue for so long. And lately worse than that. Please write her a letter and please visit us soon so you can see her in the flesh. If you can tell me it's nothing, that it's entirely in my head, I promise to relax. But your father is no help. If I say his daughter's sad he says of course she is, how not? and past that doesn't hear a word.

Come home soon. It isn't far. You can be here by Saturday supper. And stay through Sunday afternoon. We'll find a way to get to Palmer if you can't catch the Rabbit. But please come.

I miss you so.

A little too easy, isn't it? Polly's ready-made villains. A nice way to keep from facing all the other things gone wrong.

Must close now. It's very late. Please excuse my complaints. I send with them some winter socks I made, which should help keep you well until spring. I hope your boots are warm and dry.

My very best wishes to you, my darling, for the rest of this new year, and all those coming after. Work hard and take care.

Your mother Sarah

31

"Darling please listen. It's *over*."
"Why so urgent?"
"Why wait?"
"So we don't act in haste."
"You'd rather suffer at leisure."
"So I don't feel like a coward."
"For goodness sake. That's absurd. As if it were hooligans or something."
"I'll ask you not to lose your temper."
"Why not pray tell? I'm not accustomed to being ignored."
"You're the one who's not listening."
"Is there something new to hear?"
"Sarah Armstrong, you were rich. With a family, a town. And expectations for the future."
"All taken now."
"You had them once. I had nothing. You won't attempt to understand. You've never set foot in Lawrence, never mind in my old neighborhood. You haven't any idea. You had this valley. I had a mother working sixty hours a week in a mill and our tenement room and the filth in the street. That was all. You don't understand."
"Now you have me. And the children. Therefore no need for this farm."
"But it's my *home*. The only one I've ever had."
"It's *our* home, David. But we have to go."

110

32

February 27, 1931

What a picture yesterday! We took the train down to Ware. The place was packed and it was suspenseful, very exciting. I think the crowd went home happy.

My parents marvel at a movie you can actually hear. They say they miss the piano player.

I suppose in the city there are lots of films to choose from, and other entertainments too. But here it's easy to decide: Friday basketball in Enfield, Saturday movies the same, wait for baseball to start up and band concerts soon after.

March 10

Saw Roy today. Just from a distance. Don't think he noticed me at all. He came out of the store with his rucksack packed full.

I guess he finds it nice enough, living up there on the ridge. From what he said when we talked by the charcoal kiln that day the old man is kind of crazy. But he likes Roy, treats him well, and has some money hoarded up. And his shack doesn't leak. That's all that matters I suppose. Roy made it safely through the winter and I am grateful for that.

I wish he'd come to visit. It would be easy if he wanted. He'd have to march up to my father and apologize, that's all. Then my father would too; then they'd be friends again. My folks would ask him to come back and he'd say no thanks, I've got my own place now, and they'd nod and get him a sandwich or some root beer. Ask his opinions about things. It would be dignified and calm. But he won't do it—he's too proud. Won't let my daddy off the hook.

So there he stays up in Prescott, just like my brother off in Boston, not so many miles away but clear out of my reach.

March 19

They started up the Ware works not long ago. I heard about it just today. They kept it quiet, I guess, or maybe I ignored it. But anyway they turned their big wheels or switches or whatever they do and started sucking water out of the Ware and sending it through that long tunnel, all the way to West Boylston. I heard the Wachusett is rising even faster than expected, a rate of several feet per week. That's some pretty fast filling.

I mentioned it to Pa while we were cleaning up from dinner. My mistake of course. Mama went on about her business.

"They murdered six men with that damned tunnel alone," he practically shouted. "They wiped out half of Hubbardston and every single mill: Wachusett Nail, Hubbardston Chair, the blanket mill and the coffin factory. And West Rutland and Coldbrook Springs."

"But Pa," I said, "we knew all those things would happen. It was decided years ago."

He glared at me. "That doesn't make it right." He looked at Mama's back as she stood at the sink, then at me again. "Have I lost you two as well?" he asked. "Am I the only one in this house who hasn't given over entirely?"

"No more dramatics, David," said my mother very quietly. "We've both heard it before."

If I hadn't known enough to keep my mouth shut after that my pa's eyes would have done it. I watched them drowning in his grief.

At least it works. They didn't kill those towns in vain.

112

April 2

I'm reading about Madame Curie. What a remarkable person. It's so hard for a woman to rise to prominence. And her husband must have been remarkable himself. But when he was gone she carried on. Not to mention leaving Poland and going all the way to France in the first place, so she could get the education they didn't want her to have. She must be unnaturally brave.

We saw a photo of them standing with their bicycles by the road. A long time ago—when she was thirty, I imagine. She looked quite womanly and sweet, not like a scientist at all.

April 16

This time it was heavy. Thick and heavy. It never came that way before. And there were terrible pains. I was frightened at first—thought there was something badly wrong—but then I said to myself oh, this is what they're always complaining about. The other girls. This is why they use those ugly names.

Of course I wanted to discuss it with Mama. Is it like that for her? What does she do to feel better? But I can't do it, you know. No way to have that conversation without getting to the part she simply can't afford to hear.

And the worst of it is it may be my own fault. This unpleasantness. For doing what I did. When my organs weren't mature. Instead of waiting and staying safe.

I know my mother and she must wonder. Why we don't—don't talk about it as we should. I've got the body of a woman but the fears of a child.

April 26

It occurred to me this morning—maybe Caleb gets to the ballpark. To see the Red Sox or the Braves. I came across an old baseball and I thought of him there. That cheers me up, just a little, to picture him in the stands. It must make him very happy. Despite both teams are so bad.

113

May 8

My father bought himself a car! Our family's joined the world at last. It's an original Model A that he got up in Dana. He claims the service on the Rabbit is sure to be cut by the end of the year. I don't know where he found the money but it's true, as he says, that he's got to get to work. I sure hope it's reliable. If he's late he could be let go in a minute.

"Pretty simple," said the mechanic down in the village, according to Pa. "Not like some they make now. Nothing fancy, it just works."

My mama was not pleased.

"You know we can't afford it," she told him in the kitchen.

"Without it we can't afford to live."

"Not here we can't," she said in a mutter. "Why don't we move somewhere closer?" But he was already leaving the room.

May 13

And now a honey extractor. Borrowed this time but he'll buy it if he likes it. Thinks maybe we ought to expand our hives and try to boost our production. There's always a market for honey, he says. The bees do the work and we pocket the cash.

He is full of enthusiasm for investments in our future.

It isn't hard to use, really. Just have to spin and spin and spin. And Pa gets the combs—my job's the spinning, that's all.

May 25

Roy gave me fur for my birthday. A rabbit skin he tanned himself. It's lovely, and pretty big for a rabbit. White and black. I'm not sure how I'll explain it to my folks.

He was waiting for me to walk back from the bus. Sitting on that oak stump near the Atkinsons' fence. He jumped up before I realized he was there. I was startled but he just held out his hands.

"Happy birthday, Polly," he said. "I know I'm early but I figured I mightn't track you down tomorrow."

I was still startled. "Thank you, Roy."

"You're sixteen now," he said.

He explained that the old man had taught him how to treat it. Among a lot of other things. He was learning to get by, he said. Wasn't going to have to depend on anyone ever again.

"I wish you'd make it up with my parents," I told him. "They feel badly, Roy. They want to know you're OK."

He shrugged it off. "Someday I will," he said. "Maybe. When I'm ready. Maybe then."

We sat and talked for a while and then walked a ways together. It was a warm, breezy day with a hundred smells mixing. The crops, the flowers, the Atkinsons' cattle. I felt closer, somehow, to the dirt beneath my feet than I did to my old sweetheart. It bothered me but it was true. I looked up most of the time—while he snuck glances at my hips—and wanted to hurl myself deep into the blue.

Then I stopped short. "You killed the rabbit."

"Well of course," he said. He stopped too and looked at me. "You know someone had to anyway." He smiled. "I hope you still like the skin."

"I like it fine," I said. I put out my hand and grabbed his wrist. "And you probably hunt all the time."

"That's right." His arm was resting in my palm.

"It's what the two of you live on."

He nodded and squinted at the distance. "Mostly." He tossed his head. "Everybody hunts, Polly."

I squeezed his arm; he pulled away and faced the valley. Not long after that he left me. Without a care in the world.

June 4

I saw a magazine story about the Louisiana flood of a few years ago. Seems they're still getting over it. And have no money to rebuild, times being how they are. I asked Pa and he said oh yes, it was very bad. A real disaster for the farmers. "That Mississippi's awfully large," he said, "and when it goes it must be something.

Half the state was under water." Then he laughed. "I guess we'll appreciate their perspective before long."

So there I was at the time, twelve years old, fretting about something that might happen when I was twenty, and a thousand miles away people were losing their farms and homes. With no warning at all. It seems like God doesn't give you the wit, really, to understand a thing like that.

Sally, who claims family there, says in New Orleans they drink whiskey at funerals. And eat breakfast after dark. She says the roads are paved with oyster shells hauled out of the sea.

June 18

Moses Moseby has come to town. A real character, Ma calls him, and I guess he is that. I know a lot of folks don't like him. But I think he's special. He's a kind and careful man.

I had never really spoken to a colored man before. I had almost never seen one. But there he was sitting on the steps of the Inn, chatting with Mr. Murphy. A bunch of other folks were listening. Mr. Moseby was well-dressed, very nicely turned out, and he's quite an attractive fellow. He has big dark brown eyes and a good-looking profile, and a neat haircut and manicure. His skin is oddly smooth and even. He made quite a picture, sitting on the steps in his waistcoat.

"What did you say your business was?" I heard Mr. Murphy ask.

"Nothing at all," said Mr. Moseby. "Not just now." He laughed. "You can call me a lazy idler if you want to," he said. "I've been called worse. But what I really am is a worn-out man looking for peace and quiet."

"Plenty of that here," said Mr. Murphy. "A good bit less than there used to be."

Mr. Moseby smiled. "I think I'll stay for a while." he said. "If there's room."

"Always room for a paying guest, sir," said old Mr. Doubleday. I wasn't sure of his intention. The stranger didn't take notice.

"I assume there'll be a cottage to let somewhere," he said to Mr. Murphy. "Somewhere out of the way."

"Surely," said Mr. Murphy. "We'll find you something you'll like. See some people tomorrow." He coughed. "How long you plan to stay?"

Mr. Moseby smiled again. A nice smile. I thought, This is a very handsome man. "Depends on how long I'm welcome."

Since then I've seen him several times. I spoke a good while to him once; he asked me for directions. He was riding in a pretty new roadster but he shut it off to talk. I think he meant to offer a ride but was afraid it would be improper. He asked where was our high school and I told him about Belchertown and that led to some words about the project. Before I knew it nearly a quarter-hour had passed and two cars had gone by. "I'd better go now," I said, and he started his engine and drove off, waving over his shoulder.

The fact is I don't know what causes Mama to call him a character. Or me to say he's different. He's not so different, really, no more than anyone from out of state. What's different is that he's colored and dresses well and has manners. His speech is refined. Unlike any colored man anyone here has ever imagined. If he were white he'd just be another wealthy tourist, that's all.

June 21

Pa was right about the Rabbit. Cut it back, just like he said.

June 24

The cat died. Of all things. I found her curled up on the hall rug this afternoon. Simple old age, nothing tragic—she was a very ancient cat, eleven or twelve years at least—but it hurt like the devil. The more so as I never stopped to think how much I cared. Like losing a part of your own body, I imagine, impossible until it happens. And then too late.

I'll miss that cat. Miss her like crazy. What on earth am I going to do?

117

33

(1922)

In warmer weather we played tag. There were so many variations. But all essentially the same: a child presented with the burden of pursuing his companions. So that he too could be free.

One August evening we played squat tag in the dimming summer light and I crouched low in the grass, I remember, crouched there waiting and waiting, hearing the wind blow, waiting and waiting, praying for sundown, wondering (it's true) if I would ever move again.

34

October 2, 1931

We got a long letter from my brother today. *Finally.* He's in New York now. And we didn't even know it! Salesman for a clothing firm. They have him working new territory in the north of the city. It'll be a tough row to hoe.

He also sent us a map of the island—Manhattan—with all the neighborhoods and districts laid out. He marked his rooming-house with an X. I have been staring at it all evening. *Chinatown. Harlem.* It sounds so exotic. *Garment District. Lower East Side.* There's even a Greenwich Village! Caleb lives down there on the Lower East Side with another young man he met, a tailor from Connecticut (he gave no word of Norman). They share a room. He says it's cheap and convenient but simply crawling with foreigners. "I try to make allowances," he says, "but I sometimes want to tell them a thing or two. However they mostly don't know any English so I wouldn't get far."

I bet it's still hot in New York City now. Hot and swarming. There are probably more people within three hundred yards of Caleb right this second than there are in the Swift River valley. There are probably more automobiles within a half a mile than have ever even traveled on East Street or on the Greenwich Plains road.

Mama doesn't like it. She didn't say so but I can tell. I don't see the difference—Boston's pretty big too—but I guess New

York's especially frightening to someone like Ma. I heard her say to Pa, "Do you think he'll be all right there?" to which he answered, "It's better than here anyway." She sat down then and covered her face with her hands so he took the place beside her and told her "Yes, he'll be all right. He has a brain and good schooling. He's an Armstrong and a McPhee."

I miss my brother very much. For some time I didn't want to admit this to myself. Because it isn't just him—his jokes, his pet names for me, his hard work around the farm—but also being left alone. Alone with the two of them. In just a very short time I've gone from not much more than a baby to a sort of companion to my parents, a person they depend on, and Caleb's leaving had a lot to do with that.

Why do I say "someone like Ma"? I'm a country girl too. I've only been to Springfield, and Worcester twice, and Boston just the once when I was very, very small. (All I remember is the candy factory—they say I tried to run in—and riding on the subway, underground, which made me cry.) If you took me to New York right now I'd probably faint away on the sidewalk, at the corner of Fifth Avenue and Forty-Second Street, just outside the New York Public Library and not far from the Grand Central Railway Terminal.

October 6

They've started digging up the bodies. What a thing to have to watch. They've done two already down in the Plains, and Virginia who lives by the Woodlawn in Enfield says they've started there as well. The bus goes right by the churchyard so every day this fall we can count the progress made.

And what's the point of it, really? I wish they'd just leave them be.

October 22

I had a funny dream last night. So peculiar, it was, I'm not sure I should put it down. But it's good practice for writing novels someday.

It was about Mr. Moseby. And he hadn't any clothes. Although below the upper chest he was sort of a blur. Like an angel, almost, but without any wings. And in fact he was flying through a part of the dream, or at least floating above me. He started in to explain things, one after another. He turned my bedroom walls transparent so I could see all the timbers. He showed me a mark on one of them he said my four-times-great-grandfather made. He told me where everything that went into my bed came from, starting with the fields in which the sheet cotton grew, and claimed the hills around Greenwich were once mountains, very high. Said he was born down in Georgia where Sherman's army had passed, the very youngest of fifteen, and left there when his father talked back to the mayor. He said there's more I have to show you, come along.

I was still lying in bed, recalling the details, when I remembered last Monday. He showed me his watch fob, from some club he belongs to. Outside the feed store in the Plains. It wasn't very much to look at but I felt called on to comment so I asked, "Are you in any others, sir? They must be after you to join."

"Some are," he said slowly, "and some aren't."

Having remembered that encounter I was able to calm down as I washed myself and dressed. But in the henhouse I thought it's a long way from five short words to a dream.

November 7

As I was helping Mrs. Fletcher at the library today—it seems to please her an awful lot and she's been so good to me—I read a bunch of old newspapers. From 1906. Quite a year for the valley.

Three wealthy sisters in Enfield got married, for one thing. *La crème de la crème.* It made the papers in Boston. They were married together and held a dazzling reception. I read all about their dress-

121

es and the food and who was there. Not only local big shots but also from Hartford and Boston, even some from New York.

Mrs. Peirce happened in and I asked her about it.

"Oh my yes," she quickly answered. "Talk of the town. Course I wasn't invited but we all went down to watch. I can still see it now: the big door opened up and the three brides stepped out, so lovely in white, and then three handsome husbands after. The whole crowd cheered them like anything. And the guests threw bushels of rice. Then they got into carriages with teams of white horses—it would be fancy autos now—and went off to the reception." She laughed but not happily. "I remember the envy. My own wedding was modest. It seemed unfair that they could put on such a show. Just because they were rich." Then she chuckled in a more relaxed way. "Imagine being so stupid," she said. "Their husbands married them for their money, in all likelihood, and I got true love with Mr. Peirce. Which would *you* rather have?" She looked at her watch. "I'm sorry, dear, I've got to go," she said, gathering up her books. "It's been so very nice to chat."

Also, late that summer, there was a robbery on the Rabbit. A gang of four men stopped it just before dark. Threw a big log on the track and waited there with drawn pistols. A thousand dollars they took, and got clean away. The police said "Inside job" but never caught anybody.

And in that very same year a big hotel burned to the ground right here in Greenwich, it turns out. In the village. No one was killed but my ma told me later it was a serious loss. When we went down to the store she stopped and pointed out the spot.

November 9

I just now read it: "discontinued." Like a line of winter coats or an automobile. That's what they say our towns will be.

November 12

Mama laughed out loud today. I hadn't heard that in weeks. I don't know what Pa said to make her take on in that fashion but she just laughed and laughed. I heard a pan fall to the floor. When he started laughing too I wanted to run and join them but then I thought, you'll have your turn some other day.

November 18

Lovely this morning. Ice storm. Last night it showered and then froze and all the trees and everything else had a crystal cover on. When it caught the rising sun it was a miracle of light. Every object I could see had been transformed.

November 24

Listen: sometimes I remember what it was like. The way it felt. His flesh in mine. The urgent motion, rough and smooth.
But other times I can't bring back anything at all.

November 26

Thanksgiving's lonely without my brother.

November 30

Prescott's empty, says Mr. Partridge. "Ghost town" is how he put it. Guess he doesn't know about the old man and Roy.

December 7

Something terrible has happened. Mr. Moseby's gone away. He was driven out of town by some people who attacked him. "Bigots," said my mama, several times. "Horrid bigots. The kind we don't have in Greenwich. They must have come from some-where else."
"Lots of Greenwich folks were impolite to him, Ma," I said. "Lots of folks didn't like him. I've seen Mr. Tibbs cut him dead."

She turned on me. "Not the same thing," she said. "Not at all. Maybe there were points about him not to like. Maybe he didn't belong here. Oh yes"—she raised her hand—"he was a perfectly respectable man who would have been welcome in many places. But we aren't used to his kind and he made people uncomfortable. That is not the same thing, however, as unprovoked violence."

"I know it's not," I said. "But doesn't one lead to another?"

The sheriff states simply that he was chased and beaten up— with fists and broom handles both—and warned to get out of town. And decided to heed the warning. But according to Maisie, who always claims rare information, it was even worse than that. She says (how would she know this?) that they told him they'd hang him from a tree, if he didn't, and leave his body in the street.

December 11

A late flood came. From all that rain. Not a big one but enough to get over the riverbanks south of the lake, where it bends and the ground is flat. It spread out shallow on either side and then it froze. All smooth and perfect for skating. But it was me that saw it first, as I was waiting for the bus, and I went over to look. I had it all to myself. A brand-new pasture of glass. I almost felt I could tuck my fingers under one edge and lift the whole thing up and see what lay underneath. I wanted to run down the slope and start sliding on my bottom, sliding across the river, sliding so fast that some miracle would happen and the ice would be unending and I'd slide on forever. Into a universe of ice—silent coldness every- where, perfectly flat, perfectly even, reaching on to the horizon. Moving swiftly across it but never ever getting cold.

35

One Friday evening I told Bill. Down at Peewee's, having a few. I'd seen a woman on the street who was kind of reminiscent—walked right past me in front of the hardware store up in Orange, where the sidewalk's so narrow—and had been thinking of her as a consequence. More than usual, I mean. Wondering where she was. If she had kids. Like that. With a lot of strong feeling surging up around my heart, as it does from time to time when I remember my parents or my buddies from the war. I'd tried to hide it from Elsa (without too much luck I guess) because I couldn't have explained. Not to her.

He listens well, my old friend, and he sat and heard me out. Pulled at his beer now and then. I kept it mostly to myself; I'd never talked about Polly before. Not to anyone. He knew it wasn't the full story but he never asked for more. He didn't care about the details—naturally enough since I was holding so much back he saw nothing special in it, just another sad story of youth he assumed, the kind you tend to tell when you get to the age where reality and time do their best to pull you down—but he wanted to know the gist. Looking for a frame of reference. It put him in mind of his Trudy, probably, back in Ohio, the one he planned to marry until her folks went off to Kansas and he let her get away instead of making a stand.

Why don't you take a drive past a few of the old places? he suggested when I'd finished and he'd bought me a beer. Go by her house. Work it out of your system that way.

I sipped my Miller.

Oh, the valley, he said. You can't get there from here.

36

April 10, 1932

The work goes on. Nothing stops it. Not even these hard times. More neighbors leave, more fences are torn down and coffins moved. Houses burn and aren't rebuilt. Oddly, though, we seem to have gained as a tourist destination. I understand the hotels and cottages and the like are getting a big play. They expect to be booked all summer. I don't suppose I understand it, really. Maybe morbid fascination. And the way this valley has been frozen in its tracks for forty years now, since they started making threats. By now we're "quaint" to outsiders, even "charmingly well-preserved." And picturesque and green and of a very relaxed pace, if you stay away from the explosives and the drills.

April 18

We've lost track of my brother. My mother's letter was returned, marked "NO SUCH PERSON AT ADDRESS." Of course she is beside herself. She's already written again. She searched our house and the P.O. from end to end, in case some card or letter dropped behind a desk or bureau. She wanted to call long-distance to the New York City Police Department until my father convinced her not to. I wouldn't be surprised if she sneaks out some night and goes off trying to find him.

"No cause for panic," said Pa as I was washing up from dinner. "I'm sure he sent his new address, Sarah, and it just got lost somehow. There'll be a letter from him soon."

Mama was standing in the parlor, her arms wrapped around herself, her head down.

"I want him back here," she said. "I can't stand this."

"He's a man now, darling," said my father.

She laughed, or maybe yelped is a better description.

"I'd like to know why you *males* always use that word when you need an excuse for the pain you cause women."

"Regardless, he lives elsewhere," said Pa.

Later on I found her sitting in the kitchen, her sewing pushed to one side, staring at the murky old engraving by the stove.

"I'm awfully worried, Ma," I said on a guess. "I know the P.O. just made a mistake, or Cal forgot to tell us he'd moved. Maybe he's on the road and that tailor changed their room without him knowing. But I can't help being anxious about it, can you?"

"Oh honey," she said, reaching out for my hand. "Your brother is fine. You know it and I do. But if we weren't a little worried I'd be worried about us." She smiled toward the parlor, where Papa was listening to the victrola. "He doesn't like it any more than we do, Polly. Maybe less. But he can't say so."

Before I got into bed I ran down to see her one more time. She was finishing up the sewing.

"I'll go find Caleb, Mama," I told her. She actually laughed and kissed my cheek, then pushed me toward the stairs.

April 23

Oh my lord, the country's in terrible shape. It's frightening—horrifying really. Can't say I fully understand why, though I'm trying. But I saw a picture today of a bread line in Boston. Went on for blocks and blocks. My goodness. At least we're eating.

April 25

A truly nice day! I'm gay as could be.

For one thing, Miss Ballou sent a note for my parents. I was nervous but I figured, what could it be but praise? I gave it to Ma and as she read it she started beaming. Then she folded it up and just sat there smiling at me, the picture of pride.

"What's it say?" I asked, not expecting her to tell.

"It says you are *extraordinary*, Polly." Huge satisfaction in her voice. "It says you are *exceptional*. It asks that we—all three of us— meet with her at the end of the year to discuss your future studies."

I drew a breath. I hadn't been prepared for all that. "I guess I might get a scholarship to college, Mama," I said.

She reached out to stroke my hair. "I guess you might."

The second thing was that she has relaxed about Caleb. On account of a digit. "Look here, Polly," she said after rereading the note and talking a little about my studies. She jumped up and went into the parlor, came back with her letter. "See here where I wrote the street number? That one in the middle? Looks just like a seven! They simply read it wrong is all, and took it some other place entirely." Her smile got even wider. "A minor error, that's the problem. The next letter will go through fine."

It looked like a one but what mattered was that she was happy.

And last, and most amazing: a package for me from Boston! She mentioned *that* as I was leaving the room. Mr. Samuel had sent word, she told me, all amused, saying come today or he would bring it by tomorrow. If I hurried I might get there before he closed.

"Pick up your father at the garage," she called out as I was racing for the wagon. "He's leaving the Ford there tonight." I knew the roads were pretty muddy; I didn't think I could make it, but I sure had to try. I wondered why she wasn't more curious, even concerned, but on the way down I realized it had to be something she'd arranged. Some sort of surprise.

I got there with minutes to spare, it turned out. And there *was* a package for me. And it was from, of all people, Moses Moseby! And it had in it, of all things, books! One novel and two histories and a collection of essays. Mr. Samuel was also amused as I stood there and stared.

"Lent those to someone, did you?" he asked.

"Yes sir," I answered. "That is, my pa did, I think."

"How come they sent 'em back to you?"

I went into the corner beyond the stove to open the letter.

"Dear Polly," Mr. Moseby had written, "I hope you will forgive my forwardness but I felt we came to know each other while I was in Greenwich. I was impressed by your intelligence and wanted to encourage it, and also to return the favor you did me in sharing your company and thoughts." I was astonished. Why would this man, I asked myself as I shrank back behind the stove so two ladies wouldn't see me, be kind to anyone in Greenwich?

"I know it can't be easy," he wrote, "for a young person—especially a girl—in the country to become educated. You will understand, in fact, that I have first-hand experience of the restriction of knowledge to certain classes of individuals. So at the risk of overstepping decent bounds I have selected some works I thought might interest you. Read them, if so inclined, and then write me at the address below—again, only if you wish to—and let me know your reactions. No need to return the books, they are secondhand copies which cost almost nothing to obtain."

"Closing up now, Polly," Mr. Samuel called out then, distracting me, but when I looked again "obtain" was the final word. "Your friend (and correspondent?), Moses Moseby" was all it said after that. His signature was beautiful and I stared at it for a while, then quickly read the whole letter again before gathering up the books and wrappers and stepping out the door.

I was so stunned by this development—so confused and even alarmed by it, partly because his reasons seemed insufficient, and partly because I felt certain Mr. Samuel would spread the news all over town—that I almost forgot my father. I was off in the wrong direction, the horse barely moving as I thought it all over, before it occurred to me to head for the garage.

Pa was talking to the mechanic. "Hello Polly," he said as he jumped up beside me. "This is a nice surprise." He kissed me and looked down at the books. "Where did those come from?"

"Miss Ballou had some teacher in Boston mail them to me," I told him. "Extra reading she wants me to start on." I whipped up the horse and headed toward the crossroads. I couldn't look at him. "She sent me home with a note as well. Mama'll show it to you. I suppose she thinks pretty well of me. Miss Ballou, that is." I was amazed that I could lie so smoothly, to my pa of all people, and set myself up to be found out later. Oh well, I thought, maybe they'll never meet her. I remembered the mailbox near BHS; I could send letters to Boston from there.

When I finally did look he was staring at me. As if he sensed I was lying.

"Polly McPhee," he said, "I always knew you'd be special. God bless you for making a sad man so proud."

When he leaned over and kissed me I came close to speaking—to admitting my falseness. But I was afraid he'd take the books.

Later on I resolved to think about it for a while, and look the books over, and then decide whether to tell them the truth. I lay there on the sofa sort of wallowing in conceit, I guess you'd call it, considering what it meant that Miss Ballou thought I was *extraordinary* and had *a future*, that Mr. Moseby respected my *intelligence* and wanted me to be well-read.

And Papa's been kind of sunny lately, and Mama just climbed out from under her worry all by herself. And personally I'm learning to relax again, to enjoy myself, to have fun. Even to look forward to things! It's been a long time.

April 30

They don't even notice I'm there anymore.
"Where do you see us going?"

"Any place, dear. Any number of places. Any place not underwater."

"Answer the question."

"How about Wisconsin? Just temporarily. With the herd and all that land I'm sure Don could use some help. And Flo says we can stay with them as long as we need."

"No charity, damn it."

I saw her almost stamp her foot. "They're family."

"No."

"Fine, David, you decide. There are a hundred possibilities."

"Well we can't sell right now, we'd get next to nothing," said my father. "Those thieves at the Commission are aware of what's happening. They've adjusted accordingly."

"Then better we'd sold three years ago," she told him, rather loudly. And very crossly. "If we wait another three we will end up even sorrier. You can't dither forever."

But he just turned away.

May 4

Finally had a talk with Roy. Bumped into each other after church—not that he was there, I don't know why he was in town. My folks were busy with some friends so I walked him around the corner.

"I've been kind of out of touch," he said.

"That's all right, Roy. Just want to be sure you're OK."

He stared at me for a while. I felt I hardly knew him. Maybe he was thinking the same.

"Yeah, I'm OK," he said at last. "Fact, I'm better than ever."

"Prosperous?"

He laughed. "Prosperous enough," he said. "We don't need much. Mostly food and tobacco."

All through our conversation we both kept glancing to the side, like we wanted to get away. When I told him I had to go I could see him relax. That was the most distressing but when I rounded the corner it eased.

May 9

I've almost finished Mr. Moseby's books. I'm a little short on sleep and I know I've read too fast but I've been eager to get through them. I'd like to write him reports but I don't have the time. What with schoolwork and chores I'd faint away from exhaustion. I've made a few notes for myself is all.

I've managed to start a letter though. I want to say how thankful I am. He did it to help me and he deserves to hear he has. As a matter of fact, he doesn't know I even received them! He's been wondering all this time.

No word from Caleb yet. But I'm not worried, it'll come.

May 15

We're not through with bad news. I've been pretending we were, but that isn't real life. Bad news is a random and arbitrary event of unknown frequency, as we would say in science class, having nothing to do with fairness or sense, and its potential is terrifying. Beyond belief, really.

Anyway: my father has lost his job. After twenty-two years. We would all be outraged if it weren't so common now. The owner, Mr. Garfield, was awfully sorry and all that, and told Pa he can't pay his own bills this month, but it's easy to resent him. I know, I know, everybody's in trouble, but there must be some businesses that saw what was coming and were a little more prudent. Why couldn't that have been Mr. Garfield? Why not Garfield Manufacturing? Well he's got to do his own books now, and I'm ashamed to say I hope he makes plenty of mistakes.

The first thing Mama said, right in front of her daughter, was that if he wouldn't sell now she would leave home without him. Just take me and her parents' and Caleb's portraits and go. All he could do was agree.

"I'll start out looking right away," he said, staring out the window at the rain that was falling on the yard. I heard hurt and resignation in his voice, and fear too. "I'll just canvass every outfit

133

from Worcester to Pittsfield, one by one." He looked back at us and then turned to the window again. No one had lit a lamp yet and the light was soft on his face. We listened in the gloom.

"When we know where I'll be working," he went on, "we'll sell this place to those bastards and find a house somewhere nearby. It'll be small but we'll make sure it's pretty."

The clock ticked on as we waited and then my father turned and sighed. "Sarah, Polly," he said softly, "I'm sorry. I know you'll say it's not my fault but I feel I've let you down." He walked away then but as he did he said quite clearly, "Time to go."

May 18

I can picture him so clearly: the uncombed too-long hair, the scar on his chest, the smile I've never really understood but love so much, want always turned to me. Wearing big city clothes. So clearly. Like I could reach out and touch him, if I knew which way to reach.

May 23

I actually caught myself whistling on the way home today. As if I hadn't a care. How can you be *cheerful*, I asked myself, what with the current situation plus old sorrows you still wake up to some days?

God knows how I managed but I've got faith back, somehow. My belief in the future. My brother will turn up perfectly safe, Roy will outgrow that old hermit and his shack, Papa will find another job and my parents a place good for fifty years more, I'll go off to college but not before Mr. Moseby sends me the book that will magically tell me, within the first dozen pages, what I want for my life's work, and we'll all get together on the shores of the reservoir and laugh about how it came out all right.

May 27

So I had another birthday. My seventeenth. It seems impossible, on the one hand, and on the other not old enough. At any rate I'd told my parents I wanted absolutely no gifts (Pa figures we have four, maybe five more months before we're broke) and would be happy with some flowers and a cake and a long walk, all three of us, and I got those. My pa is quite tense from the refusals he's been hearing and my mother very glum from piecing through our possessions—and I don't guess any of us goes an hour, twenty minutes, without thinking of my brother—but they relaxed and even brightened as we walked along the road. For a while anyway. It was a lovely warm night. We walked until it got dark. Papa went to light his lantern but the moon was three-quarters and up well above the trees and Mama held his arm. So he hung it on his belt and took my hand in his left one and my mother's in his right as we came up our drive.

June 11

I got a nice letter from Moses. (I picked it up at the P.O.; I've been checking pretty regularly. Fortunately, Mr. Samuel, the postmaster, is keeping the whole business to himself, just why I don't know.) He apologized for the delay and promised more books as soon as he could find them. "I am impressed, but not surprised, by your embrace of new ideas," he said in closing. "The hallmark of an able mind." I can't wait for his next shipment.

No birthday wishes from Caleb.

June 15

I can't believe we're leaving at last. Five years, it is now, since the announcement. A long vigil but soon to end.

Nothing's come up yet for Pa but he has a new idea: he wants to sign on with a mill that has yet to relocate. At least one will be needing a new accountant, he figures, and he'll just offer to go wherever they want him.

135

It will be strange to cross the line for the very last time and look back on our valley. But I'm glad our turn has come.

June 19

We had our meeting with Miss Ballou. There was nothing unexpected; what mattered most, besides the happiness her praise gave my parents, who are very distressed right now, was her advice about college. She knows an awful lot about it and had written up some notes. When I thanked her she said it was a pleasure to help, and would we write to keep her apprised.

Once again I felt the tension I'd been struggling with all day. About saying it was her who'd sent the books. By some miracle we'd gotten past it the first time. My father mentioned "all you've done—extra attention, extra reading—" but she didn't even notice, or didn't seem to. And I managed to sit silent despite my urge to confess.

But with the reference to letters I felt I had to act quickly. "I'll never forget you, Miss Ballou."

"Nor I you, Polly," she answered, taking my hand.

As we left I had the impulse to run back and tell her, to explain the whole thing, but I stifled that one too.

June 25

She tried to go after all. I heard them talking in the parlor. She bought a ticket and left a note but at the last she lost her nerve. I've been avoiding certain questions but now she's woken me up. Two months! Why have they waited? Respect and trust are well and good but can be taken too far. I can't imagine them waiting this long to look for me.

It woke my father up too. "We'll go together," he said. "You can't possibly have imagined I'd refuse to come with you? Or thought it wise to go alone?"

136

"Do you suppose..." It sounded as though she could hardly speak. "Do you suppose he's just run off?" There was silence between them. "So many young men go their own way these days."

Papa coughed. "I can't believe it," he said. "He is not that sort of son."

"You'll really come?"

"In a week. We need to arrange for the farm; Polly can handle it with some help. Then we'll head down there and find him."

But later on I heard him mutter, "Maybe we ought to leave him be."

June 27

A long letter from Edna! With a snapshot of their house. I wrote back right away. How I wish I could see her.

My childhood's half-dismembered now, cast out widely and drifting. I hold tightly to the rest.

"The town of your youth—"
"No longer exists."
"Of course not. They're all gone."
"Not like mine."

The river shining in the sun; the endless whispered greens of June; the way the smoke clouds hang so round above the chimneys on a clear still freezing day—I'll miss all that.

39

July 2, 1932

Today is the very middle day of the year. You might guess it was yesterday but you'd be wrong. Most years there are 182 days before July 2nd and 182 to follow. Leap years have no middle day but I'm choosing to celebrate anyway. First day of the second half instead.

I know it's childish but I'm enjoying this made-up holiday of mine. This is a pretty rotten year and at least it's halfway over. We have a chance to start again. Maybe they'll bring Caleb home in a couple of days. Maybe Pa will find a job. Or maybe not, but as I've observed I have to have some optimism. It's almost foolish how many hard things have happened in my life, and it's got to improve.

I almost informed my folks during dinner tonight but they weren't in the mood. They would have told me to save it. Or said please Polly the way they do. Or just gone on chewing the carrots. Maybe tonight I can tell them how it's the start of something new.

July 3

What happened is my mother died. My father woke and she was gone. He must have checked to make sure but it was hours, we think, before dawn, hours and hours, so he knew right away and no mistake. Then he came to get me. We sat together in their bedroom for a while, watching over. Tears drenched me but he was dry. We held hands and were silent but we knew each other's minds and I am sure if desperate wishes could raise the dead we'd have had Mama back. We agreed after a time that it wasn't going to happen. He asked if I would watch her while he went to get the doctor; I said I would. When he left I almost up and ran after but you're a grown girl now, I thought, if not a woman you are grown, and you've got to stay by her. Even that early the day was warm, although a slight breeze spread the curtains. I pulled the coverlet up from the foot of her bed all the way to her chin—I thought at least she'll never be too hot or cold again—and smoothed her hair with my hand, then went back to my seat.

The doctor didn't have any real explanation. He looked at us in sorrow but he couldn't say why. Pa mentioned a few small things that had been bothering her and he stared into the corner and muttered, "Maybe diabetes"—but then he stopped and said, "Listen, David, Polly, I just don't know. I won't pretend to. If you want we can try our best to find out but I'm too shook up myself to speculate right now." He touched my father's elbow. "The important thing is to do what's needed for Sarah and take care of you two." Then he fell back into a chair. "I'm so sorry," he said. He pulled out a cloth to dry his eyes.

"Forgive me, Polly," he said to my face, "but we played together as children, your mother and I."

"That's OK," I told him. "I'm just as glad you're crying too."

"I was sure she'd be around for the rest of my life."

"So were we," said my pa.

After he left on his way to the Atkinsons and then to town to get things started Papa turned from the bed. "I can't look anymore," he told me. He stood and stared out the window. "It's a sin to take good farmland like this," he said. "It's not like there's so damned much of it out here."

After a while we knew the doctor had made it to town because we heard the bell ringing. Five tolls for a woman—a man is more, a child less—and then a pause and forty more, for her age. I understood that everybody had it narrowed right down on account of

141

this information and were wondering who exactly, just as I have myself in the past, and I wanted to run and tell them. I longed to be the one. Only the knowing it was impossible—that they would all have heard the news before I could ever reach them—kept me from bolting out the door.

July 4

Independence Day. For Polly at least.
She's really gone.

July 5

The service is at noon. It's too hot to wait longer. I wish like hell I could reach Caleb but given that I have no idea of how there's not a thing to be gained by putting it off another day.

She can't be laid to rest in Greenwich. A new rule. No more burials in the valley; only up in that new place, back of Great Quabbin hill. The one they've been carting their grim boxes to for the best part of a year.

Of course it would be idiotic to put her in the ground just to dig her up again but poor Mama. Poor dear. It makes a sick horrible pain. That she can't sleep on here, in the town of her birth. We felt sorry for the old ones but we never imagined it would affect one of us. I'm sure my mama saw herself side-by-side with her husband in another ancient churchyard in whatever place they went to, in the shadow of a steeple like our own here in Greenwich. Not in that new "park" they've laid out over the hill. I know it makes no major difference—except the distance we will have to go to visit her, of course—but it seems so very unfair. If it was flooded already that would be something else again but we'll pass by her empty place, her rightful place, on the way to see the new one. The dirt that waits for her body, that has been waiting forty years.

Why do I write this? I don't think I could say. As I read back it all seems so easy, so free from pain. The truth is that I weep and

142

weep and comfort my father and weep some more and call out her name and those are the only things I care to do, and when they run out temporarily—when my system is dry and he needs to be alone—I sit and write in this diary. That's the third thing. There's nothing else. For a while they tried to get me to eat but since I shrieked at Maisie's mother when she came at me with some corn-bread they have left me alone. I haven't bathed either, or even brushed my hair. Crying and holding Pa and writing: God bless those occupations, else I might expire too.

I went to see her just once. I told Pa my intention and he cleared some women out. The undertaker from Enfield had done a couple of things to keep her fresh for a while but Papa and I decid-ed—*I* decided and he agreed—that what she would have wanted was to be left alone, to lie in her own bed and be buried as she was in her nightgown and her sheets. As I sat on the edge and looked at her tired face I remembered reading in one of Moses's books that the Jews bury their dead before sundown the same day. If that leaves them just an hour then they find a way to do it. It seemed a sensible idea and I was taken by a fierce desire to have her in the ground. I wanted to run and start digging right then at that mo-ment. It seemed the only way to ease my own intolerable hurt. The fact of her death and of my loss came to me then, in its truest form for the very first time, and what I'd thought of as pain was com-pletely washed away in a new and unbelievable misery.

I threw my body on her full length. I was wild for a moment, almost in a frenzy; I wanted to strike her for not coming back to me. But then I found—I was astonished—a way out of my panic. A way to reach a place of calm. As I grasped her cold body I had a vision of my own baby, grieving for me—my own lonely little girl at seven, at fourteen, at thirty-two—and the worst of it passed on. I sat up and away from her and as I straightened her bedclothes and refolded her hands I knew I might have died first, that it might have been she mourning me, and the fact that she'd avoided that was actually a comfort. I remembered how she'd worried about Caleb and the image of her standing over my dead body, or his, was enough to make me happy—truly happy—that she had passed away first. She should have had thirty or forty years more but at least she didn't have to bury me. My chest filled with relief. Darling Mama, I whispered, I will love you forever. And had a minute of peace before my tears began again.

Then I opened the door and let some new ladies in.

July 6

I was enraged. So was my pa. We didn't know what to do. They mixed them all up together—my ma is nowhere near her kin. And no one told us until we got there. We asked them why not but they can't do it, they said. There are sections for old and sections for new and her family are installed already with no spaces around them. What kind of cretin, my father wanted to know, decided to combine all the graveyards that way instead of laying them out as they were, with room for additions? The man in charge was embarrassed but he chose not to answer. He didn't *have* any answer, except that maybe it was him. So there was this hole in the ground, next to some grandfather from up by Soapstone we never heard of who had a heart attack or stroke last spring, and all the people waiting for us to put her into it, and there was nothing we could do. What was our option—to refuse it? Wait till they dug us another? There was no Armstrong plot available. There's no such thing anymore! But Papa swears he won't rest until he has the satisfaction of telling those responsible what they've done.

"Just save the space next to her, that's all," he said to the man, looking him in the eye. "Think you can manage that much?"

The Reverend Howell's words, though, were affectionate and kind, and then my father spoke up too (which he hadn't at the church). He thanked all the mourners, not only for their help since Mama died but for caring for her and providing her such joy while she lived. I was awfully proud of him, as much as possible in my woe. Every single person left there feeling treasured by my mother. She was generous even in death, thanks to Pa.

So all my anger was gone when they lowered her down which was just as well, really, because when I realized she was on the verge of leaving me forever I simply couldn't accept it. That was a very bad moment. I jumped forward and Papa caught me and held me tight to his body and I somehow made it through. He nodded over to Larry Sherman, who'd come all the way from Otis, and it was him who shoveled the dirt on. With our blessing. The workers tried to take over but Mrs. Schuble came up and grabbed the spade from one of them and then Mr. Partridge and it was Mama's friends and neighbors who filled her grave in. My pa and I just watched.

July 7

I saw my brother coming toward me. At the gravesite. I saw him coming and looked around and then saw him again. But he never arrived.

40

I imagine me and Roy walking quickly by the tracks. From a station near a city in a country far away. Paris France, Brussels Belgium, even Budapest or Rome. Walking quickly walking briskly on a raised-up rail embankment, past a field of foreign flowers. The farmers ask where are we going, why dressed so strangely, what do we want with that old railroad? They holler out to us in tongues. Come work the land and we will feed you. Come down and play with our children. Come tell us all about America, America the kind, if what we've heard of it is true. But we can't speak— no common language—and we have faith it's just as well. We've got to move. No stopping now.

(Ten thousand weary miles away a man stands leaning on a switch. His muscles tense; the crowd gasps.)

A big black roaring locomotive rushes ruinously by. Roy grabs my arms just in time and pulls me out of its path. We stand and watch as many cars full of cattle speed past us, staring into helpless eyes. The last one whistles and is gone. The sun behind us lights the way as it crosses the horizon, the alien rim, with its cargo of souls.

(The switch is thrown; the crowd sighs. It has a mind to move forward but the damage is done. From somewhere down out of sight the sound of eager water gushing.)

After endless walking on we come at last to the ocean. We stand high on a bluff. Roy nods and tosses in his kerchief and it washes out to sea.

(A train slides into the water. The crowd is silent as it drowns.)

41

August

I guess we're staying. It's what he wants. He's given up looking for work. Says there's no work to be had and there's some truth in that. More important, he says, he won't abandon the farm because it's all he has left of Mama. There's some truth in that too. It would be different without our deadline but there it is; soon enough we'll be forced but for now we have the time to recover. Or he does—the setting's not conducive for me. But no matter. I can always do it later.

In the meantime we have to put food on the table. With the growing tourist trade we might manage half-decent money, I think, if we concentrate on specialty items, like the berries and honey and candy. It needs lots of hard work and ideally a loan from the bank (fat chance!) but we can do it. Or we can try. There aren't a whole lot of choices. He won't let me ask for help—I can't imagine why not, half the state is getting some, half the country—but I will, sooner or later. I have to make sure he eats well and dresses warmly and I have no intention of depriving myself either. We'll need to pay the doctor from time to time and make repairs to the property, and keep the car running so we can visit our friends and Mama's grave and get to interviews when his outlook improves. If we don't use the money we can always give it back but I am going to apply. Behind his back if need be.

I haven't written down a word for more than a month. Haven't read at all either—a package arrived from Moses in mid-July, the poor man would feel awful if he knew of the timing, and the books are still sitting on my bureau where I put them—and haven't missed it a bit. Grief and chores and my daddy have kept me busy and even content, if that word is not offensive. What I'm saying is that my circumstances dictate my occupations. Not so long ago in days but forever in my mind I was still a young girl who was waiting, it seems, for her duty to come to her out of the sky, out of some stranger's mouth or pen, but by now I'm a woman who sees what must be done. As was my mama I suppose. I'm to miss her and to try to find my brother if I can and care for my father and go to school and run a farm and earn a living. There's not much room for any more. There will have to be room—I have got to have writing and reading and I know it, I *am* missing them tonight—but I have yet to work that out. I will do what is required.

September 2

And college will have to wait. I simply can't leave my pa.

September 4

Finally looked at those books from Moses. I was surprised at myself. Before it was like handling objects of awe, religious articles or maybe artifacts of history. But now they're just books. I left them scattered on my bed. One in particular seems good, by a woman called Stein, although she seems to take liberties. But mostly liberties I like.

Afterwards I wept about something other than Mama for the first time in months. I was looking at the handful of volumes he'd sent and envisioning my life here for the next several years and it came to me how much there was to read and how little I would get through by the time I was twenty years old. They'll assign me some at school and maybe I can handle what Moses sends but I won't manage much more. There are so many books. Millions. And

I have so little guidance, so little extra time. It made me terribly sad and I sat there and cried. Felt sorry for myself, to be honest. Nothing wrong with it either. I haven't fully indulged, it seems to me, since Roy was sent away, but I'm entitled. About time too. Saint Polly I'm not.

September 12

Hey Caleb, God damn you, why on earth don't you come home?

September 17

Roy came by and brought me money. Lots of it. I didn't ask where he got it and I don't think he would have answered. "I figured you could use this," he said. He held it out to me and though I didn't want to take it I wanted less to refuse so in the end I let him put it in my hand.

"I heard about your ma," he said, "and about your pa's job. I'm awfully sorry, Polly. Just as sorry as I could be. I wish twenty bad things had happened to me instead."

"Why weren't you at the funeral?" I asked.

"Cowardice," he told me. "Pure cowardice. And stupidity. I'll regret it until my own."

I turned away and put the cash on the shelf above the sink, then thought better and tucked it underneath the clock.

"She wasn't my mother," Roy said, very softly, "but she came closer than anyone else ever has."

I offered him tea and we talked for a while. It was very relaxed. He told me what he was doing and asked a lot of questions about the farm, about Papa, even about school. He made some excellent suggestions for improving our business next season. Maybe it was the months with my weak and silent parent—I'd finally gotten him out of the house by himself and down to the Inn to see some of his gang—but I found Roy almost glowing with life and energy. I was happy, I think, to be with a capable man. And a man

150

he was, without question, all grown up and big. I was surprised when he told me he had no girl. Ridge runner or no he was attractive and strong.

And I was friends with him again. Just like that. Without trying. The warmth of our early years. And faint whispers of something more.

When I could bear it no longer I stood up and went to him. I sat in his lap and kissed him. Astonished? Maybe. Nervous? A bit. He opened his eyes and we stared at each other as the kiss carried on. Then I pulled him to his feet.

"Where's your father?" he asked.

"Forget him," I said.

Not in my body. I couldn't. Oh no. But I wanted to give him pleasure. He kept trembling more and more. To tell the truth I was pleased by his lack of control and my own firm containment. While his eyes rolled in his head I kept my presence of mind.

That I led while he followed: it seemed to be what I wanted. At least once I'd seen all of him again. Before that maybe more, something larger, something worthy, but not after. One good look was enough, like a dull shadow falling.

While I was standing there thinking where to hide the cash from Pa he sat on the floor stroking me, murmuring my name.

"Give me my money back," he said a little later, as he buckled his belt.

I smiled and shook my head. "Forget it, Roy Ralston," I told him. "It's mine now."

"You're no whore, Polly."

I stepped back behind the table. As opposed to slapping his face. "We really need that money," I said, "and I am deeply, deeply grateful to you for your thoughtfulness and generosity, and you did not purchase a thing."

His frown broke then and he laughed and kissed me and headed for the door. Before he got through it he stopped and turned. "You're really something," he said.

Then I was ashamed.

September 25

Pa was singing today. For at least an hour this morning, walking around doing chores before going for a look at the berries. "Brother, Can You Spare a Dime?" I don't know where he even heard it, much less learned it; down at the Inn I guess. He sang it with real feeling. When he got to "Hey, don't you remember?" it was practically opera. I was amused and glad and puzzled. Maybe it suddenly occurred to him that he's surrounded by misery in every direction, and that made him feel better. (I intend no sarcasm or disrespect when I write this; Lord knows it helps me.) Later on he was back to his grim silent self.

Maisie says lots of folks are on relief. Both those still here and those who have moved. She exaggerates of course—trying to scandalize, I think—but there must be more than a few. In the best of times you'd expect some valley people to be idle on account of the project so it stands to reason, with a third of the country out of work, that we'd be doing very poorly. And there's a bad smell that goes along with victimhood, which is part of the problem; add that to being last in line in other people's towns and the lack of jobs here and where could we be working?

Not that I have objections to our taking public money. Not this household nor any other. The state can damn well bail us out if need be. I have no lively concern for the unemployed in Boston— let them shift for themselves—but we're entitled to some help.

September 29

Off to New York any day. Pa's a little stronger now and I've been gathering my nerve. Best before it gets too cold.

October 4

It turns out Mama knew about Moses and his books. I found a letter from him in her box. (I am finally able now to look at some of her things. Poor Papa, of course, couldn't even hope to manage; he's still sleeping in the parlor.) He wrote to her way back in February—very respectful, very serious—asking if she would like his "assistance" in "broadening" my "outlook." What she would have made of that I can only try to imagine, but she must have told him OK. And kept it from my father. I never in a thousand years would have guessed this—in fact, I would have figured she'd go to the authorities—but then I still have a lot to discover about her. When I next write to Moses (I sent a note about her death) I'll ask exactly what she said.

Afraid to bring it up with Pa—don't want to make him cry again. We never mention her nor Caleb. I know it's wrong but he's so fragile, I allow him his preference.

Oh Mama. Dear Mama! I miss miss miss miss you so very much, so tremendously much, I'm so completely unable to keep going on my own. Please, *please* come back. Please do! Your little Polly is lost, Mama, fading away.

October 12

Maybe I'll quit high school. What's the point?

October 22

There is comfort in caring for the animals, at least. They depend on me but their needs are simple. With the help of Pa and a couple of his friends I've reorganized the barns and sheds and feeding is much easier. Sold off one of the cows (not Clara, of course) because it's only two of us and extra milk is just more trouble than it's worth. We're very efficient now. So I have a few moments to pause, every morning and evening, and enjoy the stock. Clara is my friend and the horse makes a fine companion—I ponder and he chews—and the chickens amuse (although one can't respect chickens). I never liked the pigs but the last one will be slaughtered any day now and that's it for their bullying and their stink. The bees are somewhat frightening but I've learned to handle everything without getting stung and there's a certain joy in that. In a way even the plants are my associates, part of my flock, and at times I feel like God, the farm my benevolent domain. It's grandiose but it soothes me.

October 27

They've picked a name for it: Quabbin. Like the lake and the hills. "Many waters" in Nipmuc or so they claim. The very first name for Greenwich, in 1739; now its eternal name as well.

October 29

Moses is silent. Caleb gone half a year. And no more visits from Roy. To my surprise.

October 30

I see a time when even the oldest don't remember. When we're all dust and mud.

October 31

No I'm sorry Roy. I'm sorry. No. Not ever again.

November 6

Governor Roosevelt was elected last week. Thank God is all I can say. If somebody doesn't do something quick the country will fall apart before they even finish that dam.

November 10

It's my dirty little secret. No one privy but Pa. It really is inexcusable; I know I'm damned ten times over. Even if I don't go— I've tried and tried but something's holding me back—there are letters I could write. People I could see. I could even send Roy, I'm pretty sure he'd be willing. But I do nothing at all.

Because I fear the very worst, I simply can't afford to know.

November 15

My pa has taken a fancy to old man Proctor. The notorious crank. They say he was a leading citizen about thirty years ago but now he just wanders the roads between the village and his farm, spouting loud extreme opinions, while his grandkids do the work. Papa says there is more to his critiques and his theories than I might realize and it's probably his family's fault he doesn't stay at home. Due to they don't appreciate him.

"Maybe they don't appreciate being lectured all the time," I said as I poked the sweet potatoes.

"He doesn't lecture me," said Pa, "because I listen. And respond to what he's saying. He's a very thoughtful man."

"You figure maybe you're the only one to listen to him since 1904?" I asked.

"You have to have the right frame of mind, I'll grant you."

I turned my attention to the stew. (He'd killed a rooster that morning.) I stirred it for a moment and looked for the pepper.

"So what've you two been conversing about?"

He laughed briefly. "Mostly the project," he said. "Of course. We have some similar perspectives."

I turned around. "Pa," I said, "I don't want him getting you all excited about that. Excuse my speaking this way but it's simply beating your head against the wall and there's no sense in it. No sense. It'll take too much out of you. Let go."

"Polly," he began, "I'm old enough—"

"But I'm not!" I shouted, throwing down the spoon. "I'm not! You need to start doing more work around here, Papa. Not stepping out with old man Proctor. *I'm just a girl.*"

We were quiet for a long time while I cleaned up the floor. I had the strongest impression of my brother in the room, standing silent in the doorframe.

"Nonetheless, I admire him," my father told me at last. "He swears he won't leave until the last dog is hung. And I agree."

November 20

Forty nights and forty years. We're all the children of Noah. Mount Pom our Ararat. But no ark will ever land.

42

(1923)

"The water's wide, I can't cross over
and neither have I wings to fly
build me a boat to carry two
and both shall row, my love and I

There is a ship that sails the sea
she's loaded deep as deep could be
but not as deep as my love for him
I know not how to sink or swim

I leaned my back against an oak
thinking it was a mighty tree
but first it bent and then it broke
so did my love prove false to me

Oh love is handsome, love is kind
the sweetest flower when it is new
but love grows old and waxes cold
and fades away like morning dew

R.C. Binstock

When sea sand turneth far inland
and mussels grow on every tree
when cockle shells turn silver bells
then would I lose my love for thee

The water's wide, I can't cross over
and neither have I wings to fly
build me a boat to carry two
and both shall row, my love and I"

43

Mama's piano waiting there. Piano waiting in the parlor. Needing only her touch her will her desire. Waiting there in the parlor across from the window next to the fireplace with her music still on. Waiting with its chips and stains. That was her voice that piano that was her vital legacy that was her instrument her motive that was her pleasure that piano. That was my mama. That was her joy.

44

March 24, 1933

There's a motto in the library down at Belchertown High. "Let these books be your adventure." And that is what they are for some, although by no means for all; certainly Mr. Doench, bless him, seems able to inspire most of his students to read, really read, and once they do they're caught forever.

But for me they're something different. There was a time long ago when I sought them out for stimulation, yes, to entertain, but I've outgrown that entirely. I don't want adventure now; I seek no excitement. I have no desire to "make my way to distant, exotic lands." Reading provides me with comfort—with companionship and support, with security and calm, all the things I badly need. In the constant brutal battle between anger and gratitude, trust and betrayal, books are my white knights; they are loyal as nothing else has been, not my childhood nor my place of birth, not my pets nor my girlfriends, not even my own mother.

I could not have survived the winter without them. The cold, the gloom, the loneliness, the poverty, the daily struggles with my father to keep him from slipping under the surface of his grief, like a swimmer going down. The images of Caleb, of Mama, of Edna, even of Moses passing back and forth like targets in a dismal shooting gallery, left to right and right to left, a little too quickly for me to take careful aim. The awkward, repugnant advances of the boys at school. (I guess I must be not too awful looking, though

Maisie still criticizes my appearance on a weekly or daily basis, something I almost enjoy.) The dreadful sameness of our meals; the total lack of happy news; the hemmed-in feeling that came whenever I went outside for air and stood looking about me, knowing that though the world went on forever my valley was getting smaller by the hour. All these things were kept at bay, if not defeated, by my candle-lit pages. By beginnings middles and ends. I survived on a ration of words set down by strangers, mostly far away, some long dead, none familiar with my plight.

The books assigned in my classes are mostly a dull lot and I'm without further guidance from Moses, who never sent another batch. But I seem to have acquired my own gift of selection, or perhaps it's that selection has become, for me, unnecessary. What I start I admire, or am taught by, or draw sustenance from; I have yet to be disappointed by what I've picked out on my own. I have the library in the village and the one at school and the assistance of Mrs. Fletcher (who sort of beams and frowns all at once every time I come in now) and Miss Green at BHS, and even my parents' small collection. All told these seem to be enough.

I find I've lost all my desire, though, to record my opinions. It's almost as if my judgment no longer matters, or at least that I'm reserving it; I'm going to read and read and read and then someday be impelled, once again, to say or write what I think. But not now. Not in this place. It's a distraction, I suppose, my opinion, or at least beside the point.

The essence of it—yes—is that a very few things have kept me whole: working the farm, caring for Pa, sleeping, reading. A blessing, a burden, release and a friend; a basic minimum set for getting through until spring.

Perhaps now life will gain some substance. Or at least admit some light.

April 2

I see Miss Ballou sometimes. I do my best to avoid her eyes. I know she has ambitions for me but I've other fish to fry.

161

April 15

I've just come from the dedication. Of the graveyard on Great Quabbin. Or rather "cemetery," as they insist, or maybe "park." At any rate forget the name; it's where my mama is buried. There was no question of not going.

My father didn't agree. He outright refused to attend, in fact, from the start, from the day I first mentioned it over a month ago. Wouldn't explain, wouldn't discuss it, wouldn't answer at all beyond the single word "no." Of all the hard times he's given me since her death, this was the hardest. I actually shouted at him twice. To no avail. He wouldn't come. I felt ashamed in the end, more than a little, so before I left I went to him (he was feeding the chickens) and apologized and called it a fuss over nothing. He nodded briskly before reaching out another handful of corn.

It was a very pretty day and the crowd was rather large, at least larger than I expected. Almost every family left has someone buried there, fresh or transferred, but there are many who've refused to even acknowledge the new location. The displacement of our burial grounds is such a powerful statement, a rigid dose of reality; if they dug up all those corpses and stuck them there behind the hill they must be serious, mustn't they?

Given this I anticipated a thin to moderate turnout, but the crowd was more than respectable. Most of the valley seemed to be there. And despite the bad decisions, the mixing up of the graves, the majority were impressed. It is a very attractive place, though I'm reluctant to admit it, thoughtfully designed and tastefully executed, down to the careful placement of town monuments and memorials. It'll be even nicer when the trees and shrubs grow up.

Perhaps this was our last hurrah. All together, I mean. Among the faces there were dozens I will never see again.

Roy showed up, of all people. When I waved he came right over. I've been seeing him around from time to time and our attitude has been…casual. I was sure he'd be back for more, or failing that would disdain me, but he's done neither. He's been friendly—

smiling friendly—and only that. A touch of longing and even wor-ship in his gaze, yes, but mostly affable is what he's been.

We stood and chatted for a while as the dignitaries assembled. I must say, he gave the most emphatic impression of liking me. Of simple pleasure at the encounter.

"I went to see your ma last month," he told me. "Cried my head off. I'll say it again, Polly—I'm awful sorry, terrible sorry. I'd change it any way I could."

Where were you last July, I asked in silence, but then recalled his own story.

A few minutes later he confided something to me. "No matter where I end up," he whispered in my ear as the band played slow and solemn, "I want to be buried here. Right here."

As some Commission man went on (he pledged perpetual care) I thought for a while about the Nipmuc. All their graves down in the lowlands. Shouldn't they have been moved as well? On the one hand they'll be staying in their own sacred ground, where they intended to rest, a privilege denied to my mother and her neighbors. But on the other it shows a shameful lack of respect. Oh well, I decided, let them have the valley floor. They don't need our sort of honor.

After the speeches I held Roy's hand for a moment and then stepped quickly away and wandered slowly, by myself, past the rows to Mama's grave, which has its marker by now. We inspected it back in town when it was finished, of course, but it was another thing entirely to see it over her head. It looked very good, I thought: "Sarah Rebecca Armstrong/1892-1932/beloved wife and mother/native daughter of Greenwich/in God repose." It is a large, impressive marker—it has to be, to say all that and still leave room for Pa—and set us back a pretty penny, the best part of our reserve. But it's a thing you have to have. I stood there next to Mama with my hand resting on it and was comforted. Truly. Began to feel al-most peaceful. As if it contained the secret of acceptance, or the hint of it at least, or the knowledge that someday the hint of the beginning of the strength to bear her passing would find its way to my brain, to my brain and to my heart, and allow me to go.

I spent some minutes looking for Caleb but this time he never appeared.

April 27

The President is a wonder. I don't pretend to understand everything he's doing. But it's clear the man has tremendous courage. The idea of being put in charge of a country racing straight to hell is so scary, I can't possibly imagine the pressure he's under. How would one even sleep under such circumstances? But not only does he appear to be calm and resolute, even hopeful, he bullies the Congress and the others like they were nothing. Doesn't just get what he wants, but obviously has utter confidence that what he wants is right, is best for all of us. That's astonishing, isn't it?

May 3

What a horrible experience. I'm still getting over it, a full week after. To think my pa would emerge from his sullen, blank cocoon at town meeting, of all places. And so angrily—so *explosively*. I was mortified, humiliated. Beyond all description. Everyone has their troubles in the Swift River valley and the town of Greenwich, Mass, but they maintain their composure; they never lose control in public. And of course he's an outsider, still is, even after twenty years. I could see the exchange of glances. I imagine they didn't *blame* him, not exactly, but they found his dignity lacking. Dignity is very important to these people, all the more so under the circumstances, and Papa let the side down.

The arguments with the officers one after another, that was bad enough, and the picking about details, but when he started with the shouting I wanted to run from the room. "What's the *point* of this?" he yelled out half a dozen times at least. It was as though he'd lost his mind. Finally Mr. Murphy called for a recess and Mr. Atkinson came over to lead my pa away. "We'll go outside now,

164

David," he said, taking Pa's arm, and it worked. To my amazement. I didn't know whether to follow or to stay—I was very badly frightened in addition to my shame—but Mildred Atkinson sat down beside me and said, "Don't worry, Polly."

Anyway that's the end. I'll be with him at the house and take walks on the road but no more going to town together until perspective returns. I couldn't live through that again, not in a million years. Tonight I'll remind him he's still a young man with the rest of his life to lead. With responsibilities, to himself and to me at the least, and Caleb too. That if he ruins all he's worked for he will one day be sorry. I may even raise the subject of departure again. What would I have to lose?

May 12

It took me days to find the courage but eventually I spoke. I was aware of his embarrassment and had no wish to be cruel but I wanted to act before he got dull again and let the whole thing fade away. Hard as it was I was able to begin for one simple reason: there's no one to do it but me.

He listened wordless to it all and then apologized. It was brief but sincere. It wouldn't happen again, he promised, to me nor anyone else. He admitted he'd spent ten months behaving very badly and said he'd known all along that he would have to rise above it. Said he was trying very hard but would need some more time. To which I nodded. He was grateful for my patience and would make it up to me.

"You can't imagine, Polly," he said, "what it was like to lose your mother. I know your grief is as deep as mine, don't misunderstand. And I suspect you can imagine more than most young people could. But you're only eighteen and you have never been married." He looked away from me and sighed. "You always know, deep down, that you'll be without your parents someday. If you're normal you count on it, at least a little. But when I married Sarah—well, I thought I'd never be alone again."

"You're not alone, Pa," I told him.

165

He faced me and smiled. "In some ways I am. You can't have any idea." To my surprise his eyes were kind, as they hadn't been since she died.

He sighed again and closed them. "Your brother's OK," he whispered after a moment. "You know that, don't you?" At first I believed he was revealing true knowledge but then I thought, more like fending it off. "The boy is fine and has his reasons. He'll be in touch when he's ready."

We sat quietly for a time—two minutes at most—and then he told me about Reenie. His mother's niece. Two years older, almost a sister, passed at thirty when Cal and I were small. Her portrait hangs in the parlor but I'd hardly known more than her name.

"She died of the influenza, Polly," he told me. "In 1918. Your brother knew her pretty well but you won't remember. I was beside myself. She was my favorite in the world except for you two and your mother. About the only part of my childhood I wanted to keep. None of us even got sick and she just up and died; we never had a final visit. I'd begged her to move out here nearby but she wouldn't leave Lawrence. Half the neighborhood had it so of course she got it too." He spoke in a tone I'd heard him use with my ma. As I watched his wet eyes I thought: If he died no one living would have known her. She would disappear too.

"I'm sorry for your losses, Pa," I told him when he paused.

"I'll try to draw the line here," he said. "Life for the living from now on."

May 22

Birthday coming. Victrola broken. Have to get it fixed for Pa. Try to pay for it with syrup, we've little money to spare.

June 5

Outside the high school last Saturday night, during the senior prom, some older boys were drinking. Boys Caleb's age, including two from the valley. Or I suppose I should say men. Though what a grown man would want with coming to a dance at his old high school and sitting by the back steps with a bottle of liquor I don't know.

I had come outside for air—it made a pleasant change from standing by the wall refusing dances, and watching Maisie spin around, and wondering what possessed me to let her talk me into attending with scrawny, silent Arnold Nugent—and I stayed to eavesdrop on them. I was looking from above. They didn't know I was there. Someone asked about Caleb and bad old Augie Roberts—he was drinking even more than the rest—said, "He's down in New York now."

"Doing what?"

"Don't know. Haven't heard from him in years. Anyone?" They were silent.

"That's the real deal, New York," said one after a while.

"That's right, it is."

"Chance to be somebody there."

"Is that so?" asked a boy I remembered from 1930. Starting halfback. Big and strong. "Then what happened to McPhee?"

Augie giggled. "Maybe the niggers got him," he said. "They got lots of 'em there."

"Wasn't he a friend of yours, Roberts?" asked the big one.

"Yeah he was," said Augie. "So what?"

"So how come you're laughing?"

"Son of a bitch," said Augie, "talk to Caleb that way." He went hard for the other but of course it was no contest. The football player hit him; he went down and stayed down.

June 10

They opened up the diversion. Under the dam down in Enfield. The final course of the Swift. The water will keep flowing just exactly as it has and far downstream—in Bondsville say—it will seem to be the same. But one fine day they'll close a gate and the river'll disappear.

June 18

Graduated yesterday. Didn't think I'd make it at times but there I was, in gown and cap, taking the paper from Dr. Graves and trying to listen to his speech. (Imagine lecturing youth about the future in Belchertown, Mass, in 1933.) All day I drifted between not giving a damn and being glad I'd seen it through—or at least assuming I would be more or less glad someday—but mostly I was happy to have the ceremony over and get out of the sun and go to Springfield with Pa. He'd asked me what I wanted and that was my idea. We'd scraped together enough to buy a pretty decent meal at a respectable hotel. He had a beefsteak and I had duck. Cleaned our plates.

45

"What a beautiful spot! Oh honey."

"Glad we came?"

"I sure am."

"Worth the walk in from the gate, I think."

"Look at all that water."

"Just like Sebago."

"And it's really just a reservoir?"

"I wouldn't say 'just.' The biggest ever. My dad used to call it a wonder. A miracle, he said."

"When was it finished, again?"

"About thirty years ago."

"Four towns?"

"Four and a half if you count New Salem."

"I'm astonished."

"I'm astonished you never knew."

"Why?"

"You grew up drinking the water."

46

July 23, 1933

A man has flown around the world. Just imagine my surprise. And the entire country cheers, as if the ability of one person to take the longest possible route from point A to point A in slightly over a week—at great expense and without stopping anywhere on the way—is in some sense encouraging. Oh, I don't doubt it's a sign of progress; soon it will be two people, then ten, then fifty, and we'll be flying off to Tokyo for Saturday night. But it's mostly a distraction. People are starving, the whole planet is distressed, and this man's having his adventures. Congratulations to him, I guess, on his ambition and good fortune. At least he's not down here with us.

July 31

Hot. Very hot. Hotter than any heat I've ever been through, it seems. I feel that way every summer but this time it may be true. And not enough rain either. Corn's doing poorly all over the state, folks in some places are scrambling to keep stock watered, fruit is becoming a concern. Maybe we'll get that prosperity they keep promising and a good drenching storm on the very same day.

Virginia's uncle's old barn—1814, she says, and in pretty poor repair—was hauled up to Deerfield last week. To a sheep farm I believe. What they want with it there I don't know.

August 5

The tunnel workers are on strike. They have complaints about conditions and of course want higher wages, and they mean to join a union. I was down in the Plains today looking for jars and heard one particularly stupid individual going on at great length to the effect that they're lucky to have work and should shut their silly mouths. I find this sort of argument so offensive. As if being human meant survival and nothing more. You might as well suggest that we should be happy we're at least getting something for our property. Or that the Germans who had to pay ten million marks for eggs should just have been glad they had the ten million.

Still I'm annoyed they've stopped working. They're two-thirds of the way from Coldbrook already. Get it finished! The sooner the better for all concerned.

August 9

I've made a number of experiments. And am very discouraged. This diary is one thing, apparently, and a story quite another. I can barely write ten lines before I want to crumple the paper. I try to prevent myself from examining each sentence but sooner or later I do, and they collapse beneath the weight of my hopes. The more I try the more I am dissatisfied and think of *good* sentences, by writers I admire. Like iron dragging me down.

Perhaps part of the problem is being on my own, for the first time in my life; no more teachers to show my work. No Mama to ask, or to run to for a hug. No Caleb to make fun. Last time I saw Roy I wanted to talk it over with him but as I watched him slinging sacks onto a freight car—he's really so stunningly virile now—I had to laugh at the absurdity of it. It was so foolish that I even gave up saying hello, which had been my intention, and just hurried home.

I wrote to Moses again. Maybe this time he'll answer, and I can send him a page.

August 17

My God I'm tired.

August 21

Blackie Simmons is dead. Killed by a cop in downtown Worcester. He was beating some smaller man senseless in the street and when they tried to break it up he turned his knife on an officer. So the other shot him down.

No one here is the least bit surprised, of course, nor feels sorry for the family, except maybe for Eddie. Poor lame Ed has done his best to be the only good Simmons and has earned a little respect, though we could never understand why he still cared for his brother. A truly loathsome individual. A barn burner in fact. No one had stood up to him in ten years or more because they knew what would happen. We all knew better than to try.

He was the worst of the lot but the rest are nearly as bad. Thieves and cheats. Braggarts. Maybe Ed had to be maimed to be different. Maybe this killing will convince him to take leave of his family. Live somewhere else, where he won't be called Crip.

August 30

Good old thoughtful Bob Atkinson has been leaving us his newspaper. After he's through with it, usually the next morning. He folds it carefully and puts it in with our mail. A small kindness but most welcome—they don't cost very much but it's still a penny saved.

It's very nice to have the news on a regular basis; it does Pa good to follow the world a little more closely. The other evening he told me he might like to see the Pacific someday. I thought that an encouraging sign.

But the best part of all is getting Dick Tracy. Papa truly loves that comic. Perhaps it's because the sort of justice it portrays is so ideal, so unpolluted, and the lines so clearly drawn. I read it aloud to him first and then he takes the paper from me and rereads it by himself.

September 3

Acceptance a virtue? I never thought so before. But it's necessity now. I am one with the wind and the tide.

September 16

My mama loved this time of year. The steady ebbing of the summer, of the heat, of the sun. The harvest gathering on the land. The hints of colder nights to come. "The world is ripe," she used to say, "I'm going to catch it as it falls," and we all knew what she meant.

47

(1928)

They asked about the scar but I never would tell them. Not a one knew for sure. Not even Augie. "Leech on your chest!" they'd call, but I'd just shake my head and dive.

48

October 14, 1933

Here's a humorous item. They mean to sue over the golf course. Claim they weren't offered enough. A couple of the summer camps have done very well and the golf people believe they're entitled to even better. Lord knows no profit-making business can be slighted. It's not some decaying old farm set up in 1738, it's a *golf course*. The Commission has got a nerve offering only fifty thousand. Was me, I'd sue for sure.

Of course the fact that they opened the place in 1928, knowing full well it would be lost to the project, doesn't necessarily imply a deliberate investment. The development made good sense, what with so many swells from Springfield looking for an out of the way spot to conduct their business scheming and drink with their girlfriends. And having reaped the fair profits for only a few short years they are entitled to be justly compensated, aren't they? Asking twenty times per acre what the farmers are getting might be called audacious, true, maybe even brazen, but that's the way the system works. It's possible the meek will inherit the earth but they sure won't be getting any fat real estate settlements from the Commonwealth.

It isn't their fault the rest of us are cowed. But they don't get any praise from me for taking on the Commission. There's no justice on their side, just cold cash.

November 9

Spent part of the afternoon with Maisie yesterday. Her pal Elissa was there as well. It seems Maisie is getting serious about Harris Coe, from our class at BHS, and felt the need to talk it over. Should she accept his proposal? Is she "truly in love"?

Well, how should I know? I hadn't the faintest idea about anything she said. She seems to set a lot of store by the fact that despite his strong desire to do a great deal more than kiss her he accepts her refusals with good grace (as opposed to that boy from Petersham last year!). He thinks she's the only woman for him and the problem is that while she likes him quite a lot, admires and respects him, she sometimes wonders if there isn't someone better. And if she does him an injustice by concealing her doubts.

"Wait a few months or a year," said Elissa. It sounded sensible to me, at least at first. "You're just eighteen now, Maisie. See if it strengthens or fades."

"Polly?" asked Maisie. "What do you think I ought to do?"

"You know it's impossible to be certain," I said. It just slipped out. "You take a chance either way."

Later on, a little past five, we listened to their Atwater Kent. It's a beauty. The cabinet is gorgeous and the sound is superb. I don't want to know how much it cost. As we were warming it up Maisie's sister came in—the youngest one, who's only nine—and insisted on tuning in her program. The "Singing Story Lady" on NBC Blue. Maisie and El acted put out but I was privately glad. I loved the show; I loved the stories she told and the things she said. Her voice was so gifted, so practiced and acrobatic. As if she could be anyone she chose.

And her laugh was a little like Mama's too.

November 28

Some things of Caleb's were returned. They arrived in a sack postmarked New York and addressed "McPhee, Greenwich Mass," and Mr. Samuel brought it up.

Several books from this house. A souvenir of Atlantic City. A certificate he earned at the YMCA in Boston. And a photograph of him. He was much as I remembered, a bit leaner perhaps.

We sat and stared at each other, heard the Atkinsons' spaniel bark. Touched the depths of our despair.

December 14

They're almost finished with the tunnel. About one hundred feet left. The other day I was out walking and heard a dynamite blast. It was muffled by the hill. I also felt it through my feet.

This project keeps surprising you, just when you think it's not possible. You believe for a while and then you slip back into ignorance–the state we mostly prefer. It's been six years already and there I was, with my little jump and my startled cry, as if I'd never heard of it. A moment earlier I would have laughed at anybody who dared to call my life normal but until the sudden blast that's what it was. I was strolling along with my feet in dead leaves. A simple farm girl in her element, that's all.

I remember years ago I had a dream about that tunnel. Or a nightmare I guess. But now I think I'd like to see it, and to walk through it if I could. Just to assure myself it's true.

December 24

Roy is going. He won't say where. Tuesday morning, he claims. We were sharing a Christmas dinner I'd made, for just the two of us. Pa was down at the Inn—I'd known he would be, they've planned it for months—and I'd intended to cook and serve for Roy without telling him. But at the last I decided to be honest. "Roy is coming for Christmas Eve," I called out as he was putting on his coat. "May be here when you get back."

"That's dandy," he said before stepping out the door.

Roy gave me his news after I handed him his plate. I was so shocked I had to sit down. Not shocked, really, but more like weakened. It was what I'd been hoping—precisely what he should do—but a little more time to prepare would have been nice.

"Tuesday?" I asked him softly, though he'd just that minute said it, hoping I had misheard.

He nodded as he chewed. "I only waited this long to come to dinner with you."

"Why, Roy?" The pheasant (he'd trapped it for me) smelled good but I somehow didn't want it. I put my elbows on the table and my chin on my hands. He kept on chewing his food; he thought for a few seconds, then waved his fork in the air.

"Oh Polly," he said at last. "I don't think I need to tell you." He took up his knife and cut more pieces from his meat, then buttered a roll. "I mean—it's embarrassing. That's all. To get into all of that."

He was handsome again, as I sat and watched him dine. As handsome as he was on the first day I saw him. Not just masculine, muscular, strong, appealing, but movie star good looking. His cares had dropped away, perhaps for the first time, allowing his face to shine free.

As I got myself some food—I could hear the wind blowing and felt a draft around my ankles and as I looked through the doorway to the tree in the parlor I thought, better fatten up now for winter—he put his cutlery down and wiped his mouth with his napkin. He was bashful at first but then caught and held my eye.

"I will come back for you, Polly," he said. "My sweetheart. We'll start again."

I believed him. Because I wanted to? For that moment at least.

Later on we discussed his old man. "What'll become of him?" I asked with real anxiety, but Roy just laughed.

"He's a smart old fox," he assured me, taking a second helping of pudding. "That son of a bitch. Don't you give it another thought. He'll take care of himself."

"And when they send us away?"

"He'll be long gone by then. He means to run off before they can buy his land from him, or take the title without a process. Tie them up in the courts. Make them search for him for years."

"My father," I said, "would appreciate that plan."

"He would," said Roy. "But I'd be careful if I were you. Don't want him trying the same."

I started then to ask him about Caleb, about the sack, about what it could mean. I had the strangest feeling he might know. But fear took my voice; I stared at my bowl and it passed.

After dinner we talked about one thing and another. When I gave him his gift—we were sitting in the parlor—I actually thought he might cry. He managed not to, though.

"I don't have anything for you."

I kissed his cheek. "Be sure to bring me something when you come back, then," I said. "Bring me something for this Christmas and any others we miss while you're gone."

I made him open the box and look at his diary and pen. He really liked them, I think. Said he'd been without reason to keep his hand in but would try to write something every day. With me in mind. Said his spelling and grammar would be pitiful and I told him, you needn't worry in a diary, no one looks at it but you.

"I don't want you to forget what you learned here," I said. "They teach those things for a reason."

And I made him happy, of course. I had to. I couldn't let him go without. It was very gentle this time, really, gentle and simple, actually loving in its limited way. We kissed and kissed a long while, then I made my intentions known. He protested but I kept on. I'd never see him again. I wanted him to remember the pleasure, and my affection. Words are all very well but touches last a whole life.

After, we waited long minutes in the dark. I could feel his blood pulse and then slowly ease and fade. We had a bond, real and true, and I was certain that as little as I wanted him to go, as little as I could spare him, he wanted less to leave me. There was

179

an idea between us that we could stay close forever. But eventually we acknowledged our necessities and released.

We looked at each other in the dark. We had no choice but we were sorry.

I'm ashamed to write this down but after he kissed my cheek and left and I closed the door behind him I was filled with relief. I was of dual expectation—that he would be back sure as anything, or that this was goodbye—but either way the tension had ended. Years of tension, *years* of it, about Polly and Roy. Fairy tale: he would come back and we would make it all right. Hard life: I'd never see him anymore. Or was it the other way around? Regardless, I no longer had reason to worry. Each ending happy in its fashion. Settled and done.

December 31

For some reason I was thinking of that baby who died. Late last year up in Dana. He took so long to be born, a day and a half, and they thought he was fine but then he simply stopped breathing. He was tired, the doctor said. From it taking so long. It wore his mother out too but she recovered in the end—from her son's birth that is. From his death I don't know.

In the city, in a hospital, that boy might have pulled through. They might have done something for him. Being tired from being born doesn't seem like good reason to stop breathing, does it? It's supposed to be tiring. But you're supposed to survive.

Maybe that was all I wanted. A living child.

Eating venison with Roy. We crouch as savages in the forest. The meat is good, freshly cooked; on our hands its grease glistens. A drop of blood runs down his chin. "Tastes better this way," he explains around his mouthful, and I sadly agree. Wild animal, wild meal, which is exactly as it should be. I send the image of its final terror spinning far away.

"Lots of chewed bones out here," says Roy as he saws off another chunk with his knife. "Old ones too. Damned old. From the Indian days." It's very easy to believe him. In point of fact there they are, not too far up the slope, under that enormous oak I never noticed before. On the ground just like us, eating their kill, biding their time, looking after the white boy and me.

We bumped into each other—almost literally, I mean—one day in 1933. Outside the station down in Ware. I had come with my father to pick up some tools and then meet his widowed sister on the four o'clock train. No idea why *she* was there. While my father parked the truck I hopped out to rush the platform (we were a few minutes late); it was a windy autumn day and I remember a big leaf nearly hit me in the eye as I hurried up the walkway. Then I rounded the corner and almost smacked into Polly. She did a quick side-to-side to avoid making contact and slowed down just a little and almost smiled at me, I think, although I may have imagined it. Certainly she knew me—I saw that clearly enough. I stopped dead but before I could open my mouth she had passed me and was gone.

She looked so sad, that girl, so sad. She looked so pale and so grim. Everyone from the valley had a dismal air by then, those that were left, but hers was even beyond that. My heart dropped into my hand. I had missed her so severely since the end of June. Wishing she would still be in high school when I started. Trying to figure out an excuse for a trip by her farm or at least over to Greenwich. And so on like that. Now came an opportunity to actually speak and she was lost in an instant, maybe not beyond reach but then she was soon enough as I stood there and stood there and couldn't run after. I hadn't the nerve. I so wanted to *do* something—about her troubles, about the project, about my silent worship of her, my innocent youth—and here I'd dumbly missed my chance. Like the little boy I was. Standing and studying the dirty old bricks that had cut her off from me.

"Wasn't that the McPhee girl from Greenwich?" my father asked later, as we were getting the luggage.

"Yes sir," I grunted. I was lifting up a trunk.

"She moved out yet, do you know?" He waved at my aunt, huddled back against the station in her black dress and veil, and held up his index finger. He checked the labels on her things.

"No sir," I told him, "I don't think she has. Her dad has been out of work."

"That's a shame," said my father, a man who always had the decency to care about others, no matter what his own concerns. "That is a rotten shame. I hope they get a new place soon." Then he picked up the cases and started toward his sister, who stepped forward to meet him, seeking his protection just as everybody did. While I helped no one at all.

51

1934

March: The Greenwich-Coldbrook tunnel, officially the
                western section of the Quabbin aqueduct, is com-
                pleted on schedule. Water will be withdrawn from
                the future Quabbin reservoir through a valve to be
                constructed at Shaft 12, on a steep slope a mile
                south of Greenwich Village, overlooking East Pond
                and beyond it Mount Pomeroy. From there it will
                travel downhill and eastward to the Ware River in-
                take at Coldbrook Springs near the Oakham-Barre
                line, and then downhill again through the aque-
                duct's eastern portion to the Wachusett reservoir in
                West Boylston (cleared of structures and inhabit-
                ants and flooded to capacity between 1901 and
                1908). A "baffle dam" to be built between the
                southern foot of Mount Zion and the heights on
                which the intake is to be situated, dividing Green-
                wich Village into equal portions, will ensure that
                inferior water entering the reservoir from the east
                branch of the Swift River must travel north around
                Mount Zion before entering the aqueduct, thereby

providing it more time in which to purify itself before falling to the east.

April: Service on the Boston and Albany's Springfield-Athol line, or Rabbit Run—so-called because it proceeds in short hops through the Swift River valley—is reduced from one passenger train and one mixed train each way, each day, a limited schedule established three years prior, to a single mixed train each way.

May: A group of naturists, or nudists, attempts to buy or rent land in Greenwich on which to establish a camp. The venture is successfully discouraged by the Metropolitan District Water Supply Commission, or MDWSC.

52

Penny candy. How we loved it. Nothing else was quite the same. All you needed was one cent, a single coin, and you could have something you wanted. Sour balls. Licorice. Caramels in cool weather. None of them made by someone's mother or aunt. Scooped right out of a jar. Not as good as a fresh batch of cookies, maybe, or Mrs. Pearson's apple cake, but who cared? They were *yours*. Your decision, your treat.

But you had to have a penny.

53

June 5, 1934

A letter from Moses. I had given up hope. He sent some books and a note in July two years ago, and I wrote him about Mama. And then nothing. Looking back I suppose I've been angry at him, and also worried. There must be plenty of people in Boston who hate educated Negroes, well-to-do Negroes, any Negro at all. And who have no respect for the law.

Now that I've heard from him I'm reassured but more resentful than not. He was "forced to interrupt our correspondence," he says. No further explanation offered. What on earth could have prevented him from sending one little sympathy card? Some suggestion that there was at least one human being outside of this valley who gave a damn that she was dead?

Well he sends me his sorrow and sympathy now, and his regret for being "out of touch," and his concern about my future, but the fact is he left me alone for nearly two years, two important and woeful years. I've grown up in that time and have moved beyond his influence, and his reasons for approaching me in the first place, whatever they were, have diminished from a wonderful mystery of girlhood to some trivial quirk. Maybe it helped him get over his rage at Greenwich. Maybe he was bored. Maybe he simply found me attractive—likely enough, I was smitten by him—and did what little he could about it, a black man at risk of his very life if he gave the slightest evidence of designs on a white teenager. He started

188

the whole thing on a whim, lost interest in it eventually, and finally tried to fulfill his obligations for stirring me up in the first place by writing a letter to a bereft nineteen year old. Offering what—more book discussions? Friendly advice? A luncheon date in Boston if I ever come through?

I plan to answer him of course. It isn't as if I'm drowning in friends. And his intentions are and have always been good, surely, and he obviously feels badly about his neglect. But I don't expect to gain much. Don't expect to still be writing in two years' time. Don't expect the arrival of his letters and postcards to produce any thrill.

It's a sorry shame, isn't it? I could use something nice.

June 17

A lot of them smile at me—actually smile—as they go on about how they love our town. Our valley. Their lack of tact is astounding.

But as long as they pay good money I don't care. I do my best to smile right back.

June 22

Today he just up and said it. Sitting piecing on the ham.

"I got us stuck here, I know, but now you're bound to stay too."

For a short time I was tempted to tell him exactly how wrong he was. *I'm off to college, just like Caleb. As I should have long ago.* But he just kept chewing so what's the point?

June 26

It's like one hundred million people in a nightmare together. Pick any place in the country and there's misery there. The same the world around, they say. The definition of *misfortune* used to be *not to me* but that is no longer valid. This is happening to all of us, even the lucky ones. You can't eat a potato without thinking of the people who might knock you down for it. You can't put two dol-

189

lars together without thinking how you ought to give one of them away.

July 11

The Boston and Albany wants to kill the Rabbit Run. Wants to kill it altogether. Not to move it or reroute it, but to pull up the tracks and erase it entirely.

July 19

In all this time I've told no one about Caleb, the real truth about Caleb. No one at all.

July 22

Rural delivery's been stopped. Have to go to the P.O. from here on. I'm surprised they kept it going until now, come to think of it. A long way between mailboxes on our hillside these days.

July 26

They got John Dillinger. Outside a theater in Chicago. Shot him dozens of times, like a mad dog on the street. A close friend turned him in. So he was taken by surprise.

He was a very bad man. You could even call him evil. He caused a great deal of distress and we are better off without him. So I need to understand how I can possibly be moved. Feel such sadness, even sorrow. And wish it hadn't happened that way.

He deserved just what he got, which can't be said of most of us. How come I'm on his side?

54

There's a professor up in Boston who says it causes earthquakes. The weight of the water, he points out. All four hundred billion gallons that were never there before. And the moisture that has worked itself deep into the ground, and serves to lubricate the rocks.

He has been going through the record and finds them much more common now. The tremors, I mean. In the areas surrounding. Although the record is incomplete.

Plausible, I say. They filled it fifty years ago. And it's a very great deal of water. As heavy, by my recent calculation, as an equilateral four-sided pyramid of iron more than half a mile high.

As to the weight of betrayal—what would a scientist know?

55

August 12, 1934

Some church ladies never change. No matter what goes on around them. I so admire them for their courage, their dedication and their strength. The Lord is the Lord and He still is our Shepherd and making hats or quilts or fans to benefit the missionaries remains just as well worth doing, water project or no. Everything here is going to pieces but when you talk to one of them you might not realize a thing.

The reds, I suppose, would call them cruelly abused, misled by tall tales of God, but whether or not one believes in the deity—I find it harder every day—the humility that comes with it is much more important.

And they never seem angry. I am but they're not. "Lord Jesus, smite the drillers" are words I certainly haven't heard. Nor "rain fire on the Commission." If I still believed in Christ I would surely be furious, but they feel it's His decision. For His own blessed reasons. Who's to say they're not right?

August 15

If I were their neighbor I would spirit them away. In dark of night if need be. Imagine waking to five tiny matching babies, the miracle of all time—and then trying to cash in. I know the Dionnes must be desperately poor but I'm a poor woman too and I'm tempted to despise them. And they claim to be devout! If ever

192

there were a gift from God it's those sisters. He must be weeping for their release.

August 17

What's this I find in these pages—a little religion creeping in? Perhaps I'm chasing my mother. Or returning to the fold.

August 18

Oh Lord forgive the engineers their trespasses against us. Forgive my mama for dying. And Roy for having been corrupted. Dear Lord forgive us, forgive us our estrangement from Caleb. Or you can see us all in hell, as you choose.

August 22

Wonderful blueberries this year. We can do a lot with these. So many big ones, deep blue, and the bushes are heavy. I've hired all the kids I can find and they may not be enough. We'll be tired when this is over but considerably enriched.

Next year at this time I'll be packing, by the way. Yes. He'll have to manage on his own.

August 28

All right. All right. I'll make sure he's looked after. He's my father and I honor him and I know my duty, yes, I do, honestly, only aren't I entitled to something by now? Like room to grow? To step out of this shame, all this muted misery, and start the life he himself wanted for me before things turned so bad? I remember the man who would have insisted. Instead of tying me here.

September 4

If there were a Lord Jesus, which I happen to know there isn't, he would bring Caleb home.

September 18

They've started the hearings about the Rabbit, apparently. With lots of lawyers for the B&A and for the Commission too. Most people think it's about what to do with the line but it isn't, of course. It's about big piles of money. The Commission's and the railroad's. It's astonishing how good at avoiding the obvious people are. Time after time.

October 3

A massive storm just bullied through. Epic might be a better word. It nearly washed us away. Nasty leaks in the house and barn, the shed by the northeast fence collapsed, limbs down everywhere and it's a damn good thing Pa rebuilt that roof over the hives. Soon as it gets light we've got to check on our neighbors. We'll find plenty of debris on the ground.

When I saw the thunderhead looming over Mount Liz I thought oh well, another storm, but this was new to my experience. I have never been rained on so hard, each drop a bullet. I have never seen the wind blow so many ways at once. Never heard such magnificent crashes. It wasn't fearsome like a tornado—I didn't think Pa and I were in danger of harm, or that the house would come apart—but I was filled with apprehension by imagination's limits. Had I tried to describe the biggest thunderstorm on earth I would not have come close.

And there were just a few minutes when I *was* rather scared, in an immediate sense. When the lightning passed by. It was closer and brighter than ever before and one bolt nearly hit the house. Our hair was standing on end. It seemed to stimulate Pa but it was very rough on me. After it struck the yard I told myself, over and over, that it wouldn't happen twice, that it couldn't, but it wasn't until the flashes passed well out of range that I could will myself toward calm. Relax my body bit by bit.

I want to live.

October 15

Heard from Edna again. It's a treat when she writes. We seem to have established a regular exchange and I hope it holds up. It occurred to me as I was reading her letter for the third time, just before bed, that I was never sure, over the years, whether she liked me. Never believed she was my friend. And what did it in the end was her words about my ma. Upon hearing the news. Not the sharing of secrets about her job and her beaux out there in Buffalo, even her quarrels with her parents, but her response to my grief. *It hurts so much, Polly. I've sewn armbands on my clothes.*

This letter was joyful and very amusing. She's having a fine time, it seems, and may be walking down the aisle before long.

October 16

Can I be sure he's gone for good? Is there no room for doubt? Or do I just prefer it this way?

I must forgive him if I can. He got away and I didn't—he is braver than I am—and it's too late to change.

October 24

Today in the Plains someone mentioned Oswald Harding. I hadn't thought of Oswald in ages, I realized as I headed up the road (the wind tangling my hair because I'd gone out without a hat). He was a sweet chubby boy taken in by the Parkers. Lived with them for many years. Mrs. Parker truly loved him, as far as people could tell, and her husband liked him too, and the other three kids. He was one of their family. Except they never adopted him, they never changed his name. He wanted it, I heard from Roy, who knew about all the orphans, and asked them for it many times, but they would never give in. Religious reasons? Respect for his parents? Ask the Parkers. But Oswald Harding he started, and Oswald Harding he remained, and when he left to seek his fortune the new grip they bought him said OAH in big gold letters, not OAP.

My father's dead. Of exposure. I found him over in the wood lot, all cold on the ground. He was splitting some logs when he collapsed from a stroke or heart attack or something of that nature, the doctor's not sure yet, and froze to death for want of help. No way of knowing how long it took.

I went to bed last night thinking he was down in the village and woke to an empty house. His bed in the parlor still made. I looked and looked, called and called, and finally discovered him after searching the barn and the sheds and even the sugar shack. He made a very peaceful corpse, lying on the leaves with his hammer and maul and split wood all around him, contrary to what you'd expect given the nature of his passing. The nature of his life. He was so peaceful I was able to sit down right next to him, on the cold wet earth, and share the morning with him as I have a thousand times. "I will miss you, Pa," I told him. It was easy to say.

It's somehow different from Mama. I'm simply not as affected in an immediate fashion. Pain is looming, believe me, but at this moment my mind is clear and my heart strong. Burdened, yes, but capable enough to take me through what is coming. All the things I'll have to do. Maybe because I'm older, maybe because I'm alone now, maybe because I'm so happy for him, so relieved, but I feel no fear at all. Not much of anything, really, except depression and regret, but those are mild enough to withstand. As long as circumstances dictate. I feel no fear at all.

Now I'm an orphan too.

November 7, later

I wish I could bury him here, on his farm. In his own beloved place. But it's not within my power.

November 10

So that's over. *Pace* David. I'm not going to describe it. I'm in a very delicate condition, I find, precisely balanced like those rocking boulders up on Cooley Hill. Press me slightly and I'll rock, back and forth, back and forth, but push too hard and I'll go rolling. Crushing things on the way. I mean it. Can't risk it. I've got to stay very still.

November 16

Larry Sherman paid respects. He was not at Pa's funeral, he said, because he was near death himself, with delirium and the shakes. When he woke up four days later and they gave him the news he wished he really had died.

I believe him of course. He loved my pa. Good thing they didn't tell him, he would have come here on his knees.

"They were so young." I said it softly.

"Prime of life." He sighed.

"I feel exactly as you did, Larry," I told him. "Looking at you now. Like I have been in a trance and am just coming out and understanding that he's dead."

"You want to bawl, you go ahead. That's why I'm here."

He held my hand, Mr. Sherman. Came over to the sofa and sat down beside me and held my hand for half an hour. I wept and wept and called my father's name many times, my mother's too, and said some things I shouldn't have said—I think part of me was trying to repel him—and he just sat there and absorbed it.

When I had almost stopped he laughed. "There're people," he said, "who would be mighty surprised to see me hold a woman's hand, no matter what the reason why."

I laughed too. I was cried out. "It's nice to hold your hand, Larry," I said. "I don't hold a man's hand very often either."

He looked at me then in a manner in which only a bachelor could look, I think. Aging, yes, but not too old. I felt an urgent need to rise and put some open space between us. Poor quiet, gentle, risky man. He knew me when I was small; I was rowed in his boat, fed at his table; I fell asleep in his arms. And now my daddy is gone and here I am, all alone.

"Will you take me to his grave?" he asked as I stood at the window. "I mean, can you manage? Would you like to?" He shook his head and looked down.

"I would like to," I told him. "It will be good for me to go. Especially with you." I took my place beside him and reached out for his hand. "But I'm not done yet." Wasn't close.

November 25

May as well stay—what else am I good for? P. McPhee, Fancy Waiting. Decisions Taken In Trade.

56

(1924)

Family came. I'd never met them. We set up cots in the parlor and had to give away our beds. They traveled east from Wisconsin just to see us. Went out there thirty years before, Ma told me, in search of opportunity. They must have found it right away—their farm near Middleton was huge. Or so they said. Three hundred acres, sixty cows, a giant orchard full of apples. Nice people too, if slightly strange.

They sat up late each night with Ma and when they left they made her promise we would visit. Soon as we get the chance, said Mama. Even sooner said Cousin Flo. We can't wait that long to have you. And Cousin Don said You bring them kids before they're grown, Sarah. They've got to come see our place.

Mama laughed. Maybe we will at that, she said. Maybe they'll ride the train out by themselves in a few years. Spend a summer there with you. What do you think of that, Polly?

Don't look so worried said Cousin Flo, stooping down to hug and kiss. She was small and somehow dry and had a funny pleasant smell. Your mama doesn't mean tomorrow! You just come and see us soon.

57

When I had made it home at last and fixed myself a cup of tea—a bitter dank and sorry day, just what he'd pick for his good-bye—I remembered the bolt. It hit our yard in that big storm, the flash-and-rumble in October. I was relieved it missed the house but Papa got all excited and kept telling me to wait—once the rain moved on I'd see. Which it did after an hour and he rushed out with a spade and started digging slow and careful, close around the stricken spot, like some Englishman in Egypt working on a pharaoh's tomb. Then he went to his knees and reaching in with bare hands pulled an object long and slender from the scorched and sodden earth. "Still warm!" he cried and got to his feet and waved it over his head. Rinsed it in the trough, stroked it, carried it proudly back. A *fulgurite*, he called it, and though I later looked it up just then I thought he'd said, "Fools go right," and wondered for perhaps the ten-millionth time what he meant.

This particular series of accidents was ordained or prearranged, I believe, so I might always recall him just that way: searching the newborn lightning-glass, taking it gently from the ground, holding it aloft, presenting it to me.

58

December 6, 1934

Lately I've been searching for a description of these days, and the way I've felt about them. It finally came to me last night from an unexpected source. Something caused me, I don't know what (an impulse, random nuance, perhaps a ghost nudged my hip?) to put down my thick Austen and go to the shelf and pick out the book on the end, one of Pa's. A volume of Frost, "A Boy's Will." The only such book he owned. I don't know Frost's work, had never really looked at it though I'd seen one or two of the shorter poems, but as is so often the case with verse—with good verse, with very good verse, by someone who not only writes well but has enough sense not to publish anything second-rate—the first piece that came to hand fit my thoughts perfectly. My thoughts and mood. My thoughts and mood and situation.

That's exactly the way to refer to it now, with the word *situation*, because this series of events—it's really quite extraordinary, isn't it, what's come to Rebecca McPhee?—has served to mix things up together with no hope of sorting them out. I can no more tell myself from my dead parents and derelict brother than I can distinguish between the project and the future, between Roy's barn and the past. I am entirely a creature of my life's sad events, committed to patience now, to endurance if nothing else. I am a part of my surroundings and they are all contained in me. Girl expecting the water.

Anyway he has it right. As I say, a competent poet. I want to copy it down without explaining any more because I can't, I simply can't, bear to think about further. About the truth that's in these lines. Save that grim consideration for another time, can't we? Please? Because I must be off to bed.

My November Guest

My Sorrow, when she's here with me,
Thinks these dark days of autumn rain
Are beautiful as days can be;
She loves the bare, the withered tree;
She walks the sodden pasture lane.

Her pleasure will not let me stay.
She talks and I am fain to list;
She's glad the birds are gone away,
She's glad her simple worsted grey
Is silver now with clinging mist.

The desolate, deserted trees,
The faded earth, the heavy sky,
The beauties she so truly sees,
She thinks I have no eye for these,
And vexes me for reason why.

Not yesterday I learned to know
The love of bare November days
Before the coming of the snow
But it were vain to tell her so,
And they are better for her praise.

1934

December: The Boston and Albany Railroad receives state and
             federal permission to abandon its Springfield-Athol
             line instead of rerouting it around the reservoir, a
             proposal fully supported by the MDWSC. The rail-
             road is to receive $575,000 from the Commission in
             compensation, in addition to retaining the ties and
             rails.

             A fire of unknown origin breaks out at Shaft 10 on
             the Quabbin aqueduct, in Hardwick. Three build-
             ings are destroyed.

60

(1927)

Brother Cal's all excited because his favorite, Ty Cobb, got his four-thousandth hit. That is a very big number, even I will agree. Caleb wrote him for an autograph last year but nothing yet. He'll probably get to it eventually—pretty soon now, I hope. My brother sure thinks he's grand.

"When you say Mass'chusetts, you mean Boston?"
"Hell no. Small town out in the middle of the state."
"Farm boy."
"Not exactly but close enough."
"Quit hoggin' and pass that bottle over now."
"Sure."
"What your folks think about you bein' in Fort Wayne, Indiana with somebody like me?"
"What they don't know won't hurt 'em."
"What don' they know?"
"Where I am. What I'm doing. Who I'm with."
"They don' know nothin'."
"No."
"When you last write 'em?"
"Couple years ago."
"Couple *years*?"
"More or less. Probably more."
"So they don' even know if you alive or dead."
"They're better off not knowing."
"Boy, you a cruel son of a bitch, you know that?"
"Is that what I am?"
"No doubt. But you so damn good looking too. C'mere, baby. C'mere."

62

I spent the morning with graph paper. With colored pencils and ruler, perpetual calendar at hand. I felt a great need, as usual, to be precise. Of course no one will ever know. Most of what I put down won't make it into the story, I suspect, and what does won't be noticed.

But it's got to be done; I understand that by now. The successes I've made I owe mostly to this tolerance I seem to have acquired, this acceptance of the process, of its perversions and demands. Neat charts on graph paper? Constant rereading and revising? Seemingly endless solitude, lonely hour upon hour? All worthwhile it seems, if not exactly to be desired. And those expensive, troublesome journeys to spacious open landscapes no matter how far away—so long as they're empty, and new—where I can stare into the static, ungenerous distance until I think I'll go blind? Listen, everybody has hobbies. It compares not too unfavorably to collecting figurines, for instance, or to tango competitions. Just a way of passing time.

Why do I do this? I'd be miserable if I didn't. But that begs the question nicely. There are many who envy me, some with good reason, but if I'm honest and fair I have to ask myself, why? Because I must? More evasion. As are my fits of self-derision. I'd like to understand it, that's all. So many years of devotion that might have gone instead to my friends, to a husband, to the babies I could have had, to all the things I enjoy and admire. So many paths to contentment, to satisfaction and hope, but I insist on searching for them in this handful of books. The way they look on my shelf. The reviews and readers' letters. Two hours of feeling powerful every other week, of feeling blessed and complete because I wrote it as I wanted. The pleasant moments and exchanges with the other crippled souls, on rare occasions when we meet, and those shot with apprehension. Try not to catch what he's got!

All incidental, in truth. Don't we know what matters most? What I create is mine forever. Despite the treasures taken from me I'm a child who has her own.

Still at times I lose my faith. On lonesome days, in dark of night. The life and its product become confused, somehow; is the work really the point or is it a means to an end?

Well either way it has some dignity, at least, and honor. The diminution of the woman without doing anything wrong. I might once have turned to drink, for example, promiscuity even, except the gutter is not a place I can allow myself to be (I am that much my parents' child). This way I fill my days without incurring any shame, any pity or debt, and find purpose enough that when I get in bed at night I can lie there and again forgive myself (and my family, and the boy, and the water) and make my way to sleep.

63

January 18, 1935

Dearest Edna,

My father's life was insured! I'm astonished. It's not a very great deal but given prices these days it will make a real difference. When I first read the letter from George Saunders of Springfield a baby could have pushed me over. I drove down there right away and the man essentially handed me a check. Said it wasn't up to him to tell me how the premiums had been paid, or since when; in any case he didn't know. He had the death certificate, he pointed out—he actually physically pointed it out on his desk before realizing I might not want to look at it—and the policy itself, listing me as beneficiary, and the paperwork complete. Therefore I would have the money. I told him I didn't think the estate had been probated yet and he said it didn't matter, it was mine not my father's. He even became a little impatient as I tried to take it in.

"Accept the money, young lady," he advised me, rather primly. "Accept your father's provision."

"This is the first check ever written with my name on it," I said.

He glanced at the portrait of his family by his elbow, then turned the check face down. "I gather his passing has left you on your own," he said in a somewhat kinder way. "I'm terribly sorry about that but there are going to be quite a few firsts from now on, Miss McPhee. If you don't mind my saying so."

I thought that over for a while. "Yes, you're right," I replied. I took the check and thanked him and started for the bank.

It's wonderful you've set the date. I really couldn't be happier. I know he's right for you.

As to the wedding itself: it's simply lovely of you to say you'll invite me but you really needn't do so. You can't afford a big wedding and there are so many others you've got to ask first. And whether I'd be able to leave here—who knows?

This has been a hard winter but I've been handling it well. The first two after my mother died were terribly frightening, as if I had no protection. As if the cold could sneak in through a cracked window pane and freeze me solid wherever I was, even in front of the stove or fire. But this year the snow and chill are more a challenge, not a threat but just a hardship to be conquered. When I go out to the henhouse and it's so cold it hurts I actually laugh—I can tell I'm alive.

Is that a horrible confession from a woman whose father froze to death not long ago? Or is it only natural? It would be easy to tell you that the cold is the enemy, that I hate it because of what it did to David, but that's truly not what I feel. More to the point is my quiet, secret wish that I could join him, I think; the part of me that says it would be easiest to go over to the woodlot and lie down on the ground and let it happen to me too. But far more of me wants to carry on than to give in—please don't worry!—so I find joy in defeating the impulse. In bundling up against the wind. In making the doors and windows tight. In spending part of that settlement on a new pair of boots before I'd even left the city, warm beautiful boots, although my old ones weren't so bad.

I'm free to look after myself now. At last. The spring to come will be mine.

COMMONWEALTH OF MASSACHUSETTS
METR. DISTR. WATER SUPPLY COMMISSION

STATUS OF CONTRACTS COMPLETED BETWEEN NOV. 30, 1933 AND NOV. 30, 1934

CONT. NO.	DESCRIPTION	LOCATION	SUPPLY	CONTRACTOR	BIDS OPENED	NO. OF BIDS	CONTRACT AWARDED	BASIS OF AWARD	FINAL ESTIMATE	DATE OF FINAL EST.
40	Removal & Relocation of Transmission Telephone Lines & Sub-Sta.	New Salem, Belchertown, Enfield and Ware	Swift	New Eng. Power Co. & Central Mass Electric Co	Date of Agreement June 20, 1933	6		Actual Cost Damages	$104,790.10 / 50,000.00	Feb 15, 1934
45	Exploration by Shovel Cut & of Borrow Area for Dam & Dike	Belchertown, Enfield and Ware	Swift	B Perini & Sons, Inc.	Feb 6, 1934	6	Feb 6, 1934	$6200.00	9,415.09	Oct 22, 1934

STATUS OF CONTRACTS IN FORCE ON NOV. 30, 1934

CONT. NO.	DESCRIPTION	LOCATION	SUPPLY	CONTRACTOR	BIDS OPENED	NO. OF BIDS	CONTRACT AWARDED	BASIS OF AWARD	PAYMENTS TO DATE
20	Coldbrook-Swift Tunnel	Barre, Hardwick and Greenwich	Swift	Wenzel & Henoch Construction Co.	Mar 27, 1931	13	April 18, 1931	$4,978,031.80	4,444,062.05
23	Making Borings	Belchertown, Ware, Enfield, Greenwich & Hardwick	Swift	Sprague & Henwood Inc	Nov 5, 1929	6	Nov 5, 1929	10,950.00	46,541.37
33	Purchase of Power at Shaft 1	West Boylston	Ware	New England Power Co	Date of Agreement Aug 6, 1931			Agreed Rates	1,767.63
35	Purchase of Power at Dam Site	Enfield	Swift	New England Power Co	Date of Agreement June 2, 1932			Agreed Rates	10,617.40 *
36	Core Wall To Sound Bed Rock at Dike Site	Enfield & Ware	Swift	West Construction Co	Dec 9, 1932	2.5	Dec 28, 1932	999,765.00	903,167.84
39	Construction of Trunk Sewer	Rutland & Holden	Ware	James J Coughlan & Sons, Inc	July 7, 1933	2	July 11, 1933	84,327.50	192,723.91
21	Construction of Portion of Belchertown-Pelham Highway	Belchertown & Pelham	Swift	Carlo Bianchi Co Inc	July 18, 1933	11	July 19, 1933	222,335.50 **	219,160.09 **
41	Use of Worcester Sewerage System and Treatment Works % Rutland-Holden Sewer	Worcester	Ware	City of Worcester	Date of Agreement May 1, 1933			Lump Sum + Annual Charge	325,000.00 * / None
42	Construction of Extension of Belchertown-Pelham Highway to New Salem Center	Shutesbury & New Salem	Swift	V Barletta Co	Aug 9, 1933	7	Aug 22, 1933	300,391.50 **	239,313.95 **
44	Construction of Extension of Belchertown-Pelham Highway North of New Salem Center	New Salem & Orange	Swift	John Tafolla Construction Co	Nov 10, 1933	9	Nov 14, 1933	779,480.50 **	735,421.45 **
46	Connection with Rutland-Holden Sewer & Disposal of Sewage from the US Veterans Hospital	Rutland (Payments under Contract 46 are to be received by the MDWSC)	Ware	U S Veteran's Administration	Date of Agreement Nov 1st			Lump Sum + Annual Charge	97,000.00 * / None
50	Dike Embankment-Quabbin Reservoir	Enfield & Ware	Swift	The Arthur A Johnson Corporation	Nov 13, 1934	6	Nov 26, 1934	1,446,655.00	None

* Proportion of Annual Maintenance Cost

** Of these amounts the State Dept. of Public Works has paid $112,879.75 on Cont 41; $82,923.58 on Cont 43 and $52,679.18 on Cont 44 covering the surfacing, guard rail and traffic signal duct items.

The above contracts were all awarded to the lowest bidder except Contract 43 which was awarded to the 2nd lowest bidder.

from the MDWSC annual report, 1934

Part IV

Drinking and other domestic purposes are the highest uses of water.

— Pierce Butler
Justice of the U.S. Supreme Court
1931

A river is more than an amenity, it is a treasure. It offers a necessity of life.

— Oliver Wendell Holmes Jr.
Justice of the U.S. Supreme Court
1931

64

(1923)

"Shall we gather by the river,
where bright angels' feet have trod,
with its crystal tide forever
flowing by the throne of God?

Yes we'll gather by the river,
the beautiful, beautiful river,
gather with the saints by the river
that flows by the throne of God.

Soon we'll reach the shining river,
soon our pilgrimage will cease,
soon our happy hearts will quiver
with the melody of peace.

Yes we'll gather by the river,
the beautiful, beautiful river,
gather with the saints by the river
that flows by the throne of God."

65

1935

January:	Bruno Hauptmann stands trial for the 1932 kidnap and murder of the two year old son of Ann and Charles Lindbergh.

James Michael Curley, assuming the governorship of Massachusetts, attempts to remove his Democratic predecessor's last-minute appointee, a Republican, from the chairmanship of the MDWSC. Eugene C. Hultman is accused of drinking confiscated champagne and spreading city-owned manure on his lawn.

February: Hauptmann is convicted and sentenced to death.

March: Dana, Massachusetts reports the loss of 208 residents from its 1930 total of 595; its new population of 387 is the smallest in Worcester County. Greenwich, down 19 to 219, and Enfield, down 2 to 495, have lost fewer than expected due to project-related jobs, inexpensive rental housing, and an abundance of available farmland. Prescott, population 236 in 1920 and 48 in 1930, is still home to 18 individuals.

Germany reintroduces military conscription in violation of the Treaty of Versailles.

The Ware Congregational Church accepts stewardship of the Greenwich Foundation, to be funded by proceeds from the sale of the Greenwich Congregational Church to the MDWSC for $23,000.

June: A Boston and Albany train makes the final scheduled trip from Athol to Springfield. It carries 115 passengers, including Otis and Arthur Hager, who had ridden the very first train on the line over 60 years before.

Governor Curley visits the Swift River valley.

The new Suffolk Downs racetrack opens in Revere, a few miles north of Boston.

Newly constructed Massachusetts Route 202, running between Belchertown and Orange to the west of the intended reservoir basin, is formally dedicated as the Daniel Shays Highway, named for the leader of a farmers' rebellion in 1786.

July: The Swift River Box Company of North Dana—sole remaining industry in the Swift River valley—relocates to Athol.

The rails and ties of the Rabbit Run are removed by the Boston and Albany. Governor Curley delays payment of the settlement owed the railroad by the Commission, pending his own investigation and reassessment of the agreed-upon figure.

August: X.H. Goodnough, prominent civil engineer and chief architect and proponent of the "Swift River plan" for the relief of Boston's water shortage, dies at his summer home in Maine at the age of 74.

215

66

"How did you find it?"

"Exhausting. Upsetting."

"Have a drink."

"I guess I should."

"Lots of valley people?"

"Just a few. A handful, really. Aren't so many of us left."

"Were you recognized?"

"No."

"And you didn't—"

"I didn't give myself away."

"That's an interesting phrase."

"Just a member of the audience. Another history buff."

"As far as they were concerned."

"One woman, one of the organizers…her name was familiar. And possibly her face. We probably knew each other as children— they must have gotten out early—and at one point I thought she might be studying me. But then someone asked about the baffle dam and she turned around to answer."

"The baffle dam?"

"There was a photograph of it. On the wall with the others. I never realized how huge it was, how overbearing. My sister told me about it once but I just didn't grasp it."

"The baffle dam?"

"Like a mountain rising up behind Partridge's store."

67

February 18, 1935

I never fixed that victrola. I'll have to see to it soon. I've denied myself for so long. And my poor father too: because I hadn't the courage he had to live his last days with no music at all. The world is full of it now and had I taken him away, somewhere electrified for instance, he could have listened all the time. Or had I simply fixed the machine and hunted up some more disks! But I didn't, and though it's a fitting enough punishment to let it lie there broken and silent it doesn't do *him* any good.

A string quartet would be nice. Or some popular songs. Why should I wander this old shell without relief?

February 22

The Danby house is gone now. Gone, just like that. They die three years ago March and their fine old home sits there all the same the whole time and now it's gone, just like that.

March 16

I find I can't avoid the memories, not even for a moment. It would be foolish to try. This house can never be wholly mine, and I feel more like a guest (or maybe even a servant) than its sole occupier. Here Mama's footstep on the stair, there Caleb's frown over the milk. Roy's skill with the plow, Edna's scorn for our furnishings, Miss Ballou's long-cherished praise. These are my companions as I drift through this mansion, this castle of regret, seeking something I can't name.

More than any it's Papa who visits with me now. Perhaps because I need him most. Or because he was last to go. At any rate I see him often, making the candy or rowing the pond, and he is always in my thoughts. All his distresses and excitements, the constant passions that inspired him, his bright and manly pride in having done what he meant to do. He was true to himself and I've no choice but to follow. Whenever the dark impulse comes—to destroy what I value, to deface what's around me, to set a match to this house or hang myself from a beam—I see him working at some task. Some task that pleased him. I stare at his back and know I can't betray his honor nor violate his trust. Cannot wipe away his limits, no matter how much I want to, and remember him truly free.

What am I doing here? What am I doing? Throwing my life away, that's what. Throwing, throwing, throwing my life, life away. As the time rushes by.

March 26

Oh my God. Now it's Maisie. Her little baby came at last and when it did she almost died. In her big new house in Amherst, imported linens on her bed. They're still not certain she'll survive.

They say she was close, very close. To leaving me and joining the others. She's got to live, she's simply got to, she must.

This is so cruel, so outrageously cruel. Stop it why don't you? You awful God. Evil monster sadist God. You stop it! You know she doesn't have to die. My mother didn't, nor my father, and who knows what you've done to Caleb?

I am surrounded by death. Why must you savage me this way? You torture me and Harry Coe and Maisie's innocent baby girl and for no apparent purpose but to see us in pain. Stop it! Oh please stop! No one else can die, please, no more deaths, please, I'm begging, no more dying no more deaths I beg your mercy. I'm asking. Please.

April 1

This one named Alyce McHenry. The Girl With the Upside-Down Stomach. A lesson there I suppose. No, not that conventional drivel about counting my blessings. I do feel sorry for her, of course, and I'm glad the operation succeeded, and I don't begrudge poor "Sunshine" the attention and the letters and the gifts from the Roosevelts and Governor Curley. But I know who's well off and who isn't.

No, what I mean is how bizarrely arbitrary I find the adult world to be. They try so hard to have you believe that your existence makes sense. Is understandable. Describable. Just so you can be disillusioned and frustrated, abused and terrified, humiliated by the dangerous, lunatic reality you eventually come to know. Look here: flooding four living towns to store water? A woman near death just from bearing a child? Not to mention millions killed in a war that changed nothing and the utter inability of anyone, anywhere, to bring prosperity one inch closer and these early pointless deaths I've been weeping about. Throw in my pa's cousin Reenie and all the others I'll never know. And some horrible person, some rapist and thief, is still hale and happy at one hundred and three.

Maybe Sunshine will be cured and very famous. Or she'll die under the knife. Or starve to death at five weeks old. Or live her life in that condition because her parents aren't wealthy enough, sensible enough to bring her to a doctor, spend eighty years in constant pain.

Maybe Caleb's well off. Maybe his old pal Augie isn't. Maybe a twister tears this house down tonight and a tree crushes my parents' bedroom. Or the one they might have been sleeping in, off in some other town.

April 7

Mama, Papa, dog, cat, Reenie, Mrs. Spiller, Jay Gatsby, Blackie Simmons and Dillinger, yes, and maybe Maisie and Sunshine too: here's something. I've been reading Emily Dickinson and isn't it strange, but if you look into work of that quality you can't help but find wisdom. It makes you angry at yourself but I suppose that's the point.

1625

Back from the cordial Grave I drag thee
He shall not take thy Hand
Nor put his spacious arm around thee
That none can understand

There's hope yet.

April 24

Moses is moving overseas. So I will never see him more. Not that I was counting on it. But it was always a possibility, somewhere in the background, reminding me from time to time that if I *did* get out of here, if I *did* head for Boston, there was an ally there with money, at least to lend if not to give. A smile at the station to greet me. And maybe comfort, maybe that—the only man I've thought about since Roy went away—and some sense of respect. To save me from being just another country girl struggling into the city, desperate for work.

He says he wrote to say goodbye. Well goodbye, then, Moses, goodbye.

He says he means to come back when conditions have improved. But that is beyond my horizon. Before I got this morning's mail he was a light in the distance, a faint one to be sure but a beacon of some kind; now he's just a dot on a map somewhere, next to one of the letters spelling out S O U T H A M E R I C A and a terribly long way from me.

May 1

Somehow it's still lovely. The arrival of spring I mean. Nature triumphant despite mankind's fierce attack. Flowers open, breezes sweep just as they did long years ago. The month of May is persistent in the face of our gloom.

I took a walk by the intake yesterday, just to see, and a worker was recounting some prize-fight he'd attended. A year ago, in Pawtucket. The whole group was enthralled. They sat ignoring all that beauty, ignoring the valley, very nearly ignoring me (though some touched their caps) to talk about who'd beaten whom, and how much blood. The way to bet. Other fighters they had seen. Their voices followed me down the slope.

May 9

I begin to have some notion of the hugeness of my failure. I was a girl but even so. I begin to have some notion of what I might have done, but didn't, and it takes my breath away.

May 18

I'm not even sure anyone knows about my birthday. Almost twenty years old and it might as well be seven, or nineteen, or forty-three.

May 26

A man from the Commission came to see me today. I wonder what kept him? It's been six months already. Perhaps they've had their hands full. He was patient and respectful, certainly, and very proper too at first, although he couldn't help smiling. "It's about time this was done," he said as he opened up his case and took out a contract. "It's just a question of the figures, is all. Of our reaching an agreement."

I had done a little checking with the neighbors and in town, so had in mind a minimum price. You can imagine my surprise when the figure he named was substantially higher, and my further astonishment when I found myself asking for more than that and he readily assented. It would give Pa satisfaction, I thought, watch-

221

ing the man write the numbers into the blanks, but then I wondered if it would.

I served him tea and cookies while we talked about the details.
He was trying to take his time. He really was very cheerful, considering his errand. He knew I didn't have a choice. "Just
business," he kept saying, and I think he believed it. He may even
have been right.

Still the pen felt very cold as I held it in my hand. And my
signature, once down, was stark and black and unforgiving. Hardly Polly's at all.

68

(1675/1736)

Ten thousand years in the valley. Then mounting death by plague. Then talk and trade with the outsider who has come to share the land. Then fear and panic as the forest is cut down tree by tree and a terrible mistake: joining strength with Metacomet, called King Philip by the English. Sachem of the Wampanoag. Hopeless hope leads to disaster: bloody battle, winter horror in the swamps of the southeast. The Narragansett are no more and though some Nipmuc have survived the word comes quickly: run away! From the English with their muskets and extinction in their eyes.

The valley is empty. Across its floor the waters run.

After many white winters new owners arrive. Descendants of the fighters, rewarded for their courage, marching out the Great Road to live on Indian land.

69

Was it too late already, on the day that we met? At the barn? When he ran? When all those choices were made?

Blame the water?

I'll never know.

70

June 1, 1935

I watched it from Mount Zion. The last one forever. As hard as I tried I could see no points about it that were any different from any other train, as Mr. Twain would have it, but it was and I knew it. The beginning of the end. We can't pretend anymore. All we built up over the decades is being picked apart and scattered and those of us who choose to stay are survivors, not inhabitants. Or maybe just hangers-on. So goodbye, old Rabbit, old faithful. You'll be missed.

The very last one, forever. Polly watched it from Mount Zion. And went home.

June 12

They dedicated the new highway. For reasons unknown I was moved to attend and thus subjected to speeches. What a pile of horse manure! A bunch of foolish politicians, not a one from the valley. Talked as if they were proud.

I can't possibly imagine what I was thinking of in deliberately exposing myself to that sort of thing. Perhaps I *wanted* to be angry. Perhaps I needed some real feeling beyond masochistic gloom.

"Mister Conkey and Mister Shays"! What do they know? Or care? The site of Conkey's tavern and Shays's rubbled farmstead lie in the condemned zone, don't they? To be erased just like my house, like Roy's barn, like Edna's parlor and Maisie's maple and the rest of our poor treasures. Those two malcontents happen to be long dead and buried but past that we're precisely the same.

One good thing happened, though: I spoke to Joe Cummings. Of the Cummingses of Prescott, later of Greenwich. His uncle and mama are dead now, I'd heard, and his sister moved away, so he's all alone like me. I knew him only to nod to. But when we saw the expressions on one another's faces we moved off from the crowd.

"They get yours yet?" he asked.

"Just last month."

"Off East Street, right?"

He is a rather plump man with a fairly funny face, and he was sweating in the sun, but I liked his dignity. More so I *appreciated* it just at that moment. His dignity and his, well, his manly strength. Plump and funny-looking but manly nonetheless.

"Mine is down the village but that makes no big difference. Just another line in some book back in Boston, is all." He glanced over at the platform and put his hand on my shoulder, turning me away from the assemblage entirely and leading me a few steps further toward the woods. I was touched by the intimacy; perhaps I should have been offended but I was touched.

"We have to stick together," he said. "What valley folks are still here. Have to help each other out." He dropped his hand.

"Do you work for them, Joe?"

He nodded. "Oh yes. Yes, indeed. I'm not ready to leave yet and I've got to live somehow. It's the least they can do."

"I don't care. I was just wondering."

"What about you?"

I smiled. "To the extent that I have needs they're satisfied by the tourists, at least for the moment. And by the garden and the stock."

When the speechmaking ended and the ribbon was cut he walked me over to my car. He inquired if he invited me to supper would I come and I said I would enjoy it. To my surprise and disappointment he did not then invite me but we smiled at each other before he turned and walked away.

Repainted the sign. It was getting very faded. And just as I finished and stood it under its tree a whole carload pulled up. I
muttered Commerce, thanks again.

I had a talk with Dr. Peeble. He's an Indian you know. He's
been caring for Enfield for more than thirty years and I imagine he
is hurting as much as anyone could. His flock dispersed to the
wind. I know he'll find a place not too far away in which to carry
on. He's the sort who'll stay the same until he's eighty, eighty-five,
and then exit in his sleep.

I ran into him down in Enfield. I was standing on the sidewalk, about done with my business and ready to head home, and
he came around the corner.

"You're Miss McPhee, aren't you?"

I was astonished. Of course I recognized him right away, anyone from the valley would, but how on earth did he place me? I
didn't even know he'd set eyes on me before.

He smiled at my surprise. "Trick of the trade," he said.

We spoke for some time. I felt a little odd that he spent so long
with me when there must have been lots of people eager for his
attention. But maybe that was the point. He talked about my parents, said some very nice things, and then he asked about my
brother. It was awkward to say the least because I couldn't, for
some reason, bear to tell him the usual lies (lately Caleb's been
working for a mining firm down in South America, did you know
that? doing real well) and thus had no answer for him for a few
very long seconds.

"I don't know," I said at last.

He peered at my face, then gently patted my shoulder and let
the matter lie.

Of course we talked about the project. "Being a physician does
lend some perspective, Miss McPhee," he told me. "If you'll par-

don the chestnut, life goes on. I feel for my patients—and I'm furious myself over the whole affair, believe me—but it is better than grave illness. If a young man I helped through pneumonia or polio lives to father his children in Shutesbury instead of Enfield, that's a fine enough result."

"Perspective," I observed, "doesn't change the basic facts."

"All too true," he said. "But in that we're far from alone."

June 29

Paying rent to the Commission. How peculiar it seems. It caused me no great distress—the amount is very small and the bulk of my neighbors do the same—but it was odd nonetheless, walking into that office, of all offices, with my envelope in hand. I had imagined myself a soldier marching off to battle, Aladdin approaching the cave of thieves, but I felt, in actual fact, not much of anything. The man looked up and I said "McPhee" and put it on the counter and started to go but he said "Please wait a moment, ma'am, until I've found you in the record," and I stood there while he did. He never checked the contents though. Just nodded and smiled and said "See you next month, ma'am," and went back to his work.

I hesitated briefly because I could not believe that was all there was to it. The first contact was pure trauma—after I signed the purchase and sale I hardly slept for a week—but this was nothing. Ridiculous in its mundanity. I suppose my corruption was already complete; nothing more to be lost.

Or perhaps it was the whisper, *As of now you're free to go.*

...

July 27, 1935

Dear Polly,

You never expected a letter from me I bet. I want you to know I can still write and am willing to. (This is my Xmas pen I am using.) Some days when I take my lunch brake, or in the evening, I think

228

about what I might be now if I had been educated. I don't believe I am stupid. I hope you don't believe it. I will probably not amount to much but nor am I going to act stupid. I mean to keep writing you and I guess my writing and spelling and all will get better from it. Let me know if they don't.

I'm working hard. How's the valley? Back in town at long last and cannot claim to be sorry thou I miss the forest too. And the farms. But mostly you. You know before I lost my folks I lived in the city and I admit I am at home here. Imagine it would scare you and maybe disgust you but there is lots of good in it.

I have a few friends. Men and women both. They think I'm too serius and don't like a good time but the way I see it life is serius. Every penny or minute I spend running around with them is not spent getting ahead. And I want to get ahead. I started so far behind I have a long way to go just to get even. Which they will never understand.

Most of my lunch times I think about you. And supper and breakfast to. There are some girls here who would like to date me but I have let them know I'm taken. They do not compare to you. We will have to figure out where we can live but we were meant for each other. I hope you think so as well.

This has wore me out. I cannot write so much like you. But I wanted you to know that you are always with me Polly and that everything I do is to get us back together. I have to save a bunch of cash and maybe get some good experience and then you will see me. Before they push you off your land. Another year, two at most. Don't go off anywhere, or if you do make sure you write me where and also leave it with the PO in Greenwich or Ware. I will be coming back to you.

Your friend and sweetheart

Roy Ralston

PS What I really mean to say is that I cry every day about all the pain you had, especialy what I caused you. I told you we could start again but I know that is not possible. Every day I feel rotten inside that we can't and that I will always be what I am to you and no helping it. I'm sorry. That is what I want to say most. I would fix it if I could and be someone else different. I love you and always have and I'm sorry. Please stay well.

...

July 6, 1935

A rusting auto in the woods. Around the Dana-Hardwick line, south and east of Pottapaug. There it was, between two trees, not even hidden by the brush. Thought I might see bones inside or other signs of foul play. But no such thing—just a car. An ex-car rusting away. That section won't be in the water so it'll sit until it's nothing but brown dust, I imagine. If it were in another town the forest might someday be cut and that hulk would have to go. But there it rests in peace forever. I stood by its side for a very long time, with one finger on the fender, before walking away.

I'm doing so much hiking lately. Flying Dutchgirl of the valley. Reflection of my discontent.

July 17

Maisie is healthy. Oh my Jesus, I'm so grateful. Thank the Lord or the devil, thank her doctors, thank good luck. I'll take whatever I can get.

July 25

Joe and I had our dinner. It's a very nice house. And he's a very nice man. Well-read, and quite thoughtful and articulate. The meal he made was tasty and the place was fairly clean.

From the start I was preoccupied—alarmed, then bemused— by my own profound response to that which should be overly familiar to a woman my age: company, conversation, the pleasure of an evening spent dining with a friend. A male friend. I was terribly moved by the experience, strong emotion rising up at the least provocation, and I thought it very humorous that this should be so.

I could be, after all, in any city or town, living an active young woman's life. Having dinners all the time.

Poor Polly. There was a moment (more than a moment, to be honest, closer to half an hour) when if he'd kissed me I'd have kissed back. Hard. But he didn't. You'd have to assume he was aware of some of what I was feeling—when you're so starved for everything it's bound to show, isn't it?—but he never let on.

So we just talked about books and the theater and the Commission. He was amusing and quite intriguing on the subject of villains and victims, "two sides of the coin" as he put it, and as the evening went on we slipped more and more into the natural but sad guise of mutual misery. I was left wondering why I hadn't taken action myself, if he wasn't going to, before the tension between us died. At least it held the promise of change, of something new. Maybe bad for us but new. Honestly, what have I got to lose? What am I defending? My honor? There's not a soul left on earth who gives a tinker's damn for that, least of all me.

But as always, I saw my opportunity only after it had passed.

Making my departure I sensed that my regained composure distressed him in some way. Could be he'd liked me better on the edge. Or that he knew I was disappointed but didn't know why. When I told him, "Thanks so much, it's been lovely," he was at a loss for words.

"This was a special pleasure, Polly," he said at last.

"I'm so glad," I said as he walked me to the road. "We'll have to meet again soon." I had to hide from his face until I was safe in my car. And when I did look it was struggling.

"I hope we can," he told me thickly.

"Why not?" I replied as I drove myself away.

August 4

Summer people. Blessed are they. Untouched by our trouble. Unmoved by our grief. Armed with their wallets, their purses, their children, inhaling our fresh air and fishing our streams. They relish our vistas at staggering discounts. If they pick the right spots they don't have to see the dams. They can pretend they're coming back. They cast no shadows as they pass. They give us money and move on. Blessed are they.

August 17

Mr. Will Rogers and that flyer. The one who went around the world. Smashed to pieces in a crash near Point Barrow, Alaska. Just dust returning to dust.

August 18

It never left my hand for the best part of a day. After I got it at the P.O. I reread it and held it and hoped it would change. No such luck I'm afraid.

I folded it, finally, and put it back in its envelope—with one last look at the postmark, a place so distant though so near, plus the memory of his eyes—and then into a drawer. And wept for a while, as I expected of myself, before going up to bed.

August 24

How about that? Isn't it something? Talk about a twist of fate. Mr. Big has been rubbed out. The General lies afield. The mastermind, you might call him, of our collective demise, but he deserves far more damning than that faint praise provides.

He set Apocalypse afoot; he too fished in our streams. Now even he is spared the end but not I.

71

"I've got some very good news."

"She accepted."

"She did!"

"I am so awfully happy for you."

"I knew you would be."

"I suspected that was it when you wired me you were coming."

"You don't mind?"

"Darling David! Why would I mind?"

"Because it means I'm...leaving you."

"I so want to see you settled. And your Sarah sounds perfect."

"You'll love her."

"I expect to."

"I want you settled as well."

"Please don't worry, dear cousin. Someone out there will have me! I just turned twenty-two last month—not exactly an old maid. And I've still got my looks, for what they're worth."

"I would have married you if they'd let me."

"You're embarrassing me, David."

"Our children. They'll play together?"

"I'm sure they will."

"All together."

"A lovely thought."

"Please come live with us, Reenie, in Indian Orchard."

"We'll see."

"You've got to leave here."
"We'll see."

72

This wretched drought is so far gone now that Dana is show-ing. With the water dropping drastically the valley's come to light. Tilted gravestones, crumbling roadway, farm equipment, garden stairs. Back among us already. After less than thirty years.

The reporters are wild for it, needless to say. The weather sto-ry had grown so stale.

If I were not who I am, I could do a lot with that. It would practically write itself.

73

September 19

Dearest Edna,

Perhaps you won't have time to read this letter right away. I'm so thoughtless to burden you—just over three weeks to go, and you must be very busy. But in truth I've got to tell someone and that must be you, I'm afraid.

Papa left me a bequest. It was never written down (as you know there was no will) but he left it all the same. To his friend Larry Sherman, who was to pass it on to me. Or to Mama, I should say, if she had still been alive. And then to Caleb and *then* to me.

I met with Larry last week, at his farm over in Otis. He'd sent another invitation. I was a little worried about it—he's old enough to be my father but that still doesn't make him so terribly old, and I've wondered if he means to propose—but this note was so urgent, somehow, or perhaps the word is insistent, that I figured I had better. So I climbed into the auto (God bless the car my pa bought) and headed west.

"I regret you coming all this way, Polly," he said after he'd given me tea. "I got something to tell you but the fact is I can't tolerate Greenwich no more. I'll never lay eyes on that town again if I can help it."

"I'm sorry, Larry," I said.

"Well I'm ashamed of myself," he told me. "A grown man making a young girl travel so far because he ain't strong enough to visit her as he should." He stared out the window.

"What do you have to tell me?" I asked.

"There is land up in Orange," he said. "North shore of Lake Mattawa. Fit to build on. I been holding it for you. He said to wait till you were twenty-one but I heard you sold out so I thought you ought to know. Before you took off somewhere I couldn't find you next May."

"What do you mean, there's land?"

"Land your pa bought, what I mean. Back in 1928. To move you all to, maybe, or for you or Cal to live on, or maybe as an investment. Thinking it'd be worth more once the valley was gone."

"Bought?" I was stunned. "In '28? With what money?"

Larry's smiled and spread his palms. "Search me, ma'am." He chuckled. "I don't know and never will."

He was telling the truth, that was plain. All I could do was to sit there, with my cup, and try to accept what he'd said.

Ma never knew. Caleb neither. Just Larry Sherman and now me. So why would my daddy keep it secret that way? He surely showed great discipline, not selling it the moment he lost his job. At 1932 prices, which would have been a big mistake. Beyond that I don't know whether to be gratified or angry. Both, I guess, or rather neither—he's six feet under the ground.

So there it is, sweet Edna. I've somewhere to go. Between the cash from the Commission and my father's insurance I might put up a little house. I plan to see it next week, or perhaps the week after. I'll see it sometime, anyway. Larry will wait until my birthday to transfer the deed but in the meantime I can do as I please.

I have a future, it seems. Ready or not here it comes.

74

Found a postcard today. Of Enfield—the old mill. In a so-called antique shop (most of it was junk, really) up in Charlemont on Route 2. One of those tinted photographs they used to use, the dyes faded down to pastel pinks and blues. I always find them so happy and peaceful, somehow. As if whatever was wrong when the picture was taken has drained away with the colors, and what's left can do no harm. Even the hand-lettered caption along the bottom—ENFIELD, MASS, Old Stone Mill—was just the dry remains of the simple way we lived then, which I remember so well but somehow can't practice anymore. Postage was a penny (good old Ben Franklin in green) and the postmark had ENFIELD at the top of the circle and MASS. at the bottom, and in the middle AUG 10 1911. Just a year before my birth but near fifty gone.

I admit my hand was shaking as I read the scribbled message but there was nothing much there. A Louise of Great Barrington told a Mrs. Howes of Sheffield that she was "out for the month" to stay with the Packhams and hoped they could visit in September. I was glad it wasn't from Greenwich. That she was no one I'd known.

But there it was, you know? Thrown in with all the others: Haverhill, Fall River, Westfield, Boston and Manchester NH. It's a fact, I confess, that those places are gone too; the Merrimac's valley from 1909 is as dead and disappeared as the Swift's from my day, and even the Public Garden, all fresh and new on its own postcard, is overhung and littered now by huge and ancient trees. But I couldn't help wondering if something, anything—a sick feeling, sudden restlessness, a suspicion of a tiny little poke at the shoulder—had come to any of the last ten or twenty customers who'd flipped through the pile when they laid eyes on Enfield. Anything? Anything at all? Because it isn't just history, like the rest. A well-kept secret, possibly forever. Just imagine: a quarter for something like that.

I thought about buying it, for a moment or two, or even slipping it into my shirt, but in the end let it be.

75

December 23, 1935

Late last month, I guess it was, I ran into Roy's hermit. I'd never seen him before but I knew that it was he. Perhaps from Roy's brief descriptions. Perhaps a lucky guess. Perhaps some intuition, some deep sense told me that here was a man who was as leery of me as I was of him, but also that we shared a wispy bond, a connection. We were the only two people in the Swift River valley who gave a damn about Roy Ralston, even knew he was gone, and there we were in frigid twilight out on Kelly Hill road.

He was old but not as old as he looked. He was dirty and unkempt, but not offensively so. Had it been July he might have smelled bad but I don't think I could have smelled an elephant standing next to me at that time and place. I had been motoring home from Amherst after visiting Maisie and felt the urge to see Prescott. Why exactly I don't know—did the pleasure of playing with mother and child, of seeing them carefree and well, require a countering excursion to Ghost Town, Massachusetts, in the freezing autumn gloom?—but I was driving on the hillside, rather slowly and aimlessly, and had come to a decision to turn around and head for Greenwich lest I be caught on the ridge after dark when I saw a motionless figure. He was standing in the center of the road, just standing there, and looked so bewildered and harmless when I got close enough to see that I put the car in neutral and climbed down to inquire.

240

"Do you need help?" I asked. He shook his head, and as he did I knew who he was. His whiskers were long and tangled and ragged, his hair greasy and curled, and his hands were very large. To my surprise he had no firearm.

"You're Roy's friend, aren't you?" I asked. He made no reply. "I'm Polly," I said. "He may have mentioned me once or twice. He talked about you all the time. It's nice to meet you at last."

His silence was all the more strange, the more provoking, on account of the interest I saw in his eyes. I was sure he wanted to know more about me, or about the wide world, or to convey something to me—a warning, a message, some fragment of advice—but his lips stayed firmly shut.

We faced each other there for a minute or more. Only the sound of the engine fought the silence. I was fearful, it's true, but never tempted to run. I was closer to the auto than I was to the man and assured myself, calmly and rationally, that should he spring I could get in and start moving before his hand closed on my coat. I wanted to give him every chance to say what he had to say, to ask what he had to ask.

And then it occurred to me: a hermit is a person who chooses not to have intercourse. Not a question of *can't* but rather of *won't*. I understood that I might stand there for a week and he would still refuse to speak. His expression was impersonal; he had probably looked that way, I realized, for many years, as his accumulating substance piled against the dam of his tongue. Like the reservoir, I told myself. Except it wouldn't overflow, but someday he might.

"Well, goodbye," I said—I'm afraid I actually sounded cheery—before I climbed back in the car. "I hope you have a pleasant winter." He was still standing in his spot as I maneuvered around him and drove away, but no longer motionless; he turned first at the waist, then altogether, to follow me with those same imprisoned eyes.

As I headed into the valley I had the most peculiar fantasy. That the man had been struck dumb on the day Roy left him and had never spoken since, would never again. That with his young companion had gone his power of conversation. Forever and ever.

Just yesterday I heard he's in a state institution. That's why I'm writing this now. I had not thought about our meeting until they told me the story of the old man who was hauled out of the woods, three weeks after a bad fall, because nobody wanted to tend to him all winter. Hauled out weeping and kicking. (And cursing, apparently; so much for my surmise.) They had to bind his hands to do it but they did and now he's gone.

...

1935

Roads through the main dam site on the Enfield-Ware line are taken out of service so that construction of the core wall can commence. Work begins on the dike at Beaver Brook in southeast Enfield, which, unlike the dam, will provide no spillway to pass water through, serving only to prevent it from leaving the reservoir.

A forest fire in Prescott destroys two thousand acres of timber and is believed by many to have been deliberately set.

The Massachusetts Supreme Judicial Court sets aside the 1933 Board of Referees award of $221,000 to the owners of the Dugmar Golf Course in Greenwich and orders a new hearing.

The Greenwich Foundation of Ware is formally declared.

...

A dog runs fast across a field. Runs and runs before the wind.

76

Spiritualists gathered there in their time, with their trances and ectoplasms. And utopians bright with hope. Both sought a certain distance, a version of escape. A rejection of that which was rooted in the cities: Boston, New York and all the growing blight out west. In the hollows and the forests, the very center of the state, on the ponds and in the hills these people found their release. From domination that oppressed them. From the grief of what must be. Heart of darkness it was, our poor humble backward valley, though not a one of us knew it. The secret heart that is no more.

77

April 7, 1936

You can't sell anything these days. Nor give it away. To valley people I mean. No one wants it nor has room. Used to be a useful object had more lives than a cat; now we're trying to figure out how to unburden ourselves. A common problem not easily solved.

When you sell to the tourists you feel like an exhibit, a historical display. The way they coo and gasp over an old gate leg table is enough to take the joy out of jacking up the price. And to an engineer, well, you simply feel like a fool. And every time you have to ask: which is better, death or still life? Do we let it end here or do we want someone to point to an old broken fiddle, for instance, that was carried in a family for three generations, and say That was made in the Swift River valley, in 1884, and then show off their new shrubs?

These are not idle questions. Each worn-out chair, each dulled dish has its own true destination. Whether it gets there or not.

April 14

You might think I would be insensible to irony by now. But in addition to being continually beset by sorrow over last month's disaster—they're already calling it the Great Flood, I gather, from Vermont all the way to Ohio—I find myself angry as well. Which I admit is perverse, if not actually twisted. We were spared, sure, and I'm appropriately grateful. But it was only because we are already of no consequence as a target for the elements; we are instead mere detail around the edges of the Commission's grand design, the reservoir basin and its pipe works, which easily absorbed all the floodwaters could do. Thanks to the water that is coming to stay forever, the water that was passing through left us unharmed.

Reports from towns westward are heartbreaking. The friendly Connecticut became a ravening monster. South Hadley Falls was almost erased, I understand. The covered bridge in Montague—something like seven hundred feet long, double-decked, with those enormous timbers—was actually picked up and washed far downstream, destroying other bridges as it went. Springfield sounds like a nightmare: folks being rescued from their rooftops while those not reached in time were swept away, thousands in shelters, looting to the point that the police were patrolling with guns in hand, ready to shoot on sight…and when the water was gone buildings, railroad tracks, streets and sidewalks in ruins and knee-deep mud everywhere. (The Auditorium was spared, thank goodness. I hope it lasts forever.)

Hard to say what would have happened here had the Great Flood come ten years earlier. But whatever damage it might or might not have done to Greenwich, Mass is immaterial. They'll rebuild Springfield, difficult though it will be, but Greenwich is gone, just like the Montague bridge; that it was nature's hand in one case and man's in the other doesn't signify. Gone is gone.

April 20

They've got a nasty name already: "woodpeckers," we call them. They are so clumsy and incapable, so far from their hard streets. They simply don't know what they're doing and if not for the Governor I'd wonder why not local men? But we all know Mr. Curley—of course the jobs went to his cronies. Not even qualified, just his pals. The machine got him elected so now he's paying off the favor, feeding cash to the machine.

What they're doing is bad enough. That they're dirty, crude and ignorant certainly doesn't improve things.

"Curley's summer camp" they call it. They can thank him this fall.

April 25

I'm bound to confess: I've started talking with Caleb. Even arguing sometimes. As I work around the yard, drive to Enfield or the Plains. Believe it started during all that rain last month, when I was stuck in the house for so long. Or maybe it was the first time I went down to look at the east branch in flood. It was so strange to see all that water overspreading the banks; it was the kind of thing that would have intrigued him mightily. A preview of when they seal off the tunnel and the waters start to rise.

Anyway, why not? Company is company. And if he were here the decisions we'd make would likely be quite different from what I manage on my own. Why not enjoy the benefit of his advice and consent? I can conjure him well enough. Of course he's much older now, yes—six *years* since I saw him, a fact I can grasp, never mind accept, only because I have to—but then so am I.

April 30

A pleasant picnic with Joe. Pleasant enough. We chose our spot carefully, up on Pottapaug hill where we wouldn't be bothered, and were sheltered from unwelcome sights and sounds.

I wondered as we drove there what would happen after lunch, but I needn't have worried. (Or gotten vaguely excited. Or whatever it was I did.) If I had his attention I've lost it. We sat on a rock and read verse to each other. He was admiring of Coleridge but doesn't hold with Ezra Pound. In any case not a single sentiment expressed by any piece we read caused him to edge any closer to me.

But pleasant at least, as I say: lovely weather and good food and he reads well, does Joe, reads much better than he imagines.

246

His voice possesses qualities he doesn't know are there. I wanted to talk to him about this, to draw him out, but then I thought: leave him alone. He's got troubles of his own.

When I got home and shut the door I was suddenly, keenly aware of my womanly frustration. For a moment or two I actually wept from desire.

I so long to be touched, only to be touched, and I just sit there reading poetry! What's the matter with me?

May 1

I saw three bluebirds this noon. It's very lucky, they say.

May 4

What I wrote not long ago, about the woodpeckers—that's beneath me. I have no cause to be so harsh. They're human beings, just men looking for work, trying to feed their families same as anyone here. What's being done to us wasn't remotely their idea.

And in truth while it does give me the shudders to watch a gang of them from a distance, when I get up close they resolve into individual citizens, the usual assortment. Some you'd want to avoid under any circumstances, sure, but others might be friends in another place and time. I even chatted with one this morning. Charlie, I heard them call him. Very much of the city but a good-looking man. Told me he was sorry about what was happening to us. When I took my leave he smiled and said, "Nice to meet you, ma'am", and as I walked up the hill I recalled my silly words and was ashamed. They're not the enemy; they're just cannon fodder like the rest of us.

May 8

Listen: let me tell you about Hemingway. Don't laugh. People talk about his novels and with good reason. They are surely worthy books, and have brought him fame and fortune, and I think that's just fine.

247

But listen to me: those stories. My goodness. *There* is confidence; there is art. How about "Soldier's Home"? And "God Rest Ye Merry"? How about those early ones, like "The Battler" and "Indian Camp"? Even his titles are hopelessly beautiful: "A Clean Well-Lighted Place." "The End of Something." "The Three-Day Blow." "A Way You'll Never Be."

It's all so very male, of course. There are things he'll never manage because women are beyond him. But maybe that's part of the effect these stories have on me. The glorious solitude. The nakedness, the isolation of those lonely empty moments. The muscle. The *bluntness*. Take the very end of "The Light of the World":

> "Which way are you boys going?"
> "The other way from you."

Never in a billion years.

May 13

The new baffle dam is a marvelous thing. Who believed they would actually have the nerve? It breaks the village in two, literally in two; it runs between Mount Zion and the knoll to the south, with another southern section on to higher Hardwick ground. Cutting right across three roads. Splitting the church from the mill pond, the Inn from the P.O. Classes held in the Grange, they took the schoolhouse to make room.

They have rent a huge gap in our fabric, this time; threads are waving unsecured and the raveling will follow. Suddenly the village as we knew it is gone. We see whose home this has become.

May 15

Maybe I'll travel—to Edna in Buffalo, to Don and Flo in Wisconsin, then across the water and Asia to Paris or Berlin. Maybe I'll study music and art. Or find a job as an assistant to some fascinating person, a sculptor or adventurer of some kind. Anything that might help to restore my broader vision. It wouldn't be necessary, of course, were I not in this position—were I off in a college, say—

248

but I am and it is. I despair of myself, some days. Of ever regaining enough of myself, of my birthright, to write as I suspect I can.

I am starting to lose sight of both the forest and the trees.

May 21

Maple and sycamore, dogwood and birch. And of course the most gracious and beautiful elm. All fall, all fall. Fall before the peckers' knives. As I've said those city boys don't have a notion but there are thousands of them here, thus our fine foliage is doomed.

The sounds of cutting sawing chopping are extremely hard to miss and bits of tree litter our paths. Willow and linden and trembling aspen. Nothing is spared, not the oldest of oaks.

In the meantime they are working to reforest cleared ground up above the water line. They have a nursery in town. New England wants to be forest and would manage by itself but much too slowly I suppose. And they hope for stands of pine they can cut in thirty years, to build houses in the towns our river's water will serve.

What we established they reverse. Replacing bare dirt with trees, erasing trees for bare dirt. A valley turned upside down.

May 27

I'm twenty-one now. A voter. A landowner. A woman of majority. I can make contracts and marry without my parents' consent. Borrow money. Buy liquor. Run for office if I choose.

I'm an adult, so they say. I'll find out what it's worth to me.

78

He held my breast. I smelt his smell. He was so near to me so near I had no hope of running away. He held my breast held and squeezed it didn't hurt but nearness did I wished him back to Cambridge to Dublin to his mama's womb his father's grave to the filthy floor of the makeshift saloon in Palmer or Ware he collapsed to Saturday night after vomiting passed out from drinking up his dollars hard-earned destroying our town lying in his supper he snored and twitched till his companions kicked his ribs and then lay quiet far from home. All this I smelt and sensed through his fingers and saw in his scowl and the scream that rose in me was short of the task and we waited we two neither ready to act he wouldn't force me in the open nor I yield to ease my fear so we waited for an accident to read to us our fates but nothing came.

79

Late in 1944 I was pushing towards Germany. Me and a whole lot of other tough guys. Twenty-five years old, more than two years since I joined and I was beginning to understand that the war was nearly over. I was going home alive. It was possible I'd take a random slug or some shrapnel but I knew just a few of us would buy it from then on and I was sure it wouldn't be me. I'd always been lucky and had never come close to any serious wound, the only one being that bad bruise on my shin where the kraut brought down his rifle before Ralphie shot his ass. The only one in two-plus years. I'd already written my father saying get the burgers ready, and the beer and the pie. And the women, oh yes. None of those French whores for me, not after the first time anyway.

So one day I went with Perlman to the quartermaster's outfit to see about some sulfa and there was this guy with a guitar. This old skinny guy with a worn-out kind of face. Hard life I suppose. The song he was playing was one I'd used to sing and we stopped to listen to him. It was "Good Night Irene". You know, you remember:

> Irene, good night
> Irene, good night
> Good night Irene, good night Irene
> I'll see you in my dreams

He had a nice way with a song for a man of his age and Danny and I listened. No one else paid him mind but we'd put in the stu-

pid form and they'd promised the stupid pills and we had no place
to go and weren't due back for a while. And his singing sounded
fine. So we waited. When he was done I asked him to play it again
and he said Got a cigarette? so I gave him my pack. Danny snorted
and shook his head but the man just said Thanks and put it into his
pocket and played the song for us again.

> Saturday night I was married
> Me and my wife settled down
> Now me and my wife we are parted
> Think I'll take another stroll through town

That voice was so sure of itself, I remember. So easy. He raised
his eyes up while he sang, as if Irene were floating there.

So we go back to our unit—Perly thought I was crazy, A doz-
en smokes for a number you already heard!—and for the next two
weeks or so that song went with me everywhere. On patrol, in my
tent, on the mess line, even combat. Every moment of every day I
sang it out loud or in my head. But it never made me tired.

Shut up, they told me. Shut up, shut up. We heard your lousy
song about six million times. But it never stopped me. I mean, I
tried—they were my buddies, I didn't want to piss them off—but it
kept coming back. At any hour, dark or light.

> Sometimes I live in the country
> Sometimes I live in the town
> Sometimes I take a great notion
> To jump in the river and drown
>
> Irene, good night
> Irene, good night
> Good night Irene, good night Irene
> I'll see you in my dreams

After a while it got to be a big joke. With the others and with
me. They started calling me Irene. Honestly. I tried hard to shake it
off, really I did. I remembered I first heard it when I was maybe

seventeen, most likely in '36, so I wrote down a list of some other songs from then. To distract me. But no dice.

We'll have you sing it in Berlin, Irene, said Ralphie one day. With your boot on Hitler's back. Make him listen for an hour or so. Before we break his fucking neck.

> Stop your rambling, stop your gambling
> Stop your stayin' out late at night
> Go home to your wife and your family
> Stay there by your fireside bright
>
> You caused me to weep,
> You caused me to mourn,
> You caused me to leave my home
> But the very last words I heard you say
> Were "please sing me one more song"

When it finally went away—and it did, to hell and gone, all at once on a Sunday evening—I was pretty sad about it. Felt like I lost a friend, like I did when short Fred got machine-gunned in Africa. Sounds ridiculous, I know: how can a song go away? You're free to sing it any time. But if I tried it didn't work. Just another tune, it was. Just another set of words.

> Irene, good night
> Irene, good night
> Good night Irene, good night Irene
> I'll see you in my dreams

It wasn't until later—much, much later, years and years and years later, when I'd become a grown man—that I connected it with Polly.

253

80

"My Sister"

My little sister is younger than me. I am now in the fifth grade and she is in second. I am happy to see her learning her lessons because I want her to have fun in school and learn. That is good about going to school together. Sometimes I watch her do her writing or sums.

My little sister is called Polly. The reason she is called this is because her real name is Rebeca but when she was a new baby and cried and cried I tried to give her a cracker. They say when I was three we saw a man with a parrot and when the parrot skwakked the man said to the parrot Polly want a cracker? and then gave it a cracker and it stopped skwakking. They say when my sister was crying a lot I brought her a cracker and said Polly want a cracker? and tried to get her to eat it. My pa says he laughed enough to bust a gut (that is what he said Miss Miller!) and after that we called her Polly. My ma says it is a much better fit than Rebeca. I do not know about names fitting nor why they name her one thing and call her another but that (Polly) is what we always call her. Everyone does.

I have enough words left to say that I love my sister and would be sad without her. She is funny and does her share of work even if she is small. Let someone try to be mean to her and they will see how much I love her. I named her and proud of it. I am happy when she smiles.

July 7, 1936

This could be my last summer in the valley. If I wanted. Next Fourth I could be any number of places. Once in a while I dwell on this, daydream about the possibilities. But mostly I know I'll be here.

July 13

I suppose it had to happen. If not to me some other woman. If not in Greenwich then Dana or Enfield. If not that particular woodpecker then one of his friends. I am tempted to write it off as historic inevitability, the product of time and place—an arbitrary but predictable accident of which I chanced to be the victim—but that is certainly too pat. And too dismissive of my pain. There are hundreds of women here. Did it have to be me?

Well, we had spoken several times and I had actually encouraged him a little, I'm afraid. So that's how it came to be me. And why I can't blame him entirely. Not that a kind word or two give license for abuse but here he is, after all, far from home for long months, living in a barracks, and *country women* a part of the inducement I imagine. The way a man thinks *far from home* means *I can get away with anything*, and who knows but he's been working up his courage for weeks.

At any rate, he thought I'd quiver at his touch and when I didn't he got angry. He has regretted it by now but his first impulse was fury. Not at my refusal, I think, but at my refusal to be moved. I was far beyond his grasp and he hated that discovery.

"Good morning, sweet Polly," he said as I approached. He'd been sizing up a spruce.

"Miss McPhee," I said, but smiling.

He leaned on his axe. "You know you've not even asked *my* name," he said. "What is it you call me then?"

"All right, Charlie. Polly it is, but please spare me the sweet talk."

He laughed and moved into my path. "There's sweet talk and sweet touches," he said, grabbing my wrist. "I can do without the one but not the other." Then he tried to kiss me.

I twisted and tried to free myself. The axe was flung to the side—I heard the blade hit a rock and thought, *tax money paid for that tool*—and his other arm went around my waist. He tried to kiss me again and found my lips for an instant before I managed to turn away. I struggled silently and he laughed.

"Sweet and delicious," he said, letting go of my wrist to reach into my blouse. "Still young I'd say by the feel of you. Young and warm and just right." I hit his face and he laughed. "And so pretty, sweet Polly." I hit again. "Take care bitch," he said.

Then I stopped fighting and simply stared at him. His face was no more than four inches from mine and his hand still gripped my flesh.

"You'll have to kill me, Charlie Irishman," I said, very calmly. "If you don't let me go this instant I swear I'll see the sheriff and tell him everything. Everything you do, everything. It's twenty years for rape, twenty years at the very least, and they don't much like tenement micks around here so it will probably be thirty. Or maybe fifty. Is it worth the rest of your life?"

He let go and stepped away. Then he reached out with his left hand and tore the blouse from my body. Then he spat on me.

"Very manly."

He spat again.

"Are you through now?"

He nodded.

I stooped to get my blouse.

"If you'd been nice," I told him, "and gone about it the right way, you might have had your pleasure, Charlie. I used to think you were quite handsome." I saw him twitch and raised my hand. "No more warnings," I said. "You've gone too far already. Either stop right now or bash my head with that axe; otherwise the sheriff will hear about this. Every bit of it." I wiped his spittle off with my handkerchief, then put on my blouse. "It will make a good impression on the judge, don't you think?"

He stood staring, breathing heavy, hands open and fingers spread as if ready to pounce, but I knew he wouldn't touch me. Not as long as I kept my mouth shut from that point on. I looked up at the sun and turned around to go back. I was out of his sight entirely, nearly to my gate, when I heard the sound of chopping. Very even, very slow.

Up to now I haven't cried. Not for an instant, not in the slightest. I'm not even angry. Bruised and sad, is all.

July 19

The Atkinsons' raspberries will be a huge help. I went over yesterday and the bushes are spectacular. Fresh raspberries are scarce in the city now, and dear; I'm told they get snapped up at any price, better even than peaches or herbs. We have never had many to speak of on our place but Clara and Bob had quite a stand.

Looking them over was like studying someone's bureau drawers. Or hope chest. Or safe deposit box. But I guess they're mine now.

"Keep an eye on them," said Bob as he showed me the berries, the day before they left. "I'm sure you'll know when to start."

"I can't pay you yet," I told him. "But I'll pay you from the proceeds, if you can wait that long."

He looked hard at my face. "You can't pay me at all," he said. Then he turned to the bushes. "Your parents didn't teach you to embarrass a neighbor that way," he said. "So why do it?"

"To be fair, Mr. Atkinson," I told him. "We're all needy now."

He laughed to keep from growling. "Needy people need their friends most of all, Polly. I hope you'll bear that in mind."

July 30

There was Charlie. In a group. Around quarter of three. They looked at me and touched their foreheads (much too hot for wearing caps) and several nodded and one said, "Afternoon ma'am." My former friend just turned away. God knows what possessed me but as I passed I paused to speak.

"I hope you are all taking care," I said primly, "to drink plenty of water and rest in the shade. It's a very warm day."

"They don't pay us to rest, miss," said one muscular fellow with a tear in his shirt.

"They don't pay you to drop from heatstroke either," I answered. "You may be workers but you're also men."

The look on Charlie's face was simply wild. That's what it was. Simply wild. I had intended to say more but that was that. One called out, "Thank you, miss," as I hurried away.

August 3

Who burned the church? That's the question. We're all accustomed to fires by now but this one bears speculation. Who held the match? No one can say.

There is talk that it was woodpeckers or some of the other outside labor but goodness me, I find that silly. Would any disgruntled worker really try to get at the Commission by burning something down? It's just a convenience for the project. Nor as revenge against Enfield, surely, or some citizen thereof; a man dismantling a town wouldn't go to such risk to hasten one building's end. And attacking a house of Christ—even a blasphemous Protestant one—would be contrary to their natures.

No, I think it was one of us. I can't imagine that it wasn't. "Better it should go in a blaze of glory than be torn down stick by stick," said Mr. Andrus.

Enfield Congregational, one hundred and fifty years on earth: may you rest in your ashes, on the bottom, in peace.

August 11

I ran into Joe in the village today and he invited me to his house for coffee. As we walked there I resolved to tell him about what happened. With Charlie. I've been trying to pretend that it didn't affect me but the truth is it's been with me ever since, all the time, dragging me down, and I thought it might help to unburden myself.

But when it came to it I couldn't. And not only because I realized Joe would insist on going to the sheriff right away, or worse yet seeking out Charlie himself. I won't say I was ashamed, but it wasn't something I wanted Joseph to know. That Charlie had his hands on me. That I'd been talking with him in the first place. That I was standing uncovered on the hillside in the sunshine, in full view, on display.

Happily I don't believe it will be bothering me anymore. Just thinking of telling was enough.

August 18

This afternoon I stood and watched as some woodpeckers on their break were approached, one by one, by a man with a mustache and a portfolio under his arm. I gather these boys do not belong to any union; this man was telling them they didn't earn enough and their conditions weren't safe and if they'd only get together they could fix all their problems. Most looked at him blankly or sullenly shook their heads but one laughed and answered back.

"These are just temp'rary jobs, chief," he said, "and there's no skills to it. They can replace us in a second. You don't make sense."

"No it's you who doesn't make any sense, my fine friend," said the other. "But as long as we're against each other no working man makes sense. We've got to end all that. What I'm telling you about is the need to *organize*."

The pecker coughed and then frowned. "Why don't you organize your ass out of here, perfesser," he said. "We're doing fine."

"Your mistake," said the union man.

82

(1920)

My daddy takes me to Boston lots of people there he says don't be scared little one but I am I am I am. Crowds of bodies and big buildings dirty engines everywhere. He takes me down the dark cellar where the trains rumble in and I say I don't want to and he says hang on Polly we will get on the train and I cry and I cry. Be a big girl says a lady I try to kick her but pa sees me puts his foot in front of mine. That smarts he says oh boy! listen Polly listen squirt we're on the train now to stay why not quit crying and have fun we will arrive before you know it but I cry and I cry. Your daddy's here he says to me nothing bad will happen to you I promise.

83

Walking back across the campus—it was after a story seminar and I was savoring the praise of my instructor and my classmates, strolling slowly in a trance of ambition briefly sated—I found myself pausing by the fountain. The one given by Mary's grandfather in memory of her aunt, a sad rich girl who fell ill and succumbed in her senior year.

"My mom and uncles," Mary had sniffed as she showed me the plaque, "were spoiled rotten, later on. So I'm told. Cars and gold and trips to Europe. But this is all poor Lilly got."

"That's what comes of dying young."

As I stared at the rushing water, remembering my teacher's words—"first-rate work," he'd said twice, as well as "masterfully done"—I thought of my own father, and of his final gifts to me.

Why didn't I hate him? For his silence. For our ignorance. Where was my anger, my sense of betrayal? He had means of significance, extra money, a safe haven, but he never disclosed them. As bad as things got. Lost his son and his wife and kept his secrets all the while.

I stood for long minutes in that lovely tranquil place, on the threshold of my future—surrounded by greenery and dusty pink brick, by centuries of grace and manners, by the children of privilege I could barely imagine—and tried to guess at his design.

84

September 28, 1936

It says they call them "chain stores." An entirely new idea. They lay the goods on long shelves, in standard packages, and let the customer decide. Then she goes to a clerk who rings it up and takes the money. Increased trade and decreased labor; no more waiting on customers or measuring things out or going out back for an item. Keeps the prices way down.

Why on earth would anyone choose to live that way? Or call it the "market of the future"? Right now, yes, of course, folks are desperate to save money. They'd stand on their heads for a break on the price, never mind pick their own sack of flour and cart it up to the counter. But when things return to normal they will find this unacceptable. They'll want to get back to the old dignity, I'm certain, the familiar respect.

October 4

Joseph tried to take my hand. Finally. Late last night, after the movie. And the awful thing is that I wanted him to, I've been waiting for him to—so we can for god's sake move on to something more satisfying—but when he did I wouldn't have it. I actually snatched my hand away. What on earth? I thought I had grown well past that sort of nonsense.

To my great good fortune we were in shadow when it happened, almost unable to see, and by the time we reached the corner and the glow of its streetlamp he had composed himself again.

"That wasn't a very good picture," he said.

"I'm just glad to be able to go at all, honestly."

"When we're shut of this place," he told me, "and living somewhere real, we'll go to the cinema whenever we please."

I put my hand on his arm, very lightly. "Listen, Joe," I said as we walked. "I've got a terrible headache and to tell you the truth I've been sullen all day. I hope you'll overlook my poor behavior. It's nothing to do with you."

"I haven't any idea what you're talking about," he said.

"Don't be courteous, Joe," I whispered. "Don't be kind. Just this once. I'm asking you to forgive me."

He took a small step away, forcing me to drop my hand, and insisted, "There is nothing to forgive."

October 8

To Enfield this afternoon, to sell my squash. After stopping at the library I went right by the church. Or I should say the place it was. Even after all the destruction I've seen, the demolitions and transportations, it was something of a blow. I had to stop and get out and wander around for a while, convincing myself that what I saw was true and real. That church had been there forever—it *was* Enfield, more or less—and I had a miserable time accepting it as gone. All the more so, I'm certain, because of what still stood around it; its sorry ex-location was so clearly defined. Any idiot could see that a church had disappeared, never mind a former congregant, never mind me.

But here is one consolation: when they've torn down the rest it'll all be bare soil, just dust and stone, and the marking of past presences will be an academic problem, very dry, without pain. Sad to think but surely so; there comes a point at which enough has been taken that what's left begs for removal. Cries out to join the departed. Enfield's not there yet but as I stared at the naked ground, the looted graveyard, I could see the day coming. The day on which we'll join together to pull down what remains. To return it all, for god's sake, to primordial mud.

As I studied that vacancy it brought to mind others. All the empty places everywhere, across the county and the commonwealth, the breadth of the nation. Roy's rented room, for example: the spot on his bureau in which my portrait once stood. Mama's place at our table. The shelf in New York that held Caleb's books and souvenir, if it still exists at all. The Danby's lot and the empty graves and all the falling down shacks of all the farmers who've fled their dust fields for the coast, the little chair in the White House in which the Lincoln boy once sat, that stinking barn and the children missing fathers in the war and your naked smeary plate when you've finished your pie. I was so solemnly aware of all the hollowness around me—of how it overwhelms the fullness, how all our frantic industry is mere vapor to its wind—that I wrapped my arms about myself and closed tight my eyes, and marched quickly to the auto without ever looking back.

October 16

There are walls in the woods. All over the state. Stone walls and cellar holes. New England was covered with farms at one time; they cut down all the forests, piled the boulders into walls. Trying to keep their bellies full.

But as soon as there was any other way to make a living— such as laboring in some dark and crowded mill—they up and left their stony fields, left the forest to reclaim them. Only a fool would stick most New England farms, working near death to pull another three ears of corn or six potatoes from the soil, if he could earn real money elsewhere. So those farms dropped into slumber and from there out of sight. And you can find their crumbling traces in the woods most anywhere. Reverted to their former guise.

This valley is an exception, of course. Most of our land is good. Maybe the ice dumped a pile of fine dirt, maybe the river spread its leavings on the plains. But it's a sin to take good farm-land, as my pa once said. It can never be replaced.

There'll come a time when we too are just old walls in the woods. Or at the bottom of the lake. Just more farmers said good-bye.

October 17

Roy's birthday.
He's twenty-three.
No further word.
Goodbye, Roy Ralston. Goodbye.

October 27

The people are going. Exodus in full throng. The town of Greenwich, Massachusetts is emptying at last. And I'm speaking of holdouts here, real holdouts, truly ornery ones who believed they would stay to the bitterest of ends. But enough, they are finding day by day, is enough.

So that leaves us waiting here—those who don't seem to mind.

November 1

I was sorting through some papers when I found the yellowed essay. How it got there I don't know, and my reasons for picking up the documents at all are a mystery to me. An inner miracle, some might say. To think it was sitting there all that time, waiting for me. To make up my mind. To get ready, I suppose, ready for something of importance; I didn't know what I might find, muck-ing around in that desk, but I surely understood that I would come across more than a handbill for the county fair in 1919.

To say that I am touched would be both narrow and glib. I am, of course—I wept hard and long and wetly with the paper in my hand and I think I would have given my arms, my legs, my very eyes at that moment to feel my brother's hand in mine and hear his voice in my ear—but there is more to it than that. I confess that I feel calmer, saner, stronger, even peaceful; my discovery is a tonic. I've got perspective back again. Not that Caleb wrote what he wrote or felt what he felt, that is no news, but the reminder that the once-firm realities of childhood and ignorance, of the time before the fall, really were in the world—no sad lie to ease the hurt—gives me courage and conviction. The sort of thing I've sorely lacked. I can miss him, all right, and my mother and father too, and my friends and my home, and I can do it with joy. I am aware of what I've lost but still possess. I won't lose sight of it again.

85

Joe was the man I might have married. If things had been different. If we had somehow come to terms. At the time it was too difficult, too far beyond my sight. Something precious got lost in the muddle we were part of. But we might have been married and I appreciate that now.

When I try very hard I can see him for a moment without the puzzlement on his face. Without the look of kind distress. And then I want to return to say Joseph, Joe, Joe, we don't need you this way. You can be anything you are. You are strong, you are angry, you are permitted to grieve.

We could have married, Joe. We could have. In a grave but hopeful service. On the baffle dam, say, or in the shadow of the dike, or in front of the wreckage of grand houses in Dana, by the common still green. And they all could have come, all those living in the valley, by virtue of resolution, of determination—of good old yankee perseverance—or if not then blind luck.

Perhaps the Chief Engineer could have given me away. Mrs. Roosevelt my Matron of Honor. With the Governor presiding, Springfield's mayor as best man. Amid big bunches of wild flowers.

I loved that man that Joe. I see it now. I was so fond. And we deprived ourselves of each other for reasons I would rather not consider now at all. Unworthy reasons. Youth's sad follies. Simple misunderstandings held too close to the heart.

It could be he's alive and well, somewhere in New England. He was of very sturdy stock and a vigorous man. That boy who gave me his seat on the bus yesterday—perhaps he's Joe's grandson. Perhaps he could have been mine. Riding along with me, holding my arm, instead of moving to the back with faint pity in his eyes.

Or the doctor with whom I spoke at the hospital last week. The one with the very short hair. Her smile was like his. Wishful thinking again?

<u>1936</u>

August: Greenwich Congregational Church is dismantled. Its bell is purchased by the Polish Catholic Church of Bondsville.

September: Enfield Depot, last of the Rabbit Run's stations, is torn down.

October: Hunting is forbidden in the Swift River valley.

Very early one morning, in a gentle waking trance, I lifted up my pen. There was a sentence carried in me that had come there in the night and would have nothing but the paper. For several minutes I resisted, lying limp beneath my quilt, all the wrongest of reasons (I'm so sleepy, it's too hard, it will only make me cry) rising up and falling down like startled birds before my eyes. When that was finished there I was, still under cover, sentence cradled in my heart but imploring its departure. Like a child I suppose; I didn't want to let it go but also saw, with deep sad rectitude, the necessity of freedom. Necessity and relief. Take the plunge, something said. Have it out or lose forever. Too much has come to you and gone.

So I got up and found my robe.

Not just a sentence, as it happened; once released it drew forth others. Had I not been so determined to pull that chain to its end I would have stopped to praise my pen, to stroke and kiss it, for I so loved its easy quickness, its suitability to my hand. I had a sense of justice then that I had not known before and may never find again, of perfect function, zero friction, balance in every respect. The words were there when I had need; all my meters ran together. A strange joy, surely, but joy all the same.

And in the end I had three pages. Not so much, I admit, very little if typed out; the beginning of something that might possibly be more. But a *beginning*—which means, when I returned I'd know the way. Not my diary and its burdens, not the uninformed attempts of my earlier days to mimic what I'd read, but a real and vital portion of a thing to be made by me.

By sunrise I was wise enough to grasp such an event. There could be no mistake. I was terribly frightened, very nearly overcome, but I recognized the truth: this was something I could do.

Exalted and anxious, exhausted and fresh, longing for someone's warm flesh to press against my own in a vain attempt at comfort, picturing myself running off through the dawn away from Greenwich, from my dear Swift River, away from those misfortunes that had made me what I was, I paced the room. And then the house. From bottom to top. What is to be done? I asked myself, what will happen? and no answer arrived. But I smiled at the question. This was everything I'd wanted, the fulfillment of my need. A chance was all, like any other, like a lesson, a job, a useful tool or homestead land. A living chance.

I stood by the open window looking at the denuded hills and gripped my arms, holding tight, and thought *I will not drown.*

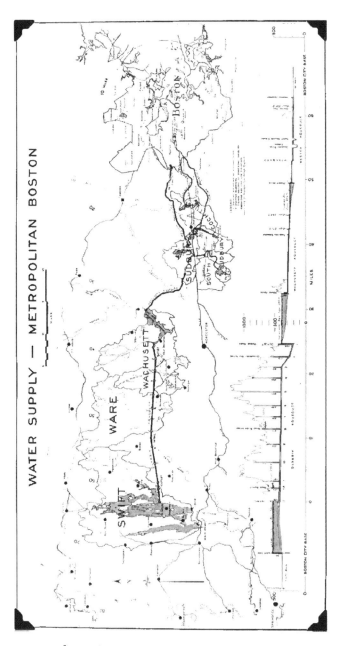

from the MDWSC annual report, 1936

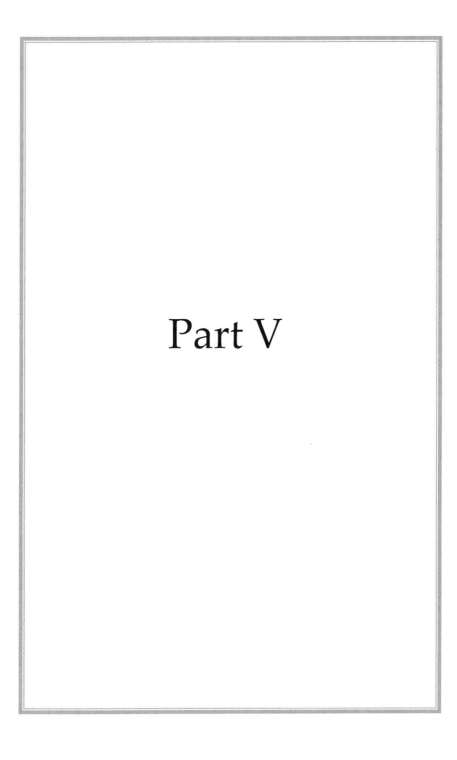

Part V

People still trusted their government then.

— Terry Campbell
Belchertown, Massachusetts
1996

88

"Get a good running start."

"Not sure I want to."

"Fraidy-cat."

"I tear my pants my ma'll kill me!"

"Chicken. Fraidy-chicken."

"I'm not afraid, I'm just not stupid."

"Who's stupid?"

"Anyone who tries to climb that fence, that's who."

"Not just *tries to*. I already been."

"What for?"

"See the dam. Water rising."

"Big deal."

"Skeletons floating in the water."

"You lousy liar."

"It's true, dumbo. They never dug up all the bodies."

"Bones don't float."

"These ones do. They still got rotting clothes and stuff. And lots of hair. Makes 'em float."

"What a load of manure."

"Suit yourself. I'll go alone. Maybe this time I'll jump in."

"What—with the skeletons?"

"Want to dive down to the houses. The ones they never took apart."

"Now I know you're stupid, Percy."

"Better stupid than scared."

89

1937

Removal of timber from the Swift River valley is indefinitely halted, although not yet complete.

90

April 9, 1937

Damn it, I didn't get enough for that syrup. Nor put up nearly enough, lazy sluggard that I am. And I think I'm so smart! If I'd worked harder and asked top dollar I could have doubled the take from Sandberg and still kept some for the tourists. As it is I'll hear them asking "Don't you have any syrup?" the entire blessed spring. "It's all gone" I will tell them and they'll come back with "Just the candy? No syrup?" and I'll be hard pressed not to shriek. "It's all gone" I'll say again, "but I've got some nice honey" and they'll look at me and wait.

April 12

If you could walk through the tunnel, from the other direction, you might come out the western end to find a different sort of valley. A valley cast back in time. Before they started the project, before white people arrived, before Miss Polly came of age and grew so weathered and wise. When I was nine or ten years old I ran across the word *pristine* and thought it the most beautiful idea in the world. Once I'd looked it up, of course. I am sure that my own life was in some way *pristine* a very long time ago but now that doesn't apply, to me nor anything around. We've all been touched by human hands. So maybe I'll drive out to Coldbrook tomorrow and sneak down their shaft and walk the dark until I'm

279

home. Maybe I'll arrive before the Indians, if I'm lucky, and have the whole place to myself.

April 14

Today's anniversary: the death of the Titanic. Exactly twenty-five years. I was a long way from born. Ma was carrying Caleb.

What I can't seem to shake is the thought of the fathers—with their "See you soon, dear" when they knew it was "Goodbye." They knew for sure, some of them did, some of the women as well, but there could be no saying. No "I love you," no "thank you," no "with you I've been blessed"; just light kisses and admonitions to stay calm. How hideous and low. What a fate. Some little girl was six then and she is thirty-one now and every time she hears a word—the very word "father," or "deck" or "voyage," or perhaps the phrase "take care"—she remembers his embrace and his reassuring tones and his wave as they lower the boat into the sea and she feels, to this day, the urge to rise up on her feet and climb the side of the ship to get back to him, back, make him come along too.

April 22

I sold the cow. Faithful Clara. To people who need her more than I do, which is little if at all. Still I'm sad.

April 27

Talk about famous disasters. They're gone now, the peckers, gone at last, but you should see what they did to our valley.

91

"Another drink, Miss McPhee?"

"Most of my friends call me Polly."

"Does your husband?"

"Don't have one."

"Have a beau?"

"Not at the moment."

"Another Tom Collins for the lady, please, and bring me a gin and tonic."

"It's funny to hear that word again. Beau. We used it quite a bit as children but it's fallen out of favor, don't you think?"

"I'm sorry. I'm feeling awkward. The fact is I'm an admirer— one of your most devoted readers—and it's a little unsettling to find you so attractive, along with your talent."

"Now I'm the one feeling awkward."

"I didn't mean to distress you."

"You meant to flatter, which I don't really mind, especially at my age. And I'm glad you like my work."

"Men must approach you all the time."

"I teach writing classes, Rob. If you're a fan I'm sure you know that. In a small town in Massachusetts, at a college you've possibly heard of. Everyone there is either 30 years younger or married. It's not exactly a gay whirl."

"I hope you're not lonely."

"Oh no. I have friends. And more than enough to do."

"Join me for dinner?"

"Why not?"

92

July 6, 1937

Amelia is lost. I was certain this would happen. I had followed her achievements and over time her intentions were clear. I don't know whether she'd have chosen to work it out just this way—the distance, the mystery, the absence of remains—but I suspect that she would. It's very simple, now, and clean: woman lost in the blue. Sea or sky, it doesn't matter. What does is that she found what she'd been seeking all along.

I'm so proud of Amelia, for her perfect escape. And for all that flying too.

July 12

God bless the chickens. Always the same. They are my only stock left—I'm not inclined to count the bees—and it is very nice to know I can rely on their discretion. They never appeal to me, never ask what's next, never stare with suffering eyes. Just peck at my toes and then the corn once I drop it, lay their eggs and mill about, make a racket and raise a stink. Sooner or later they'll be in the pot—I will not, will not, will not be taking them with me to Orange, I can promise you that—but they are wholly unconcerned. They have no thought for the future and don't ever wonder why.

July 20

The height of summer. So familiar. I could hardly forget. But it stirs in me the need to find a means of expression. It's not enough to just remember. It's not enough to be smug.

What if I were to be shipwrecked in Ceylon or Kamchatka? How on earth would I describe our New England July? Bad enough that words are all I have to reconstruct this glory; worse yet that I'm still baffled by them, still so anxious and inept; and the most awful thing of all is that I don't even try.

See above what I've written. *The height of summer. I won't forget.* Fine reading, yes?

A memory's a treasure, sure, but currency it's not.

July 29

I haven't seen Joe in ages. Since last winter, point of fact. I don't even know why. And I bet he wouldn't either, if I asked, which I surely will not do.

It's ridiculous, isn't it? The pleasure and comfort we could have been giving each other, all this time. It makes me very angry. But I have no idea at whom.

August 12

About those empty empty houses: they tell the kids they're full of wildcats. To stop them falling through a floor or getting a rafter on the head. But of course it doesn't work—they just love to sneak in. To them it's rare fun.

They'd run like hell around the yard, round and round, almost endlessly—my sister giggling, the dog barking, the chickens hustling out of their way and then (stupid chickens) walking right back into it. Every so often she'd stop, turn around, face the dog and shout his name. Then she'd spin and start running again, the dog barking wildly and right on her heels. Sometimes I'd see Mama looking from the kitchen window, a smile on her face but a little worry too. Sometimes Polly would catch me watching her and stop just like that, her cheeks red, breathing hard, and go back to her chores or head into the house.

I suppose if there is a heaven, which I'm precious sure there's not, and I get there, which is even more farfetched, the best part of it for me will be watching that damned kid and that damned dog going round and round and round, giggling and barking, loving each other, going round.

I dreamed I met an old gypsy. Her name was Mrs. Boba. She had a brightly painted caravan, all golden and green, and when I told her she laughed.

"You think that's something?" she asked. "You lousy miserable something? You try living like me!"

"But it's my home," I dared to say.

She approached me as a tiger, a saucepan held high. "You stupid English," she said. "You try living like me!"

I was certain she would strike.

But Mrs. Boba dropped her weapon and stared a long while at my face. Then she gestured to her trailer. "Get in girl. Get in. Time to go."

"This is the last of it."

"Yes."

"Our last moment here."

"Yes."

"Let's wait a minute."

"It doesn't matter."

"There's nothing much I want to do, mind. I know it's time to get moving. But I can't."

"Not yet."

"I just can't."

"Soon you will."

"This was our home."

"Yes."

"And now it's nowhere."

"Perhaps that's true."

"All right then. Get in."

"You're sure you're ready?"

"I said get in."

96

August 21, 1937

Dearest Edna,

What a gift! I couldn't thank you if I tried—not sufficiently, that is. If I live to be a hundred I will never forget all your warmth and your kindness. Being welcomed to your household. Jacob is a perfect darling; he has that courtesy of manner some men are born with, I think. And he loves you so much, and he adores his little girl. And she's so happy and calm! I am weeping all over again thinking of it now, just as I did on the long ride home, about how pleased I am that such a family's in the world. There *is* decency under heaven, if you know what I mean.

(And on the ride I also giggled at the memory of your heft! You're a sight, old school chum. Hard to believe it's still six weeks to go.)

You didn't think I'd make it, did you? Even after my telegram. Don't try to deny it; I saw the amazement on your face as I stepped from the train. And was very well-prepared, having brought your letter with me and studied it closely on the way. You were right in your assessment—it was a little hard, that letter. Not your reference to past invitations nor your offer to pay the fare; those lapses from convention flew over my head. But your directness—*bluntness*—about my personal situation. Like a wet rag across the face.

"Sit by the deathbed for as long as you please," you wrote (this from memory, I needn't look anymore), "until they carry you

288

away." Well perhaps that's right, dear Edna, harsh but right; that may be just what I am doing. I thank you for the description. Because I learned from it too.

But what I need to say is this: it was a wonderful joy to be part of your life, to *see* your life and know it's out there lending comfort and light, but it isn't my own. My circumstance is something different. And as much as you care, as much as you feel my sorrows, we inhabit different nations. With miles of water in between.

"Look to the future, won't you"—I love your firm courageous hand!—"and think of all you might do." I want to tell you that I will. "You're only twenty-one and you have got to make some plans." And that is where the border lies. Somehow I want to convey to you that planning is the single thing I can't afford now. I don't want to—that's the truth. You may call it what you will. I can't tell much about my future but I know about my present and it has settled down right here in Greenwich Mass USA. I have to be here, don't you see? Have to be here while I can. Time will pass and then deny me, I'll be required to move on, and attention will be paid to all the questions you raise. But for now, as of this writing, I have other concerns.

As you must know I'm getting ready. I am Polly in control.

"And then the man comes along and he is very very sad and the boy says let's go! and the man says OK but he still is very sad and the boy give him a candy and he's happy! He is. Then they go to see the puppies and *along* comes a woman and *along* comes a woman and she's the mommy with her baby. The baby wants to have some bottle and she gives it to she. Then they all go to the puppies and they were very very poor and the king took their money so they were very very poor and the boy says to the woman can we keep them they're so sad! and the woman says say please because it's *not* a good idea to say stupid and it's *not* a good idea to say idiot. It isn't. I won't do it anymore."

"That was a wonderful story, William. I love to hear you tell stories. I'll listen any time you like."

"I want my juice now Aunt Polly."

August 24, 1937

"Leave the bicycle and the buggy." I imagine that's what they say. "Just leave them there in the woods. Get in the car. Get in the wagon. Leave all those things and come along. The water can take them, they're not ours anymore. Just leave them there and come on."

September 19

I know. Yes I know. I don't write much here these days. Perhaps I'm gathering my strength. The time is coming, after all, when Miss Rebecca McPhee will record her own departure. The final emptying of the valley, the demise of her home. Transformation, cataclysm or the withering away. And though a voice in me says Let some other fool do it the fact is I'm not reluctant. Some burdens are acceptable, if not at all welcome; I understand the term *devotion* and like all the strongest words it carries costs with its rewards. A burden's weight is as nothing compared to the reasons for its bearing, even those still concealed.

And who else is there but me?

September 25

For some reason I walked up Mount Lizzie today—wanted a bird's eye view, I guess, of the condition of things in our neck of the woods—and rested a while on the open ledge near the top, facing east. The one that looks down on the farm. As I drowsed in the sun I pictured all my young men. Roy of course and Caleb too, and Jimmy and Tom and the others I've known. Even Joe. Playing baseball, I imagined. The dog frolicking between. It was sadder than I can say.

In the past *left behind* has more often than not been the whisper in my ear, the lump in my throat, but this was something else again. They had not left me behind; it was I who'd gone on. Or at least off to the side, or one step up or one down. To a nearby but different place, a different world, where I could see them running round and hear them shouting for the ball but never get them to hear me. Nor pay me any sort of mind. They played their game in brilliant light—I swear I smelled the spring grass—it was very real to me but I existed not at all. I felt my own hand pinch my flesh and heard myself saying You, real is you, oh Polly Polly real is you. And as I left them I waited for a cry of supplication but nothing came.

September 29

"What have you got?" I was asked by the man.

"I beg your pardon," I said.

"What have you got?" he asked again. He gestured to his truck: H. Herbert Parkman, Household Furnishings. From out of his jacket came a huge roll of bills. "I deal in curios and antiques," he said. "Mostly from estate sales—rich people with no heirs. Or sometimes the heirs prefer money to bric-a-brac. Anyway, I came out here because I figure you've got plenty. You people. Plenty you aren't taking. Maybe to you it's just old tables and chairs but in the city, believe me, it'll fetch a pretty penny. So you just tell me what you've got and we'll negotiate our terms."

I smiled sweetly and folded my arms. "Covering the valley, are you?" I asked.

"I know," he said, almost confidentially, "it ain't that big a truck. Well I'm sort of picky, lady. I'm not buying it all, believe me. Believe me. But there's plenty worth buying and when the truck gets full I'll just drive on to Boston and come back the next day. Until I've got all I can handle."

"Most of the families are long gone by now."

"So I'll see the ones that aren't."

"I don't think I have anything worth your while."

"Let me decide that, will you?"

I smiled at him again and put my hands up in my hair. "Wouldn't you rather just sleep with me?" I asked.

He looked me quickly up and down. Then he smiled too, and whistled. He said, "Honey, you're not bad. I'd be more than happy to take you upstairs and give you the works. But first of all I don't think you're serious and second I'm not the type to put pleasure before business. Reason I can take a doll like you out first and show her a good time—I don't just walk up and slobber on a woman, not my style—is because I make a good living. Take care of business is my motto."

"Mrs. Parkman must be pleased."

"She's got no complaints."

I stopped smiling. "I'm not ready yet," I said. "Come back next spring." I turned to go inside the house.

"Next spring I may not bother."

I turned again. "Your loss," I said.

"No honey," he told me, "it's yours."

99

NEW ENGLAND NEWS BRIEFS
Boston Globe, May 18, 1996

OLD PALMER DAM THREATENS TO BURST

 PALMER—Town officials said they are concerned about the safety
of an old dam by an abandoned mill in Bondsville. Selectman
Elaine Nikodem said Thursday that the high water in the Swift
River and continued rains this spring have town officials worried
about losing part of a recently expanded fire station and other
property if the old dam gives way. (AP)

100

November 9, 1937

Fratricidal war in Spain. Germans torturing their Jews. And now this villainous invasion of huge China by Japan. I'm amazed I have attention for such things but I do. And I've learned a great deal. There are words I have read, photos I've studied, scenes I have witnessed in the newsreel that will stay with me forever. Along with the woodpeckers, the baffle dam, the church reduced to ash. Papa lying by his wedge.

If it were me wearing a star and getting spit on by children, if it were me being raped by foreign soldiers in gray, if it were my goats blown apart by bombs dropped from overhead I'd have more company than I do. Twisted thought, isn't it though? Unworthy of the noble martyr. Well I'm not noble anymore. I find nobility overseas, or in a few of my neighbors. Not in this full-grown McPhee.

We're of the same race, those far-flung victims and I, and I reach out my hand.

November 18

I said enough is enough and went down to call on Joe. Waited through the afternoon and into the evening on his porch until he arrived. He was a little surprised to see me but not very. He just greeted me, invited me in, made tea, brought out some ginger cake. We talked as if nothing had happened, as if a gap of nine months

295

was perfectly ordinary. He looked leaner and stronger and was really quite appealing. I admit I felt some stirrings. But I dampened them with vigor. As I say, enough is enough.

He asked me to Thanksgiving dinner next week, with some other folks he's having. Believe I'll accept the invitation. Valley folks talking gratitude ought to make for quite a party.

November 29

There goes dear old Ernest with his titles again. "To Have and Have Not"—is that memorable enough? Even if the book's no good the name will last forever.

December 7

I had never imagined I would see them anymore. Not in my most peculiar dreams. But there they were standing before me, having knocked on my door. A lot older, a lot grayer—after all, thirteen years!—but very much as I remembered. Standing in the twilight in the pouring autumn rain.

"We're so sorry to disturb you," were her very first words. "You are Polly, aren't you?"

"Oh my goodness!" I said. "Come out of that right this instant!" I stepped back and they did; I helped them take off their slickers. "I'm so delighted to see you!" I exclaimed, almost shrieked. And it was no lie, I was.

"We're darned happy to have laid eyes on *you*," said Don, "believe me." He had gone almost bald except for patches above his ears. Still big and manly, though. "We didn't even know if this house would be standing."

"Or if it was, who'd be in it," said Flo. "Look at the mess! We've made a puddle in your hall."

"Go ahead and make five more." I embraced them in turn. "I take it this was unexpected, or you'd have written ahead."

Don sighed and looked embarrassed. "It's a long story, Polly, which we'll be very glad to tell you, but first off let me say we're as sorry as could be."

"About my folks?"

He nodded. "And for not being heard from."

Flo reached out and touched my arm. "I hope you'll be able to forgive us."

I shook my head and smiled at them, amazed that I could speak of the departed, even briefly, and be so unperturbed.

"You're heard from now, that's what's important."

"You don't know the half," he said.

Though puzzled I took their hands. "Let's get you some tea."

Once we were seated in the kitchen I could see how much they'd aged. Nor had time alone done it.

"You've had trouble," I said.

"We have," said Flo. "Mourned our children to begin with."

I stared, aghast.

Don hung his head down, glanced across at the stove. "Lost the farm as well," he told me, or perhaps my missing parents. "Nearly everything we had." His speech was soft. He turned, this stooped midwestern Job, to gaze to his wife, as if expecting her correction—it was all a dream, Donald, your life never turned so sour—but she had nothing to say.

"We're on our way out to Erie, Pennsylvania," he explained. "Got a line on jobs there. We've been down by Litchfield the last two years or so. Thought we'd double back and look for you before we went west."

"So close?" I asked, a little shaken though I fought it. "Right there in Litchfield all this time?"

Flo smiled thinly. "That's what he meant, Polly," she said. "Who knows what put us off at first? Maybe we just couldn't bear it. And after a while, you know the way—you don't do something and don't do it and don't do it and it doesn't take long before you *can't* anymore. Because you didn't before. Seems like a problem you could fix by just getting up your nerve but it isn't that easy. I'm pretty sure you know the way."

I was ready to reply but she started coughing then, loudly and violently, coughing and wheezing in an alarming fit that lasted more than a minute. Don got up and went to her but all he could do was hold her shoulders and hand. I thought This woman is not well, not well at all, and was filled with fresh sorrow.

"I'll be better," she assured me when she could get her breath again. "I finally found a smart doctor, back in Connecticut. He told me just what to take. I'll be right as rain by spring."

"Cold out that way," I said. "Hard wet winters. You take care."

"I'll see that she does," said her husband.

"So now you're going," I said. "Well. Better late than never. I assume you'll spend the night and eat supper with me. I have some chicken and some squash."

They looked at each other. "Be pleased," said Flo.

I won't say our meal was jolly but it was certainly pleasant enough. We talked mostly about happier times, although it was understood between us that trouble was common ground. I was gratified to know they shared my distress without sharing my circumstance; equally so to lend a knowing ear to these poor mistreated souls, to be conversant with grief.

Late in the evening, as we were finally clearing the table, I realized they hadn't mentioned Caleb. Not once. A wild and chilling thought came: maybe they knew, knew something I didn't. But I pushed it aside.

It was awfully close to midnight by the time we went to sleep. At the very last moment, after Flo had gone up, Don turned on the stairs.

"You should be angry," he said.

"You've done me no wrong."

"We kept away at a time when you badly needed family."

I tried my best to consider that fairly, objectively, from his point of view. "I don't know," I said at last. "I don't know what would have happened if you had come to see me then. It's a mystery." He sighed; I shrugged my shoulders. "But you didn't and I'm not angry. Maybe I should be but I'm not."

The gas flame was set low but I could make out his smile, his first real smile of the evening. It went away just as quickly. He came down a single step and stood holding the banister.

"I guess better late than never, as you yourself said." He was looking past my face and I wanted to embrace him but as I heard the floorboards creaking under Flo's tiny weight I saw the shape of his regret.

Don slowly resumed his climb. "Pleasant dreams, Cousin Polly," he said, almost fondly, as he was taken by the night. "It's nice to be at home again."

101

1937

(another year growing old)

A plan for the eventual taking, by eminent domain, of any land not yet acquired is filed by the Commission. June 30, 1938 is set as the absolute final departure date for all remaining residents.

The final harvest is gathered in the Swift River valley. Planting of new crops is prohibited.

The former owners of the Dugmar Golf Course of Greenwich accept a reduced settlement of $150,000 from the MDWSC.

(another year going out)

102

I walked straight in, set down my bag. It was a good house, I could see; they had done a good job. Small and plain it surely was but well and carefully accomplished. And to the letter of instruction, near enough. I hadn't counted on success, aware that things can go awry even under careful watch and here I'd kept myself away. Never saw the trees cut, the well dug, foundation laid. Never touched a window frame. So it surprised me that the end was almost what I'd expected. I had been granted, for once, the institution of my vision, the earthly power of my dreams.

I'd been afraid to see the land at first and had prayed so for its beauty and when I'd dared, finally dared, to travel north and set my foot the site had almost overwhelmed me. Breeze so cool, lake so fine, sun so ready and so calm. And I a traitor to my past, standing breathless by the shore—*you could exist here, you could stay*—before the shame the impulse raised washed it out onto the rocks. By then I knew I would return.

And now the cottage: further grace. A place for me. It looked so fresh, with clean bare walls and vacant floors. It smelled so sweet. It was a vessel to be filled.

CASES SETTLED BY AGREEMENT

November 1, 1937.

Company	Located on	Diversion Covered by Settlement	Amount Paid	Date of Payment	Estimate of Commission's Engineers	Claims of Owner	Remarks
Ames Sword Co.	Chicopee	Ware & Swift	$ 2,500.00	2/7/34	$ 7,000.00	$ 15,000.00	Settlement, made by Office of Attorney General after jury was impaneled, includes purchase by Commonwealth of real estate and water rights
Barre Falls Reservoir Co.	Ware	Ware	4,800.00	12/5/36	....	7,500.00*	
Dana S. Courtney Co.	Chicopee	Ware & Swift	10,000.00	5/9/34	8,500.00	16,000.00	
Chicopee Mfg. Corporation	Chicopee	Ware & Swift	250,000.00	8/10/33	300,000.00	375,000.00	
Dwight Mfg. Co.	Chicopee	Ware & Swift	295,000.00	12/2/31	275,000.00	275,000.00	
Indian Orchard Co.	Chicopee	Ware & Swift	375,000.00	9/28/34	393,600.00	425,000.00	
Northern Conn. Power Co.	Conn.	Ware & Swift	30,000.00	8/1/34	20,000.00	201,000.00	
Quinnebtuk Company	Chicopee	Ware & Swift	140,000.00	7/12/33	135,000.00	183,000.00	
T. E. Rich Company	Ware	Ware	3,250.00	6/26/33	5,000.00	5,000.00	
A. G. Spalding & Bros.	Chicopee	Ware & Swift	12,000.00	8/9/33	12,000.00	12,000.00	
Thorndike Co.	Ware	Ware	25,000.00	4/28/32	32,500.00	172,500.00	
Geo. W. Wheelwright Paper Co.	Ware	Ware	35,000.00	5/24/33	18,000.00	75,000.00	

*For damages only—does not include real estate

VERDICTS OF MAHER & DUGGAN CASE

November 1, 1937.

	Amounts of Verdicts	Amounts Paid (Finding, interest, etc.)	Maximum Damage Estimates Reported by Commission's Engineers	Claims of Owners	Trial Expenses
FIRST TRIAL. MAHER & DUGGAN (Finding returned 1/25/34)	$221,000.00	Hearing before Board of Referees. Retrial ordered by Supreme Court.	$57,000.00	$400,000.00	$14,192.63
SECOND TRIAL. (Finding returned 7/28/37)	150,000.00	Finding, including interest from 9/15/33 - 7/29/37 at 5% per annum. Finding $150,000.00 Interest $29,041.67 $179,041.67	57,000.00	365,000.00	29,664.69

from the MDWSC annual report, 1937

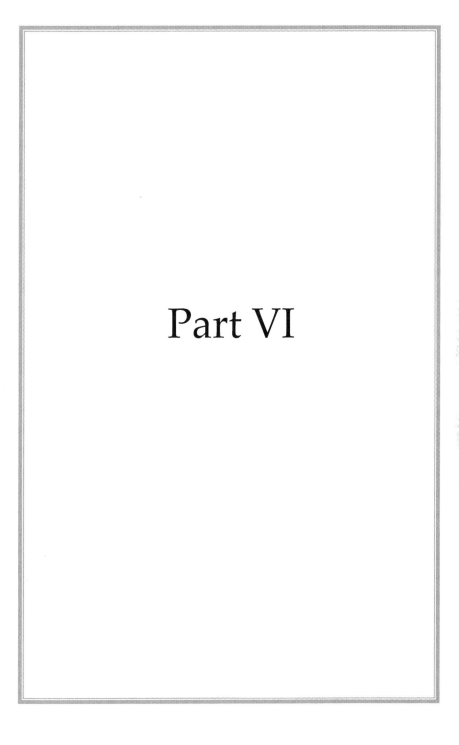

Part VI

You can't step into the same river twice.

— Heraclitus of Ephesus
Fifth century B.C.

103

1938

January:	MDWSC Chairman Hultman predicts flooding within nine months.
(the end)	
March:	All land still in private hands is taken by eminent domain. The Commission controls the valley.
	Dana holds its final town meeting. Officers are elected to their customary terms. Municipal funds are sufficient to preclude terminal debt.
(is now)	
April:	Enfield holds its final meeting.
	Thousands of sightseers view the dams.
(in sight)	

104

January 27, 1938

They want us out by April 1st but Joe insists I can stay. "They won't bother you," he says and I know he must be right. They'll let the kids finish school and families sell their effects and secure their new deeds, he tells me, and summer will be more like it. April 1st is just a push before the final all-out shove.

And why would they bother to remove me? Why would they even care? Before long they'll be sending detectives and enforcers, perhaps the National Guard. Some old crank is sure to stay until the very end and will have to be hunted down. So why should they notice someone lingering now?

I will do as I please.

February 8

It's pretty funny. My mind wanders. A tranquil confusion, else I'd worry for my sanity. It must be like being old, perfectly strong and sound but old, and for this reason gives me comfort. When they close up the diversion and the puddle starts to form I'll continue with my youth, pick it up where it left off, but for now old seems right.

I will be walking out the door and believe that I am seven. Mama calling not to spoil my dress with company coming soon. And then I'm thirty-six with children, growing children of my own, and I scan the roadway waiting for them walking home from school. Oh no I think not now they said they're staying for the game. *No no* I think you fool you have no sons, you are not seven, that's not your pa kneeling by the snowbank fixing a flat. You never saw that at all. And then: I've watched my husband. I helped him once. When we drove out in that storm.

February 17

I have become a fiend for lists. What a soothing activity. I've little else to work on now so why not be prepared? Why not think for a while about what I'm going to do with the sheet music, the engravings, the lanterns and the beds? The fact is of course I'm going to take every bit—no I haven't got started on putting up that cottage, haven't even seen the land, over two years and I've done nothing so I'll have to find some storage for all this Armstrong and McPhee—but why not know what's entailed? I read as much as I like and visit with Joe and take care of the house (to the extent I have the heart) and still there's plenty of time.

Suppose Caleb comes back. Suppose we hug and kiss and cry and spend a week in joyous embrace and then he says to me Hey Sis—that baseball picture. My old chest. Papa's ties! Will I tell him I'm not sure?

They are our lives, those possessions, and deserving of account. Someday they'll be my remains.

February 26

Oh hurry up you stupid spring. Hurry up hurry up. Let's get this show on the road.

105

Out of the night the yankee ghost, his features far from distinct. As are his other indiscretions: the dates of his birth and passing, his name and woes and ragged fields, the way he beat his children and gripped his wife's scanty flesh.

But a yankee no doubt—that is brilliantly clear. Wheeler, perhaps; Carlisle, perhaps; Gibbs or Nevins or Blodgett or Patterson, Stebbins or Shumway or Townsend or Trask. Of a family old when the nation was young. Of a family debarking gaunt in 1652 without a shilling to its name. A former fighter of the French and of the Indians, no doubt; perhaps he holds a musket ball as spectral now as he.

I know you she says.

Well you ought replies the ghost.

What do you have for me? she asks.

Or you for me?

I have nothing.

You have news.

You'd rather not.

Give o'er young miss.

Your fine new England—it's dying.

An evil falsehood.

To be more honest it's near dead.

As she watches him weep she wonders little about him. She would have liked to protect him but he asked the wrong question. It is true he has no heart but he is still required to know.

Don't think me cruel, if you please, she instructs the apparition. I am no different from you.

106

March 2, 1938

Gentle Polly,

Confident as I am that you expected never to hear from me again I hope most sincerely that you are glad nonetheless. There were moments during my Colombian sojourn (a disaster almost from start to finish, if I may be so frank) when I bolstered my courage with thoughts of you. That may seem strange but you must believe, despite my grievous negligence, that I am fully aware of the hardships you endure. That hideous water project and your mother's tragic passing and heaped upon all of it, as I prepared to embark, I received your brief notice of your father's sad end. To be orphaned of parents and home altogether at such a young and sensitive age is a very great trial and more than once I thought of you, suffering and surviving, when I had to find the patience to last out my own misfortunes. Being poor, after all, is nothing to being bereaved; being ill is certainly bad but I knew that if I recovered I could sail home and visit my own aged mother, could at least go with her to view the tiny ruined shack in which she raised me. I thought "If Polly can shoulder her burdens, so can I" and that helped to see me through.

It was as I say a disaster and I returned with little beyond my name. Since that day however—I will not bore you with the details—I have seen my opportunities and done rather well in making the best of them. Extremely well, I should confess, given

I'm a Negro in the U.S. of A. Not only have I managed to stave off the jealous white men who have tried to wreck my business but last week I signed a contract with the state of Massachusetts. With a white bureaucrat of considerable power! I dare say I am the only black man in that position, not only in the commonwealth but perhaps in all New England. I have reason to be proud.

But I did not sit down to crow. I want only to share my prosperity, if you wish. Consider the forgoing explanation. Knowing as I do that you must thoroughly resent me for my inconstant ways I want to offer all I have. I want to help you if I can. I am alone in the world except for my mother; the fact is I seek a family. Oh no, not that Miss Polly!—liberal though you are I could hardly expect you to consider a Negro. And I am aging, and not inclined to wed. What I wish is to have someone to look after, a young relation who can benefit—a niece or nephew, shall we say?—and you are the closest there could be.

My dearest Polly: education. You know how I esteem it. I would be glad to provide this for you. What do you think? What are your ambitions? I yearn to know.

I can do nothing but pray that this reaches you safely. My address appears below; I expect to remain here for many months to come. Ask and you will receive, to the best of my ability. It is as simple as that. Should you need help please ask.

They'll have to clear it all again.

That wind blew everything down.

If we'd been there we would have suffered. No doubt at all about that. They kicked us out just in time. Hundreds of dead are left in its wake and so many homes destroyed nobody wants to try to count. In 1928 it would have ruined us, wiped us out.

But ten years later it arrived to find a blank spot in its path. No towns at all, just rubble and trees. Their precious basin must be a mess.

Unimagined in New England. Caught every last soul by surprise. They will talk of this hurricane for a century or more but it missed us by three months. Who'd have thought through all those years that it was coming, coming on, like an angry bull or a downhill train, and they were pushing us out of the way?

1938

April 21:	The last town meeting in the Swift River valley takes place in Greenwich. Charles Walker is appointed to select a tree from what remains of the town's forest to be replanted in Quabbin Park Cemetery in memory of his brother Stephen, sole Greenwich casualty of the Great War. It will be joined by a memorial to the town itself and all its war veterans, for which $2,000 is appropriated.
April 25:	A bill to effect the disincorporation of Prescott, Dana, Enfield and Greenwich is passed by the legislature of Massachusetts and signed by the Governor. New Salem, Pelham, Belchertown, Ware, Hardwick and Petersham are awarded new territory, and Franklin and Worcester Counties are enlarged. Hampshire County receives the sum of $55,000 as compensation for its losses.
April 27:	The firemen of Enfield host a grand ball in the municipal building. The hall and the streets around it are filled to overflowing.

April 27, 11:58 pm:

> The orchestra stops playing.

April 28, 12:00:01 am:

> Four towns go out.

109

March 27, 1938

No more sugaring for Polly. The endless boiling and stirring. It's over now; confess I'm glad.

Poor sacred hens. Don't know they're doomed. They'll be my dinner by and by. If I space them out just right I'll feast on chicken till the end.

March 30

They finally took all the land. They got the first in '27 and here it is, a decade later, and they've purchased the last. It would have been better for everyone concerned if they had grabbed it all at once and marched us out under the gun. Like the Seminoles from Georgia. Got it over with clean.

April 5

Passed Larry Sherman's place today. I won't bother with sad descriptions, no point in that anymore. But as I went by the gate I remembered his horseshoes (you can still see the marks where each one of them hung) and the day—nine years ago!—when he told us he was leaving. I was a bit shocked to realize that I haven't heard a word from him in a very long time, since the Christmas before last. I do hope he's OK. I thought briefly of my fears that he was after my maidenhead, when he called me to Otis; I was afraid he would propose, really I was, and now it seems I am forgotten. Along with my relief I feel a very faint regret, that he gave up so easily. I didn't mean for him to have me but the asking would have been nice.

April 14

The latest word: July 1st. With "good reason" they say.

April 20

Everything is breaking down. All inhibitions are in flight. When I approach an old acquaintance I can't predict what she'll say. Men fail to remove their hats, are unresponsive to my greetings. The remaining children look as though they're being raised up by wolves—not their cleanliness or clothing but the wildness in their eyes—and are clearly unbalanced by the chaos around them. They've been riding their bicycles in some of the larger buildings, I'm told, for months now, even in winter, and you can see them throwing stones at empty structures most every day. On the roads all courtesy has been abandoned, every drive is an adventure. No one splits wood when they can pull it off a wreck. And I find myself wishing Mr. Parkman would come back; some of this year's scavengers are breaking into houses and those that don't are horrendously rude.

The strangest tale I've been told is about a girl named Shirley. Who wanted to open her father's coffin. As long as it's dug up and on its way to the Park, she figured, why not introduce herself? My God, it's like the judgment, the end of the world, except my neighbors are going to have to adjust, sooner or later, to the world still here.

Of course some order remains. Those Enfield ladies held a close-out, for instance, a last *rendezvous*, and had the sense to meet in Ludlow where it's sane. They could have let their institution die slowly of neglect but wisely chose to kill it instead. And the sun falls and rises and the river still flows south. And town meetings right on schedule—that makes me proud.

What a wonderful party. I expected a wake but it never came close. I had my doubts about attending but just before five o'clock I looked in the mirror—at the lines on my face that wouldn't be there if I'd been born in Lexington or Chatham, at the hair that hasn't changed since I was four years old, at my eyes grown very pale—and thought, This is ridiculous. You'd hate yourself all your life. So I took out my best things and drove down to Enfield to find the place choked with cars! I had to park a quarter mile from town hall. Apparently everyone in the valley showed up, including Commission people, and a lot who used to live here and a whole bunch more just curious. There must have been two thousand at least. I can't tell you how perfectly perverse it was to see such a crowd in Enfield—with its buildings half gone and some of the rest falling apart—after watching the thinning for so long. It seemed a waste to simply socialize; I almost wanted to leap onto a fire engine and declaim a stirring speech, like Henry at Agincourt.

I hadn't thought about eating but the Grange was serving sandwiches so I stopped for a bite. It was like being at a fair. Fortunately it had been a bizarrely hot day and was still very warm so people could mill comfortably in the streets. I stood on the sidewalk sipping my coffee and watching. To my amazement tears were rare, almost absent—despite the sound of earth-movers over the hill. There were warm cries of pleasure as friends encountered each other, and constant laughter, and children running through the crowd. That was most of it. I thought for sure there'd be a fight between some gawker and a resident, between a reporter and one of Enfield's nearly ex-officials, but there was nothing like that. It was jolly, even festive. And when I went into the hall—I was glad I acted early, after a while they sold out—it was exactly the same.

Even junior hermit Polly saw some people she'd missed. Friends and acquaintances of my parents, classmates from BHS, all sorts of individuals I had written off forever. It was fine to see them, shake their hands, share a story. And at one point Dr. Peeble—the center of attention, maybe the most important man there,

with people pressing round him and hanging on his words—
spotted me over a row of heads and winked. He winked at me! I
wore that unexpected honor as a prize the whole evening.

The air was thick, spiced by sweat and by the beer they were
dispensing in the basement. Along with the bunting there were
trimmings of black. And the tickets and programs had a black border too. I hadn't known black could be gay.

I danced with Joseph, of course. In fact as soon as I saw him I
wished we'd come together. Maybe he was one reason I'd been
planning to skip it but once I'd spotted his bright-eyed grin all I
wanted was to hold him. He didn't see me despite my gestures so I
pushed my way through the crowd until I reached his left elbow.
He was involved in conversation but I pulled on his arm just as the
other turned away.

"Sweetheart," I said. "May I have the next dance?"

His smile broke my heart.

"Are sure you want to, Polly?" he asked. "There must be
someone better here."

My hand went to my mouth. I couldn't help it. Was that what
he had been thinking? Was I that badly confused?

"My dear friend," I said, after a moment for composure (I had
to shout, actually, over McNelly's orchestra and a thousand chat-
tering faces), "I know we've let each other down but I wish you'd
understand it's neither your fault nor mine. It's the state's if it's
anyone's." I took his hands. "Now here we are, the music plays,
our little town has hours to live. So won't you please give me this
dance?"

He thought that over and smiled again, but with less pain.
"All right," he said. "Although I'm not very good."

"Neither am I."

We waited our turn—it was two numbers more before we
could find enough space—and danced together in the crush. I held
him, he held me, we didn't stamp each other's toes and it was pretty close to heaven. If I'd had two hours to live I wouldn't have
minded very much. Joseph's body, his warmth and muscle, and his

manifest desire were like a source of infinite strength, perhaps even salvation. I resolved to start again, to do much better, to restore the chance we'd thrown away. Maybe I'd cared for him more than I could bear; maybe he'd been paralyzed by some demon or haunt he'd imagined on his shoulder. All I was sure of was that he was being cheated, that I was being cheated—as was everyone in the room, Commission engineers and all—and I felt bound to be fair.

In another thirty minutes I had abandoned the future. Not a thought for tomorrow. We stayed together for the rest of the evening, holding hands and sharing punch, and I felt like a feather. My worries dropped away.

When Dr. Peeble stopped the music grief finally broke through. As it had to. There was sobbing as midnight struck; even the children were crying. Then they played "Auld Lang Syne," which was hard but appropriate, and further comfort was forsaken.

I'd thought of my parents a time or two during the evening but it wasn't until midnight that I remembered my brother. And instantly wished I hadn't. Thank God for Joe's comforting arms.

The ball went on for two hours more and our spirits picked up, although beyond that dreadful moment it was never quite the same. The concluding selection was "Home, Sweet Home"; it set many of the older women weeping again. Joe and I said a hundred goodbyes and walked back to my car.

"Come stay with me, Joseph," I whispered as I hugged him.

He drew back and shook his head.

"Is there no way to persuade you?"

He kissed my cheek and walked away.

So finally and at last it's just a hole in the ground. I left my parents' house in Greenwich and returned to it in Hardwick but that's a flimsy legal fiction. Our home is now the hole that they determined it would be.

R.C. Binstock

May 19

The car is done in. It has failed me at last. It was old when Pa bought it and it's much older now and I'm grateful it ran all this time without a hitch. The man in the Plains who checked it over— I'd never seen him before, I guess he moonlights from the Commission—made a silly to-do. "It's a relic," he declared more than once. "How'd it ever last this long?"

"Abel Fuller, now of Maine, is a very fine mechanic," I said. "You would have to ask him."

The man grinned. "I'm sure he's real good, miss, but I don't think there's been a car like this in Boston for a couple of years anyway. It wasn't what you call a late model."

"It didn't have to be."

He shook his head just a little and turned to the engine again. "Well whatever it was it's through," he said. "If you tried to start it now the motor'd go all to pieces." He shut the hood and faced me. "I got a couple of junkers I could let you have cheap, if you need something to get around in." As he pulled out a handkerchief and blew his pointed nose I smelled oil in the air. "They'll just be hauled out and wrecked when they close the place down so you can give me twenty bucks and have your pick."

How small of him to squeeze me for such an unimportant sum.

"I don't have twenty dollars," I told him as I rose, "and I don't want another car. Now what shall I do with this one?"

He was about to ask for money again, I could see it plain as day, but then he thought better and sighed. "I'll put it with the others and they'll carry it away when they get around to it," he said. "Happen to know that's what they'll do."

Guess who helped when I was stranded between the village and the Plains? See if you can guess. Eddie Simmons is who. Eddie Simmons Lends A Hand. He came by in his truck and stopped as soon as he spotted me—stopped before he could have known who it was—and hobbled quickly across the road. When he saw my face he smiled.

320

"Need a tow, Miss McPhee?" he asked. "Happy to oblige you. No charge."

"Well yes, I do," I said, "but Eddie, I don't want—" It was too late. He was sitting in his truck, turning it around, backing it up in front of my car before I had finished my sentence.

He hopped out and hooked them together. I was still standing and watching—a little nonplussed, I suppose—when he rose up and said, "The Plains, I assume. Come on and ride in here with me. Isn't safe in your car."

He told me four or five jokes as we drove slowly into town, and I laughed at every one.

1938

May: Memorial Day ceremonies are held at Quabbin Park Cemetery. The Walker Tree is planted. Veterans' exercises are also held, for the last time, in Enfield, Greenwich, Dana and North Dana.

June: Valley schools graduate their final classes.

The Enfield and Greenwich Grange chapters jointly dissolve, surrendering their charters to the state Grange master. Members vote to donate their treasuries to the fund for a new Grange building at the Eastern States Exposition grounds in West Springfield.

All valley post offices save Enfield are closed.

///

Joe's wagon is standing in the middle of the road. Piled high with everything he owns. After all these years of watching people leave I still can't get over what a house contains. And Joe has known this day was coming for more than a decade. But the wagon is full. I want badly not to look.

"Well, Joe," I say, "it seems this really is the last." Standing there and studying that kind, courageous face I am filled up with my gratitude. His companionship these past years has, I'm certain, saved my life. I don't know how to describe it but he's been everything to me. Or everyone, rather, in his own too-modest way. Father, brother, suitor, all the men I don't have. I am moved to embrace him but I hold out my hand.

He won't take it nor meet my eyes. "For God's sake get out of here, Polly," he tells me. "Let's none of us do this anymore." Then he turns and walks away, back to his house, slapping at the side of his wagon as he passes. Disappearing through the door.

The sound the blow makes is very loud, very strange—it echoes all the way to Connecticut, where he's bound—as if he'd hit something larger instead.

The sun is fierce as I make my way back to the farm. Beating down on my head—I can feel it through my hat—and glaring into my eyes. Time to go, it tells me harshly. Clearly time for you to go.

"The last dog is hung and I seen it! Time to go."

113

The sky was blue the trees green the moment solemn but not for me. A silly song sung inside. Memorial Day, Memorial Day, that's really all Polly wanted to say. Goodbye Stephen Walker I'm sorry you died and sorrier still you can't sleep where you lied. Goodbye Mama Papa goodbye others too I won't soon be back to bring comfort to you. Take care village hedges so long village lanes au revoir valley hills fare thee well valley rains.

Memorial Day, Memorial Day. In memory of us. In memory of trying.

Memorial Day.

Everything goes away. Human beings most especially, and all the many living creatures. But every other thing as well: sunsets, snowfalls, seasons, years, mountains, oceans, stars, the universe itself, all someday to disappear. And once gone, never were. We speak of the dead as if still in the world but that's a passing reprieve; when we die they die with us. And so forth unto forever.

Listen: I hold knowledge. I hold memories. These are mine, all mine, all that can truly and ever be mine, and while I breathe they are real. As real as anything there is. My mother's face serenely smiling as I bring her her slippers; my brother naked in the bathtub, shining smooth but for his scar, dark hair in unexpected places. These things are as bright and as solid and proud as the slope outside my window, the pen with which I write. Precious treasures held inside, that wait so quietly and well.

And when I die? When I end? Gone, all gone—Ma gone, Cal gone, Papa gone too, town and schoolmates and thunderstorms gone, dinners and sermons and evenings on the lake, all gone gone gone with Polly, gone away. Gone with the love I hold, with the fear, gone with my breasts and feet and backside; gone with the feel of his hands and his weight and his flesh on my lips and all that pleasure cut with pain. And what I've shared of me gone with the deaths of those who shared it, and then sooner or later Polly's current is no more. Blood becomes history, sadness pale nostalgia, the days of a woman brittle numbers on a page. This month in such-and-such a year: she was Polly then yes. And in these other seasons too. But before this moment no, and no later than that either. The limits of a term that may as well be struck to nothing because once ended it can never be reclaimed.

Still there is this: no change can harm you. No sudden hurt, no disappointment can ever worsen your condition. Valley gone, loved ones gone—what small distinction shall I make? The trivial gradation of my losses over time is a game, a purposeless folly; in the end it doesn't matter. A life begins and goes on and at a certain time is over. And then it simply never was.

This is the source of all grief.

115

June 14, 1938

School's over forever. That was the last Greenwich class. We all went down to applaud and it was remarkable, really, that it was so like any other. Like brother Caleb's or my own. They'll be widely scattered soon, from White River to Altoona, but the children were untroubled. They danced and sang a class song.

Proud and happy to have made it, is all, and to be free. As we ourselves were in our day.

June 21

This is much easier than I thought.

June 24

Hey look at me, Ma—I'm gone.

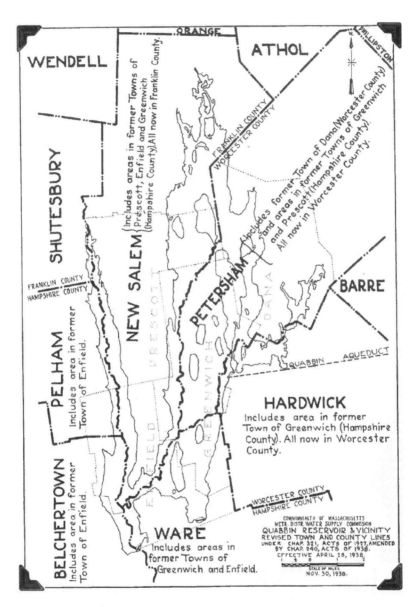

from the MDWSC annual report, 1938

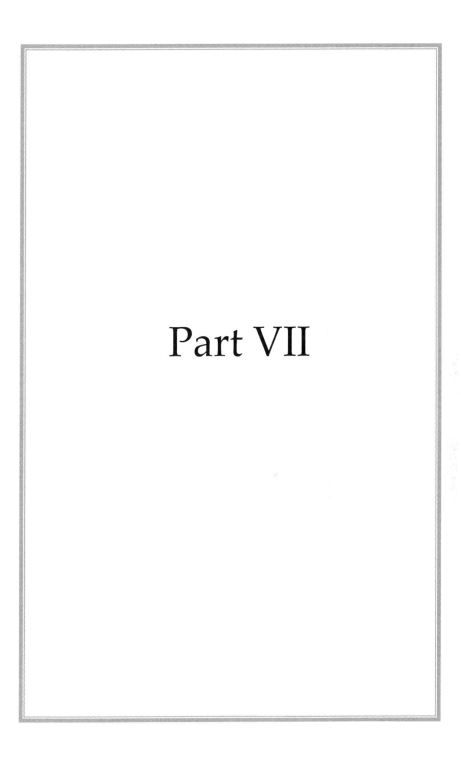

Part VII

We are the victims of an unfortunate necessity.

— J.H. Johnson
selectman of Dana, Massachusetts
1922

116

Early in September of 1938 Cecil Beecher of West Halifax, Vermont, is discovered in the pantry with one of the Rideau girls by his mother-in-law, Margaret. Although he hears her coming just in time and manages to pull his hand out from under Brigitte's skirt before she arrives, he dislodges in his haste a jar of tomato preserves from a shelf behind him and it smashes on the floor. Brigitte, as amused by their faces as she has recently been by Cecil's need to feel her buttocks, flees quickly outside with fresh red stains on her ankles. Cecil stands tall to confront his accuser, already calculating the price of her silence and finding it acceptably high.

In the Swift River valley an auction of public property features books and other school supplies, office equipment, Enfield's fire engine, and various municipal buildings. Enfield town hall, being constructed of brick, brings $550, but the nearby Grange building yields only $35, about half of what is paid for the fire engine. Dana's town hall is purchased for $90 and the adjacent schoolhouse for $110.

The Great Hurricane devastates New England on September 21st, killing more than 600 people and causing destruction whose entirety will never be successfully described. Its path takes it over central Massachusetts and thus over both the Swift and Ware Rivers. While twenty million board feet of timber are blown down in the now-uninhabited Swift River valley, the structure that will be known as Winsor Dam is unharmed.

R.C. Binstock

In October the telephone exchange in Enfield, Massachusetts goes out of operation after forty-one years. A radio broadcast on the 30th, "The War of the Worlds," haunts a nation at peace.

117

What if we were there? We might have ended up dead.
Though I had lost them anyway. Would I have chosen, if I could, to
have them live until that storm and then be struck down all around
me?

(Dark forests tumbled into streams)

I wonder about the house. They might have flattened it last
month. Surely it was smashed to bits by one of our big trees if there
were any still standing. Either way there's nothing left.

(The forests tumbled)

What if we were there?
I looked out on the waters.
I visited in my dreams.

118

It wasn't just the fatigue, or the shock. Of course we were tired—I know I'll never, ever be that exhausted again—and sure as hell shocked. No one from the captain down was prepared for any of it. I mean any of it. For the first twenty-four hours we didn't even discuss it between ourselves. And when we did more than one guy talked in a strange, squeezed voice that didn't sound like him at all.

But it went way beyond that. We were so far from home, living a life so unnatural, so full of the unfamiliar and almost empty of what we thought we knew. It all blended together into a sort of daze of anxious anticipation—of getting shot at, of explosions in the middle of the night and incomprehensible orders, of another hour, another day spent dirty and cold, of sergeants going nuts over small things they'd laughed at the first hundred times, of guys admitting to the most awful, the most twisted deeds back home and drinking and whoring to a fault and fighting viciously over nothing, of German prisoners who looked more or less like us, only dirtier, colder and younger. Of friends being killed. Of thinking of their families sitting at home, hoping they're OK. Of thinking of your own.

And now we had to add to that something no one, no one anywhere could have possibly imagined. Except the people who did it. We were completely overwhelmed. It meant there might be anything coming, *anything*. We knew we had to get prepared but we didn't know how.

So the second day after we got there I was sitting in the mess tent they'd set up, staring at a blank V-mail. I'd had a brief impulse to write to Roseanne, but to hell with that. I didn't want to write to anybody, as far as I could tell. Especially not by V-mail. At that moment, I realized, I didn't want to talk to or even look at anyone I'd known before I shipped. But there I was, sitting and staring.

Finally Pinkowski came in. He almost smiled when he saw me—almost. Smiling really wasn't on anyone's agenda for the time being. But Pinkowski, being of sounder mind and more likely to laugh than pretty much anyone in the regiment, could come close.

"Lot of that going around."

"Lot of what?"

"Trying to figure out what the fuck to say."

"Haven't gotten that far. I can't even figure out who to say it to."

"I know," he said, sitting down on the facing bench. "It's a bitch. 'Dear Ma, I hope you are fine, guess what the krauts have been doing to all those people they locked up.' I think not."

We sat for a while. He gave me a cigarette, bless him, and for a couple minutes we could focus on the pleasure of the smoke.

"So let's go find DeSousa and see what kind of royal juice he's come up with," he said hopefully, after tearing down his butt. He stood up.

"You go ahead." I touched the front of my jacket, gently; Augie's letter was still in the pocket. "I'm just going to write a quick note."

"A *note*? To who?"

"My sister."

"Heavens to Betsy. She'll enjoy reading all about it, I'm sure." Then he got all indignant. "You been holding out on me, dog boy. You said no family."

"Everybody has family, idiot."

"No, damn it, you said, quote, and I remember this very fucking clearly because we *thought* those fucking Panzers were coming for us any minute and it was true confession time, 'I don't have nobody left, no family at all, zero,' end fucking quote. And you have never in these nine months said a single fucking word about a god-damned sister."

"Well, I got one."

"Does she have a sister?"

For a second I was truly confused.

"I know," he said. "They don't work around here. The stench kills everything." He headed for the flaps. "Catch me up later, OK?"

I took the letter out and studied it for the twentieth time. And there it was again, still, in black and white. There was nothing holding me back.

I can't tell you how or why. Mysteries of the heart, I guess. All that suffering, the disbelieving horror, the tears of panic and rage had shaken something loose, something that had been stuck for years and years in a very bad place, and I was able to do, at last, what I hadn't dared—hadn't wanted—hadn't known how to do for so long.

I kept it short. Which seemed wise. And hurried out the instant I was done, to get it into the mail sack at company before I changed my mind. And find Pinkowski before he drank up all of DeSousa's booze. I needed a drink—or two or seven—worse than I ever had in my life, but I was light as a feather. Lighter, I swear.

119

In 1939, the last valley post office (Enfield) is closed.

MDWSC Chief Engineer Frank Winsor dies on the witness stand while testifying in a suit brought by the A.A. Johnson Company charging Commission engineers with deliberately providing misleading information. As the contractor's attorney asks him to read a memorandum ordering the substitution of false data and carrying his signature he enters cardiac arrest, expiring where he sits at the age of sixty-nine. He is succeeded by Karl Kennison, an influential contributor to the metropolitan water supply effort for nearly twenty years.

Extensive burning of brush and debris begins.

Dynamite transforms the old mill in Enfield into a rough hill of stone.

The last three resident families depart.

Roads into the watershed are closed. Guards are posted.

Final clearing is complete.

August 14:   The diversion tunnel is partially sealed. Flooding begins at half a million gallons a day.

R.C. Binstock

September 1:   Germany invades of Poland.

October 6:   Fuhrer Adolf Hitler denies any intention of making war on France and Great Britain.

October 24:   Benny Goodman's orchestra records its signature tune, "Let's Dance."

In 1940, the Chandler Mansion of Enfield—MDWSC laboratory and last surviving building in the Quabbin flow area—is torn down.

120

I sneaked in. They are burning. The valley is full of smoke. They are burning the trees. I sneaked in to see the valley full of smoke and flaming wood a conquered land. There's nothing there. They are burning. There's nothing there but piles of ash. Gray ash dead grass and cellar holes barren fields and asphalt roads. All my suffering peaks and slopes. I went to look at the naked ground. I went to see the farm but when I tried to climb the hill the intake shaft rose before me and I turned and started down. Retched and started down the way. The naked ground they saw me there they scowled their scowls and showed their backs. They would not see me did not want to. Through the smoke I approached at a distance they wondered and then no more. The bitter smoke the naked ground.

A voice called out I stood and turned is that you Mama is that you? Is that you Mama that you Mama that you Mama is that you? A lullaby a gentle voice I stood and sank into the mud. Is that you Mama are you here do you love me is that you?

I sneaked in. They are burning. The valley is smoke.

/2/

A world at war the cycle of seasons babies born copulation ha-
tred jobs in the plants bodies burst by bullets and shells and vans
in the forest filled with carbonmonoxide His Excellency Governor
Leverett Saltonstall of the Commonwealth of Massachusetts of the
United States of America turns a wheel in Southborough water
flows through a tube and is welcomed in Weston to slake Boston's
thirst the reservoir is off limits will not be seen for five long years
fire-tower on Great Quabbin and swarms of planes move east to
bomb a tropical harbor twenty thousand enlist at Brooklyn coffee is
rationed murder is mechanized young men die and die and die
desperate millions without homes blown apart starved to death
cities brought to flaming ruin miles of beaches soaked in blood the
last of the bodies is laid to rest at Quabbin Park Cemetery Hultman
dies Hitler dies a flash in the desert the watershed lands are reo-
pened to all the valley is gone.

122

I looked up from my work and there she was. Standing wind-blown and tranced-like, staring down into the valley. I somehow had the idea she'd climbed the hill without knowing. Without see-ing the ground. She was standing on Mount Lizzie but a part of her was elsewhere and another part (the strongest) was nowhere at all. She was standing looking out in the direction of her farm and as I watched her all my shame at what I was doing came flooding up into me, choking and sick, and made me want to just vomit. To vomit out my wounded soul. I desperately wanted to damn it all down, to tear the day to pieces; to pitch my shovel and march to the office and spit on their wages. I swear I felt like Judas, taking money for a friend.

I had never seen anything slightly like her as she stood there and hope to God I won't again. Her face was sweeter than I re-membered and her figure made me ache. Having come so close—so close—to loving a woman a month before I was at last in a posi-tion, I believed, to truly want her. To guess what it might be like. Lord Jesus I wanted. But to grovel at her feet, that also, you under-stand—I was dying for that too. I wanted to beg pity, to find out where she was living. I'd heard what happened to her family and wanted to know was she taken care of? Had she means of support? I wanted to kiss her, to surround her, to send myself far away. But all I could do was watch.

She turned slowly, slowly turned, looking out over the valley, staring at Mount Zion and Mount Pomeroy and Prescott's ridge and at Little and Great Quabbin and at the Beaver Brook dike—she couldn't see the main dam so that left only the dike to fix herself on, I guess, the dike they'd just named after the dead old engineer who started all this rotten business, and I imagined she was trying to figure just exactly where the turnpike would be dropping into the water—and over at Ware and then at me. By luck or by design she had turned counterclockwise so I was the last. I was last on her list. Standing there all filthy and tired, stripped to the waist because I thought I was alone, a sweaty smelly beggar with the weapon in my hand. Like a knife above her heart. Please forgive me, please do, I wanted to say, I know this isn't my land but she hardly even saw me. Won't you please come stay with us I'm sure my dad would welcome you were the words that rose in me but they never got said. She never once met my eyes. I know she saw me, all right—like a rock or a tree, like an innocent bird, like another caved-in homestead or a burning stretch of fence—but then she started her turn again.

June 22, 1946:   The Quabbin Reservoir fills to capacity.

It was a pleasant summer evening when I saw the shooting star. A darkened sky like any other; so I assumed as the sun went down. I'd heard the radio news and though I'd known it for a year I *believed* for the first time that it would end. That we would win. Truly believed we would win. I prayed for our men and for everyone threatened, that they would make it to the finish, overcome their luck, survive. I sat on the porch as the light slowly dimmed and thought a while about my brother. Saw him fighting the war. South Pacific? Burma? Paris, London or Rome?

His letter rested in my hand. Little more than a greeting and my proof he was alive. I felt my heart pulse inside me as I told him my goodbyes. Goodbye and bless you, darling Caleb. May you soon be at peace. May you never be in pain.

It was then I saw it fall. My eyes were fixed along its path. Just an accident, perhaps, but I saw that meteor drop from the zenith to the hills. I hadn't time to sit up or even stretch out my hands; I saw descent and fiery flare but in the seeing was its passage, urgent journey to no more.

To have and to hold: it's what we most want to do. But all we reach for we lose. Brother father mother friend…and all the others and the virtues and the burdens they bestow, the love we take and we give. Swept away, swept away. And lost from sight.

Except the voice that is mine: the words I speak in it I own. Forever more.

A wave laps gently at the shore.

"That's the limit, all right. And just exactly where they said."
"Imagine taking seven years."
"But it'll be here forever."

A road descends into water. From overhead a blue jay cries.

after

I encourage all readers, but especially those who live or have lived in greater Boston communities served by the Metropolitan Water Resources Authority, successor to the MDWSC, to visit the Quabbin Reservoir when opportunity arises. At the Enfield Lookout near Winsor Dam you can survey the sites of Enfield, Greenwich and Prescott and get a real sense of how much water that 400 billion gallons comes to; from Gate 40 on Route 32A you can walk or bike to Dana Common, still recognizable as the site of a typical Massachusetts village, and then on to the shore, where the road to Greenwich really does descend into water. As with meat from the supermarket and electricity from the socket, it is best to know where your water actually comes from.

The history of Massachusetts's Swift River valley and the Quabbin reservoir as portrayed here is, unfortunately, all too real. I believe this portrayal to be generally accurate, although accounts differ and as a novelist I have not hesitated to shift a date or alter a minor fact when it suited my story. For my Quabbin education I am indebted to many sources, but must acknowledge in particular author J.R. Greene; the Commonwealth Museum at the Massachusetts State Archives and its former director, Bobby Robinson, and staff photographer, T.C. Fitzgerald; the Friends of Quabbin; the Swift River Valley Historical Society of New Salem and its former president, Elizabeth Peirce; and most importantly Lois Doubleday Barnes and the other former valley residents who contributed, directly and indirectly, to my understanding of what happened.

The characters and the events of their lives are entirely made up. I trust that no reader will entertain the slightest doubt about this.

In between my own creations and the sad grand outlines of the period described are a few real and public individuals to whom I have referred. With one exception, however—that of the year-book essay quoted in Chapter 5, which was written by Madelaine N. Haesaert of Belchertown High School's class of 1927—I have refrained from incorporating anyone else's writing into my own without immediate acknowledgment.

The following piece is entitled to be included and I gratefully enlist its help in bringing this work to a close. According to the SRVHS it was "found on a scrap of paper". I would be pleased to know more about its author, although there is probably nothing to be learned.

> Once it was a village
> Now it is a lake
> Blue-bright in the sunshine
> Black in falling night
> Church and weathered farmhouse
> Store and village green
> Wine-glass elm and garden
> Graveyard loved and trim
> Once it was our village
> Now it is your lake
> An old New England village
> Someone said you could take.
>
> – Beals, Enfield

thank you

First and foremost: my beloved and lovely wife, Maja, who caught my dreams when I threw them away and sheltered and nurtured them for me until I was ready to accept custody of them again. Without her gentle but persistent support and encouragement this novel, begun in 1996, would still be sitting undisturbed on a hard drive in my desk drawer. She kept after me, year after year, until I finally cracked and admitted I was not yet finished as a writer. And even after I started revising *Swift River*, I couldn't imagine how it could actually be published; the grand vision was hers. I cannot possibly say how grateful I am to her and how much I love her.

My talented and adored daughter Kasia, who already had plenty to do in her busy 22 year old life, nonetheless agreed to create the cover and illustrations, with fantastic results. For whatever reasons it was very important to me that this work be done by someone close to me, and I couldn't be happier that it was one of my four delightful children. I thank Esther, Halie and Tomek as well for providing the daily joy and ongoing support that gave me the strength and courage I needed.

Book lover and blogger Luke Sherwood first encouraged me at a critical moment; with a few words he may have tipped the balance from despair to hope. And he has backed me each step of the way since. He did it for the work's sake, not mine, but I deeply appreciate it.

R.C. *Binstock*

Luckily for me and for *Swift River*, my teacher, mentor and dear friend Ann Beattie read it at just the right time and helped enormously with her insight and wisdom. Thanks to her I was finally able to appreciate some fundamental aspects of the work that had eluded me for many years, not to mention roll back a revision that had gone a bit too far. The novel is much better as a result.

I was also terribly fortunate when old college pal and palindrome buddy Stephen Morillo volunteered to help with the internal design. The pages of this book are far more readable and appealing than they would have been without him.

Finally, there are the wonderful and generous people who backed the Kickstarter project that enabled me to pay for publication. Far beyond the financial resources they provided, these folks, by showing their support in this concrete way, gave me the courage I needed to continue. I salute them!

Rosey
Celia Applegate & David Blackbourn
Barb Bryant
Bari Brodsky & David Gunther
Marcia Landa & Josh Goldman
Marylee Klinkhammer
Ellen Touart-Grob & Larry Grob
Debra Wise
Lauren Walker
Jim Haber & Susan Larson
B. A. Bean
Jenny Binstock & Gabe Smalley
Sarah Horowitz
Gregory Maguire & Andy Newman
Joshua Lubarr
Heidi Tompkins & Tal Gregory
Susan McM Tucker
Geoffrey Day
inzenity
Mary Kerins

Liza M.S. Patnoe
Adam Grossman
Jean A. Roberts
Carolyn Morillo
Susan Wadsworth
Steve Weiner
Avril Horn & David Klein
Joel F. Richman
Luke Sherwood
Amy Munsat
Ann Beattie
William Critchley
John Reilly
Williams James Bryant
Ken Carson
Adriana Gutiérrez
Owen Andrews
Michael Resnick
Yoko McCarthy
Dave Mitchell

Eleanor Andrews
Amy Cohen
Lynn Binstock & Hugh Klein
Rich Zeliff
Katie Touart
Anna Swan
Jane Wolansky
Andrew Lear
Mary Lou Touart
Betty Munson & Marty Blatt
David Feingold
Linda Lipkin
Bonnie McKeating
Julia & Probyn Gregory
Russell K. Jones
Karen Erb
Bernice Moy
The Whiff
Dan & Helen Horowitz
Stephen Morillo
Bill Carbonneau & Denise Corbett
Kinsey Wilson

Martha Binstock
Kent Carter
Muriel Klein
Judith Perlman
Theresa Levinson
Joanne Zeis
Elizabeth T. Binstock
John A. Shetterly
Elizabeth McCracken
Julia Werntz
Joel Feingold
Linda Mui
Laura Argiri
Rob Siegel
Mike Stockman
Kathleen Mahoney
Bruce Pardee
Robert E. Downing
Suzanne Ennis
Mary Mccluskie
Recreator

Betty Munson/Linda Lipkin

R.C. Binstock lives with his family in Cambridge, Massachusetts. At Harvard College he studied writing with Ann Beattie, Monroe Engel, and Grace Mojtabai. His story collection, *The Light of Home*, was published in 1992, followed by his novels *Tree of Heaven* (1995) and *The Soldier* (1996). The publication of *Swift River* represents the beginning of a renewed effort to write and be read.

Find R.C. Binstock on the web at http://rcbinstock.com.

35430278R00206

Made in the USA
Charleston, SC
10 November 2014